Tinnitus

To Nicola,
Best wishes
3rd July 2013

Tinnitus

A ringing or whistling sound in the ears.

Bob Samedi

Library of Congress Control Number: 2013910036

ISBN:	Hardcover	978-1-4836-4810-1
	Softcover	978-1-4836-4809-5
	Ebook	978-1-4836-4811-8

This book was printed in the United States of America.

Rev. date: 06/11/2013

To order additional copies of this book, contact:
Xlibris Corporation
0-800-644-6988
www.xlibrispublishing.co.uk
Orders@xlibrispublishing.co.uk
306202

For Luisa

Chapter 1

Theodore Grouchier's surname suited his character, as he was no philanthropist. A sullen child, a sulky teenager, a grumpy science student (B.Sc. hons) specialising in entomology, he matured into a curmudgeonly adult. He wasn't the sort of grumpy middle-aged man who had some characteristics that engendered sympathy, like Victor Meldrew played by Richard Wilson. Theodore didn't really have *any* redeeming qualities.

During his fifty or so years, his most memorable love tangle was with a fellow student, and that entanglement petered out in embarrassment and almost caused them to be sent down.

A reserved man, with thinning hair and carrying more weight than his height, would offset; he had a complexion that was earned from a bad diet (a face that had lunched on a thousand chips). These factors contributed to people feeling uneasy in his presence. Being in his fifties, he had long ago resigned himself to bachelordom. The more insouciant children in the avenue where he lived called him names (Gimpy Groucher, Greaseball, and, on one notable occasion from an obviously better read youth, '*Piggy Sneed, piggy, piggy, piggy, piggy, OINK! WEE!*'). Well, you get the picture. Whilst not unhygienic and speaking in more than grunts and oinks, he certainly was not garrulous. He didn't put much effort beyond a regular, but not enthusiastic, brushing of his stained teeth, a washing of his face, and a weekly shower when he shampooed his receding but still dark hair. He occasionally grew a beard that seemed to grow in a straggled manner with brown or sometimes ginger patches randomly seeded in it. He abandoned this practice after the grey patches started taking a firm hold and a dose of impetigo settled into his face requiring an antibiotic cream to cure it. The nurse at the health centre had donned a pair of surgical gloves before examination, and he caught her look of distaste as she parted sections of his beard during diagnosis before turning away to key the prescription into the computer. To make matters even worse, he had recently needed reading glasses for interpreting text, purchasing these at a bargain price from a supplier of assorted cheap goods in a nearby town. While reading glasses did not improve his attractiveness to any extent, he could now peer over them in a somewhat supercilious manner at anyone who chose to impinge on his personal space.

Employment as a chief scientist at a laboratory in a small research facility enforced his insularity. There was robust security, and the few current employees were work-conscious and not particularly gregarious (apart from the marketing research team), which suited Theodore fine. He pedantically and promptly corrected anyone who addressed him by a short version of his first name or mispronunciation of his surname, which he insisted ought to be the French version. Although no recent antecedents had originated from, or visited, the country, the surname allegedly originated from the nurses who took in his grandfather found howling on the steps of a hospital as a baby, according to a story propagated by his father, a teller of tall stories if ever there was one.

In addition, Theodore hated being called by his initials and even objected to people who used initials in correspondence. This, in his opinion, was the prerogative of royalty and not for the common man. Such principles did not endear him to his colleagues, nor did it dissuade them from using familiar versions of his name. It was this sort of attitude that ensured an invitation to the traditional 'Poet's day' pub visit was not extended to include him. He wouldn't have accepted anyway, especially when it was explained that Poet's wasn't a recognised holiday and that it was an acronym for Piss off Early Tomorrow's Saturday (thought to be a marketing research team invention). Theodore Grouchier lacked a sense of humour and eschewed coarse language.

In fact, he was a bit of a prick.

However, with this insight into his character, it probably wouldn't surprise you that he could be irritated easily, by lots of things.

But nothing brought him to a boil so quickly and then kept a steady simmer bubbling away as the invention of the personal stereo, especially the way that people who owned one managed to tune it, *as if with the specific purpose of setting a fire under his virtual saucepan.* He possessed a portable transistor radio with a single earpiece, whose predecessors were played at school where it was permitted to listen to one during breaks (either with the speaker pressed to the ear or via the use of a single earphone), but only when a test match was being played. And anyway, other cricket games were seldom broadcast ball by ball, and other broadcast sport was restricted to evenings and weekends.

Given his lack of tolerance, it was a bit of a paradox that Theodore was a bit of a cricket obsessive. Test match cricket is a game for the cool and easy-going, apart from the occasional bursts of adrenaline that occurred during a match. Limited-overs cricket matches may appeal to the less patient, but Theodore was traditional and old-fashioned. His love of the game was initiated by his school days even having only made the school eleven on a few occasions, as a third-choice opening batsman. He possessed a masterful forward defence but had few attacking strokes, an outcome of the limited extra cricket tuition available at his school. The first lesson of the course was free, and during lunchtime, the subsequent ones were after hours and parents were required to pay a contribution. Given the stretched budget in the Grouchier household, further tuition was not an option. Anyway, Theodore's cricket tuition aside, if a pupil was caught listening to anything other than test cricket, but especially popular music, the normal punishment would be detention after school or sometimes a hundred lines of 'I must not listen to fatuous music programmes on my transistor radio, and certainly never during school hours'. (I expect these days the offender would type the first line into a tablet and copy and paste it; after seven iterations, the job would be done in less than a minute, before printing it off and handing it in. Well, why not email it?) Schoolmasters on break supervision were tasked with the not-cherished chore of checking pupils' transistor radios; listening to BBC Radio Four occasionally earned the pupil a reprieve. Such punishment was much deserved in Theodore's view; he wasn't fond of pop music and found disc jockeys' commentary utter drivel, and as for the trite jingles, how could people listen to such poppycock! (He wouldn't have used the word poppycock if he realised that the expression stemmed from pappe kak, Middle Dutch for soft faecal matter as he could be a bit of a prig as well.) However, the modern equivalent to the transistor radio was much louder, in stereo and practically universal.

It was the personal stereo that caused Theodore Grouchier, for the first time in his fifty or so years, to foray into the world of deceit and criminality, a world for which he had neither the experience nor any natural flair!

Theodore Grouchier seldom drove a car. Some collisions, several near misses, wet weather, and abuse from the local youth had caused him to stop cycling to work. Not being close enough to walk, he was virtually forced to use the bus to commute. He was actually more at home using the bus, not meaning that it felt like a family gathering, but there seemed to be wider spread of people that one couldn't conveniently label as typical.

This was underlined by the fact that senior citizens travel free in Wessex and although they only have age in common, their characters traverse the whole spectrum. A bus journey is seldom without at least one eccentric as a passenger, being a senior citizen or not.

It was the combination of being a season ticket holder on the bus and the number of people who occupied themselves with the output from their personal stereos that would light the blue touch paper.

Theodore also invented nicknames for his regular fellow travellers. This was not an exercise in amusement or intellect; it was more to relieve the tedium of a regular commuter journey. He started doing this on a typically grey miserable rainy late autumn morning where the windows had misted up and the rain meandering down the outside meant that any stimulus external of the bus was either not visible or difficult to discern. To Theodore, there seemed to be more of this type of day in recent years. He disliked autumn, the oncoming long nights, the lack of domestic cricket, and the approach of that most false of festivals, Christmas. His father once said to his mother when he thought Theodore was not in the vicinity, *Christmas isn't just for Christmas. It is for the two effin' months before that.* Apart from his genes, the dislike of the winter months and the artificiality of the Christmas festivities was something else that was inherited.

Theodore's first and probably most pertinent on-the-bus christening (given his career) was 'the Mantis'. The Mantis was a lady of uncertain years who had a triangular face that she periodically inquisitively cocked to one side or the other, which one would associate more with the characteristics of a bird. The fact that she didn't have a pleasant and chirpy sort of countenance meant that a bird was not a suitable comparison; hence, the nickname was settled upon. The Mantis, after sitting down and adjusting her personal stereo, would invariably open a packet of snacks and with thumb and forefinger (little finger slightly cocked) select a morsel. The selected victim would be inspected, rotated, and examined one last time before finally being crunched between the mandibles, with no obvious savour of the flavour. Every time Theodore saw this, he could picture in his mind's eye the sorry look on the face of a locust having just been seized and bearing an expression of resignation that seemed unaltered during the act of being consumed.

Then there was Scooter, who was named thus because of the Lambretta cap he wore, no matter what the season. The cap was gradually fading, headband up, because of the sun and also the salt from the sweat that had seeped into the headband. Theodore admired Scooter because he never sported a personal stereo and seemed like a polite young chap who alighted at the college. Theodore guessed that he was IT support although this didn't seem to fit the stereotype, who normally wore their hair long and often in a ponytail, old jeans, trainers in winter, flip-flops in summer. They would talk in clouds, petabytes, and name the servers after characters from science fiction television series or that genre of feature films.

Tory Boy one (TB1) and TB2 were named because of the slightly greasy and floppy hairstyles and serious countenance, confusingly coupled with schoolboy puffiness. They could be imagined spluttering and pontificating in the Houses of Parliament whilst condoning tax avoidance and persuading old school chums to sign off the less than compliant expenses. Although their appearance suggested this, their presence on a bus in the county of Wessex while Parliament was in session precluded it.

Little Red Riding Hood regularly wore a flame red anorak on her journey to the college and almost always with the hood covering her hair that was surprisingly lush (Theodore wasn't quite sure why she should wish to cover such a mane or what role she played at the college, but her hair condition, the early start, and lack of sloth indicated that she was most definitely not a student). Also there were Angels 1, 2, and 3 because they were nurses at the local hospital. Angel 3 was especially endearing because she had tended to Theodore when he had last been knocked off his bicycle and required a few days in one of the wards. She had tended him with Philippine charm, an accent that made him smile, compassion, and a flower worn in her hair. This was more endearing because she was named Doris, according to the name tag nurses had to wear these days. It probably wouldn't surprise you, for many reasons, that she wouldn't recognise Theodore on the bus. Theodore wouldn't contemplate addressing her, even using her real name; he, anyway, preferred Angel, and she was only Angel 3 because she was the third nurse that boarded his bus. Theodore wondered whether she still donned the flower or was disillusioned because of the cuts in the National Health Service and no longer bothered. He didn't intend to break more bones or be involved in any more accidents to find out. It wouldn't occur to him to attend hospital under false pretences, such as impersonating a doctor, and even if it did, it wouldn't fit with Theodore's character, maybe because romance didn't feature highly on his order of priorities, or possibly because his motives would be suspected and didn't want 'Stalker' or worse 'Porker Stalker' as one of *his* nicknames. Theodore wasn't a lucky man.

The weekend brought out a different set of passengers, but just as easy to christen. There was a man in his senior years, of doubtful hygiene, who would vocally abuse any male passenger as the passenger alighted the bus (admittedly from a safe distance), although Theodore seemed exempt from a vituperative outburst. To Theodore, this was quite an obnoxious characteristic, and hence, he became the Deeply Obnoxious Old Man or Doom. However, if you were to imagine making a comment to Theodore like 'prepare to meet thy doom', then Theodore's reaction would be to look at you with a frown which may be of irritation or puzzlement. Humour did not come easy to him.

Another weekend feature was a little old lady who was often waiting on the bus stop on a Saturday. Theodore would help her board by carrying her shopping basket. As he stooped to lift her wheeled basket, he would catch that unmistakable aroma of embrocation disguised with a dab or two of eau de toilette under each ear, which seemed to cling to old ladies, like a pheromone identifying them as a distinct specie. Escorting her to her seat wasn't as straightforward as it seemed because she would insist on sitting at the back where she '*could see everybody*'. This made Theodore wonder whether she thought she was going to be attacked, on a bus! Did she imagine somebody rising from a seat and turning round to assault her? She was so frail. What could she do anyway? Theodore came to the conclusion that probably she just liked to watch people and you couldn't do that if she were seated in front of them. Well, at least LOL (Little Old Lady) didn't plonk herself in his favourite seat, which is the one adjacent to the fire exit with the extra leg room.

Passengers who hadn't been suitably categorised were named New Boy/New Girl with a number until they either became more regular when a formal mental christening was given or the number was reset. He never used a name that he thought would be offensive or abusive (he didn't think calling someone a mantis was offensive or abusive because he was fascinated by insects), so the portly Asian man who got on at the stop before the college and then got off at the entrance was just nicknamed LazyMan (LM) with a number as per all people who got on just for a single stage. LM1 obviously worked in security at the college because he wore a crisp shirt, satisfyingly taught at the waist, which was embroidered with 'University of Wessex—Security'. Security officers didn't feature highly in Theodore's list of good companions (although not many people qualified or would want to qualify for this honour). A security officer's life was predominantly one of boredom, and the only time it would become exciting was when one was in danger of physical harm from serious villains or, even worse, amateur ones.

A new weekday regular recently named was a short man with tattooed forearms who spoke in a voice a few decibels louder than necessary and an octave higher than expected. He also had a habit of discarding the free newspaper on to the nearest vacant seat after superciliously flipping back and forward through it for a minute or so, without seeming to read any of the articles. For some reason, this annoyed Theodore immensely. Theodore nicknamed him the Uvula (Latin for a little grape) after the clapper-like lobe of flesh that dangles in one's throat with no apparent reason for its existence, apart from annoying a partner by adding a rattle to a snore. Theodore also considered maggot (professionally he would have preferred larva, but maggot would have been more apposite), but he settled on the Uvula as it sounded more scientific. It was while he was quality reviewing his naming process that he realised one of the jokes at the office was at the expense of his initials and grumpiness: '*Well, TG, cheer up, it's Friday!*' There was a double pun here as well because Theodore knew that his mother had chosen his name from the classical Greek, Theodoros (Θεοδορος) that translates as gift from God. Theodore's father would have called him Sid or Zak. Theodore was glad his mother had prevailed, as he would have hated possessing a monosyllabic first name. Theodore's appearance, but more importantly his character and demeanour, meant that he was not, however, God's gift to women.

As mentioned earlier, bus passengers possessed almost universally, possibly with the exception of *some* of the senior citizens, a personal stereo, and whilst a good majority of travellers kept the volume to a reasonable level, i.e. you could hear the occasional cymbal-like dental (adding a 'T' to make it 'Tsss') hissing sound, but little more, there was a sufficient number however who insisted on sharing their taste in noise (and to Theodore, this was noise, not music). In some ways though, Theodore was consistent; he would never request anyone to reduce the volume, no matter how he seethed internally. The reasoning behind his logic was pretty sound. He decided that if he didn't have the courage to confront a 6 ft 5 in muscle-bound thug, then why should he tell a teenage wimp to control the volume, which surely would be hypocritical? So he pulled the corners of his mouth downwards in the most outward display of disapproval as he could muster and just sat there and seethed as he simmered, occasionally rustling the free newspaper. Mind you, he wasn't averse to nodding approval while pushing his lips forward in a sort of pout if another passenger requested the owner moderate the volume, providing this was done politely and not as on one memorable journey, in the format of 'if you don't turn that fing dahn, it'll be come a firkin suppository'. It was probably that this suppression of his expression (he would have loved to tell someone that their personal stereo may shortly become a personal suppository, even if you can't get an impersonal suppository) was the catalyst to designing a project that would moderate the noise without the confrontation.

One grey and overcast Saturday morning in late autumn, when Christmas was approaching like an unwelcome relative (although Theodore had no relatives who visited him), he started planning. He knew what he would embark upon would probably contravene criminal or civil law and would likely entail police involvement (not that the police had the time or resources to investigate every breach of regulations). Theodore was sure that any investigating officer assigned to his crime would be logical and would reconstruct any incident by timeline, as Theodore would do, were he the officer assigned the case. Theodore did not want nor intend to be traced, caught, prosecuted, and probably sent down; he would sedulously construct his project leaving little or nothing to chance. As mentioned, Theodore was not a fortunate man. The thought of prison and the type of person detained there almost caused abandonment at the outset; as well as not being lucky, he was not overly adventurous. In cricketing terms, Theodore was a Geoff Boycott, not an Ian Botham.

Chapter 2

The first observation he made was that personal stereos were of various makes and models: Some were telephones that had media playing as an additional function, others were pure personal stereos, some were minute and some more bulky, and some used one format and some another. In short, he was bemused by the plethora of technology that resulted in the similar susurrus that irritated him to such an extent. Being of a technical nature—some might even label him a 'geek'—Theodore was aware of various devices that could be deployed to attack computers without contact, and we might as well face it the personal stereo was a closer relative to the computer than the gramophone (record player to the younger amongst us; stereo to the even younger). In fact, the effect of magnetic pulse (EMP) on electrical equipment had been known for some time. The magnetic pulse from a high-altitude nuclear test known as Starfish Prime caused damage to the electrical circuitry in Hawaii, at least 900 miles away from the detonation point, which included the knocking out of at least 300 streetlights, setting off numerous burglar alarms and damaging a telephone company's microwave link. This happened way back in July 1962 when the electrical circuits were far more robust than the micro-circuitry of the modern age.

Whilst instigating a high-altitude nuclear test on the spur of the moment may seem a little overkill because the volume of someone's music irritates you, Theodore was interested enough to research further. He discovered that there were non-nuclear electronic magnetic pulse weapons (e-bombs) that had been used to destroy certain fragile electronic control systems critical to the operation of many ground vehicles and aircraft. The details of the construction of such devices were not available in open scientific literature, which is hardly surprising. In the United States, the declared strategy is on maintaining sufficient spare components to repair infrastructure after an EMP strike, rather than spending time and money developing a shield against the effect. In the Wessex branch of the Territorial Army reserves, the strategy is to rely on the enemy not deploying such an unsporting weapon. Further research showed that magnetic pulses could also be used in a more benevolent manner by reducing tumours, malignant or otherwise, which is particularly useful if the tumour happens to be in a place that makes surgery life-threatening. During his research, Theodore found a product in Canada called an MPG (magnetic pulse generator) that could be purchased without prescription. He noted that the unit was powered by a 12-volt battery. In addition, it bore a caution attached not to use within two feet of electronic equipment! Theodore's heart skipped several beats, and his stomach performed a slow roll, the first gymnastics his body had performed since school. However, his joy was short-lived; other cautions warned against use when the owner was pregnant or had a pacemaker, which somewhat took the wind from his sails. He wondered if it could be made directional so it could be beamed at a target rather than flooding a radius. He wanted his disruption to be against the equipment of the ignorant and insensitive, not the vulnerable or venerable members of society. Anyway, being a bit of a skinflint, he was reluctant to part with the sum of money the device cost. At the time, he wouldn't realise how much tangible and intangible cost he would incur on his decided course of action. This device may well have been the preferred option in hindsight.

It seemed that high-tech sabotage by interfering with software using digital barriers or magnetic pulses to interrupt transmission or corrupt the rotating or static disc storage was at least sidelined, if not out of the question. To top it all, the effect would be instantaneous. Theodore would like something more subtle, anonymous, and with a delayed effect. This would allow him to escape any repercussions. Well, if you consider the fact that suddenly all the electronic devices within a certain radius ceased to function and there was one normally morose middle-aged man furtively smiling, whom would you suspect? Theodore also realised that if he succeeded with a blocking or a storage corruption system, he may cause a problem with the engine management system of the bus as a side effect, not that the Wessex bus company deployed top of the range, sophisticated coaches. The buses that Theodore travelled on were old and hissed and spat like ill-tempered dragons, with exhausted damper systems that caused anyone not of sufficient suppleness to wince in pain and probably resulted in bone fractures for little old ladies with osteoporosis. The doors would often stick or suddenly slam shut, entrapping limbs that were not speedily withdrawn; the brakes would howl, screech, and judder as if the same dragon had caught its tail in a bear trap, further adding to its ill humour. The lurch of the bus as it belched and farted diesel exhaust reinforced the metaphor. One of the wags among the bus drivers once apologised for his tardiness and the age of the vehicle by saying, 'Sorry, I'm a bit behind, you'd never believe it, but this bus was new when I left the depot'. One senior citizen, whose speed of thought had not degenerated at the same rate as his body aged, responded, 'You're not a bit behind, you are a total arse'. Quipping OAP's apart, the quality of journey by bus almost cost-justified the extortionate fares the rail companies charged for train travel.

Curiously, he overlooked his field of expertise for some time, or rather, he didn't realise that his field of expertise would come into the equation, until it dawned on him that there was one item in common that all personal stereos required. To boot, this single point of dependency was also obtainable at very low cost. It was the headphones. Prices of headphones ranged from around a pound to upwards of thirty, and the design range was also as varied, although the jack plug was standard. Theodore thought that he would market his own brand of headphones with a device embedded that he could cause to fail remotely, but how to persuade people to own such a product when they had something that worked perfectly already? The style-conscious would obviously prefer the pricier range of headphones. Would anything persuade them to replace headsets for a pair of headphones that had no standing in the market place? In addition, supposing he could deploy his own brand of 'interface', what mechanism could he use to cease the sound on demand? A miniature shutter which closed subject to a certain frequency being received? Surely, he would not be able to design, build, and fit such a mechanism into a headphone, unless it was the traditional bulky version, rather than the daintier, lighter type that sat in the ear. Anyway, how would he activate such a shutter remotely with a signal when there was music passing through the headphones simultaneously? Then if the headphones stopped working, the youth of today would simply cast them aside as landfill and purchase a new set. Theodore dismissed the microelectronics and mechanism relatively quickly. So physics and mechanics were discarded. How about another approach using a different science?

Theodore's ongoing main project at work had been on a method to combat the nuisance of Cochliomyia hominivorax, or the screwworm fly to you and me. This little charmer lays its eggs on domestic animals, and the larvae feed on living flesh rather than necrotic or dead tissue as per normal maggots. The female fly lays eggs close to a wound so the maggots can dive into the food source; this wound is caused by the usual sufferings of domesticated animals, namely branding, castration, and tail-docking. Other accidental wounds such as barbed wire lesions or bites from other insects also attract the female. The screwworm fly had been a nuisance in the Americas for some time, causing misery for stock farmers (and also much agony for their animals). It was one of Theodore's heroes from his university studies (Edward Knipling) who pioneered a technique for controlling this unsavoury pest. This technique involved the release of sterile male flies; the sterilisation of the males was done by the use of a very small scalpel (only joking, they were irradiated, a bit like the process to give supermarket fruit the additional shelf-life coupled with a wax-like appearance of artificiality). As a result of mating with a sterile male, the female would lay unfertilised eggs, and given that the female only lays one batch of eggs in her life time, this was very effective. This technique removed the pestilence from Florida and gradually throughout Central America.

However, the reduction in the cost of air travel combined with an increased resilience acquired in the fly's gene pool resulted in the insect making the transition to Africa and thus providing another source of misery for impoverished African farmers and yet another contributor to famine. Theodore's company had been provided with funding to breed Cochliomyia hominivorax, then sterilise the male flies, and batch them ready for release in North Africa. Releasing them at regular intervals in North Africa would prevent the pest crossing into Europe, a key consideration when providing aid to Africa. Theodore was in charge of controlling the breeding of these delightful members of God's creatures; after the imago emerged, he would separate the males and assign some of them for sterilisation and retain some for further breeding subject to strict control. The separation was done in a refrigerated unit and had to be manual as other methods such as identification in the pupal stage was not as successful as Theodore's dexterity. The security procedures were strict to prevent any escapees; although the screwworm fly preferred a warmer climate to the UK, any slip would provide a tabloid newspaper's scaremongering material for a long time (hominivorax is derived from the Latin for man-eating). Given the fact that the larva, if not provided with its dinner on a plate, so to speak, can also make its own entry wound and takes a lot of antibiotics and care to counter its infestation, headlines would continue for weeks. It was while nursing a batch of eggs that Theodore had his Eureka moment. Combine the single common interface (headsets) and Theodore's field of expertise (entomology), and while Theodore preferred a shower to a bath, there was a brief moment of similarity between himself and Archimedes, well, two actually, if you consider Archimedes's screw and Theodore's screwworm.

It didn't take much of a search on his computer to locate a company a mere 15 miles from where he lived. This company would supply custom headphones (and other paraphernalia pertinent to personal stereos, mobile phones, etc.); all one had to do was submit the design, and with a sizeable deposit, they'd turn your design into production, probably by submitting it to a Chinese manufacturer. They would also supply a standard headset in a choice of colours for a reasonable price per unit, variable with volume ordered. According to the advertising blurb, this service proved popular with airlines, seminar organisers, and so on. Having found a supplier, his problem would be breaking the trail linking the company supplying the headphones, to him, especially if he ordered a batch and had the package delivered to his own address, or the one at work. He decided he would open negotiations with the company after setting up an email account that forwarded responses to yet another email account; he would then close both immediately after delivery. Theodore would put a lot of effort into the footers of the email account that he would use to correspond with the company for added authenticity with the right amount of pompous buzzwords to make it sound like the dialogue heard in a management consultancy type of business. It was Theodore's nature to be so meticulous even if the fabric of his ruse was as thin as gossamer, he would try and nail it down as much as possible, probably thinking six-inch nails as being suitable. In his imagination, there was an army of police officers on standby with a back office team of forensic scientists just waiting to leap from a coach or blacked-out truck with plain livery, on the slightest clue that he left. The Scenes of Crime Officers (SOCOs) would be armed to the teeth with swabs, test tubes, evidence bags, surgical gloves, microscopes, and exhibit labels.

The management consultant option he'd chosen was based on the theory that the type of males who worked in marketing research, being far younger than Theodore, would provide a more credible alibi. He would present himself as a consultant to an airline owner who was regenerating the brand of his airline which had to be kept confidential until a coordinated launch could be arranged. Anyone who asked the airline whether a rebranding was occurring would get a response of 'don't know anything about such an exercise', which wouldn't gainsay Theodore's ruse and add credence to the confidentiality. The eccentricity of the airline owner would account for the fact that Theodore would insist on cash payment of the thousand-pound price for the fifty customised headsets, reinforcing the confidentiality, but would raise an eyebrow of suspicion as surely no one dealt in cash anymore? It was intended that the headphones would only be supplied to customers in first class and this batch would be for day one of the launch. He would send some designs incorporating the new logo via email, which he sketched and then photographed digitally; these he assumed would be much improved by the company before being returned for his approval, whereupon he would approve the design he thought most fetching. He was assured that a subsequent batch order would be fulfilled within five days of an order by email, unless the volume exceeded so many units. Theodore stated that he would collect in person from the outlet and hand over the payment in cash as *that is the correct way of doing business, dear boy.* All this activity had been conducted remotely by email, but collecting in person would mean face to face, and therefore, he must rehearse as if it were a play. He did at regular and opportune moments and secretly. Theodore was enjoying rehearsing his persona for the transaction. He might even buy a new suit! The only question was whether even he was *slimy* enough to be a management consultant! As far as he was concerned, management consultants provided advice in respect of matters that were technically legal but definitely amoral, such as tax avoidance (tax efficiency) justified by having a cupboard in Luxemburg, yet all your employees were UK residents who paid the full UK rates, which doesn't seem to make sense to ordinary people. The quid pro quo was that the consultancy firms would provide staff free of charge for political officials, thus stifling any outrage in the Houses of Parliament. Yet what is definitely undemocratic is that there is no flexibility for ordinary people within the Pay As You Earn system. While Theodore was definitely not a political animal, there were certain matters that would cause him to sympathise with political protesters, no matter how strange their hairstyles or unwashed they appeared. Anyway, a management consultant he would become for his own protest. He practiced by listening to some of the management-speak that went on in the marketing research offices adjacent to his laboratory or that he heard being spouted down a mobile phone on street corners or public transport. He then regurgitated the phrases when he was at home. Words and phrases he often heard comprised things such as 'across the piste', 'getting traction and leverage' (leverage pronounced in the way someone from the United States would say it), 'I'm passionate about the xxxxx' (where xxxxx was a business, a business process or the latest business philosophy), 'We need a more blue-sky approach to "Outside the box with monitored flexibility"'. Such expressions seem to lose their sell-by date very quickly because there appeared to be new ones surfacing at regular intervals, some of which were rewording of old clichés.

Theodore practiced assiduously in front of the mirror. Fixing his face in an earnest, open manner, he recited, 'Regarding our recent electronic communications', 'there is zero flexibility in the promotional timetable of the project', 'actual cash is necessary as the confidentiality is preserved within the ledgers'. 'I am pleased with our transaction and look forward to additional similar transactions occurring in the near future. I bid you good day.' He would probably have done better being his usual morose self because putting on such a fake charade would make him more memorable than just being 'normal'. Businessmen (and women) didn't really care about noticing or pandering to the customer unless it affected profits, or it was necessary because of regulatory pressure. A whole consultancy industry had been created based on teaching businesses pithy presentations full of buzzwords and also supplying them with the latest pithy acronyms on how to 'Treat The Customer Fairly' *(Fairly What?)*, including such parables as 'Teaching the Gorilla to dance', meaning that once you've taught the gorilla to dance, he then controls you. So not only is this insulting to the customer (being put on the same platform as a gorilla), but also some sort of cruelty is implied. Imagine if they'd used the analogy of a dancing bear? Of course, once you've demonstrated compliance with the consultant's guidelines, they would kindly allow you to purchase a plastic plaque that you could nail up in your business premises. This sort of plaque would normally bear a wreath or a scroll with something like FECK (Federation for Endorsing Customer Knowledge).

He'd been laying foundations and rehearsing only for a few months when he decided he ought to start moving from feasibility into initiation. Admittedly, his research had been sporadic and rehearsals occasional, but he hadn't lost sight of the end game, which justified the decision. A lot of projects never reach fruition because too much time is wasted on having woolly meetings and the fluffy front phases of projects.

It was while rehearsing in front of the mirror, trying to be his own interpretation of a management consultant but strangely confusing it with the manner of a bodybuilder, that he noticed just how plump he was getting round the midriff. A couple of little jumps saw the adipose tissue juggle for position above the belt before settling with a slight overflow. He sucked his paunch in and held it for a few seconds, flexed his muscles, and grunted like the incredible hulk. A button on the belt line of his trousers pleaded stress and ricocheted off the mirror and fell at his feet, rattling on the bare floorboard before coming to an accusatory halt. *Oh botheration*, he thought (an expression often used by his mother), as he picked up and examined the button that had been neatly cored. He must consider dieting, or he would be forking out for a new wardrobe. He made a serious face as he stared at himself in the mirror. 'Right, no more takeaway curries and burgers, and any junk food is out of the question from this day forth. My second clause is that if I go to the fish and chip shop, I will only have the fish, and I shall not even eat the batter. Third clause is that I will buy fresh fruit, salad, and vegetables.' He changed his sad look to one of stern concentration into the mirror, jowls slightly jiggling, as he made this vow. *Might save a bit of money too!* the skinflint side of Theodore whispered in his ear. It took him an hour to locate a suitable button and sew it roughly in the position from where its predecessor had ejected. He was glad he hadn't opted for practicing medicine; he'd have trouble stitching a wound or rather making a neat repair of a wound using sutures.

The next day, being the earliest possible start he could make to his new regime, saw him go out during his lunch break to the greengrocers and stock up on apples, oranges, honeydew melons, mushrooms, onions, potatoes, tomatoes, walnuts, bell peppers, and jalapeno chillies. The old greengrocer, on seeing the size of his purchase, offered to deliver free of charge, which Theodore gratefully accepted. It dawned on Theodore that his mother had been a regular customer and that the greengrocer obviously remembered and respected this. Theodore felt somewhat embarrassed for some reason, possibly because he remembered the meals his mother had cooked from scratch and how since her death, he had seldom prepared any of his own food; well, now things would change. The initial change was easy; there were hundreds of quick recipes available for free, and all he needed to buy, in addition to the ingredients, was cooking oil, spices, and maybe some soy sauce or something similar. He would need to blow the dust off his mother's favourite ancient wok (at least it was well sealed). He started to look forward to a new routine and thinking up dishes that would appeal to his own palate. His attitude towards food had taken a 180-degree turn; before he just stocked up on cheap fuel, now he wanted to gain pleasure from meals, the trouble being that healthy food did not have the instant gratification that junk food seemed to possess or maybe healthy eating wasn't so addictive.

During the following week and subsequent weeks, conveniently as spring was developing, instead of sausages, bacon, and doorsteps of bread and a hefty late evening takeaway, Theodore snacked on fruit and prepared a simple evening dish, sometimes without any meat and certainly no sausages nor processed meat. Anytime his stomach or brain complained about such a swing in his diet, he picked up and ate a piece of fruit or a handful of walnuts. He would repeat this until the offending organ was mollified, or at least complained less; again, there was this conundrum about healthy food lacking that instant gratification. To some people, missing out on a full English breakfast would be tantamount to giving up the ghost. Theodore probably never really enjoyed eating; it was a simple fuelling exercise. As a scientist, he was intrigued by his body's reaction to the change of diet. Eating fruit is fast food (providing there is sufficient stock), but this sort of fast food doesn't work every time for ordinary people although Theodore definitely wasn't ordinary. Theodore hadn't visited the doctor for some time, but if he went now and explained his change of eating habits, the doctor would have been ecstatic. However, a dentist would have whinged about the citric acid affecting the tooth enamel and therefore recommend an expensive brand of paste that had been specially formulated with a corny-sounding scientific name like pro-anthracite, dento-myte, or enam-a-tyle. This new regime brought Theodore into conflict with the refuse removal or recycling arm of the Wessex County local authority. He now filled his minute 'food waste only' bin to the brim with peelings from vegetables and fruit, and if he overflowed or put the foodstuff in the 'landfill' bin, he would get a barely legible note on the headed stationery of the outsourced company threatening not to recycle anything from his address if he *refused* (sic) to comply. Theodore blew a gasket; this even exceeded the infuriation caused by insensitive people with personal stereos. Here was a local authority obliged by law (he believed) to collect household refuse who were not meeting statutory requirements. It was bad enough making you sort and collate items into a myriad of differing receptacles, yet the men collecting the stuff seemed to inspect the content like a schoolmaster checking your homework. Next, they'll be requiring you to dig a separate landfill area in your back garden and supply your own paper and cardboard pulping machine, the output from which they would charge you to take away (unless you built your own paper mill, of course). Well, bang goes for certain that Christmas six pack of beer (which he never remembered anyway). He found an envelope and notepad on which he penned the following response. 'Thank you for your undated note left outside my premises, if I may make the following suggestion. Please make it softer and more absorbent.' The force with which he made the full stop almost penetrated the notepaper.

Chapter 3

A weekend in early spring, the first time that Theodore actually noticed the weather brightening (it had been a long, damp, dark, a typically Wessex winter). The sun was braving a brief appearance and causing warmth and goodwill. He set out on a journey using his season ticket to cover part of the journey to the Wessex coast. Here, he sourced a second-hand mobile telephone with a pay as you go subscriber identity module (SIM) card from a seedy shop at a seaside resort some twenty miles away from his home. This telephone also had the ability to play audio in mp3 format (sadly, he knew that the extension came from the Moving Pictures Expert Group). Also in the store was a head with no features, normally used for displaying wigs, or more appositely headsets. This went into the bag with the phone. He had to pay a little bit more because the head was not an expanded polystyrene model; it was wooden based and covered with material, so more likely for wig-making, then. He left the shop and made a point of avoiding a greasy spoon cafe, where he would normally have treated himself to a fry-up, being a full English breakfast, sausages, eggs, bacon, and mushrooms, all fried in the same grease. This came with a mug of tea and cost only £3.50, which at 0.1 p a calorie was a real cholesterol bargain. Instead, he picked up a couple of oranges for 50 p (nearly 0.5 p a calorie!) at a nearby greengrocers; the sun peeped from behind a cloud as if in disbelief. On his way back to the bus stop, he purchased some cheap business cards via a machine in the local railway station that produced a batch for £5. After spending some ten or so minutes selecting a template, tinkering with the design layout, and double-checking that the number on the card matched his mobile phone number (despite the odd sigh from an impatient person behind him, why anyone was in such a desperate hurry to get some business cards was unknown), not adding any other contact details, he paid and printed the cards, which read as follows:

Kevin Sedgley-Ahern,
Freelance Management Consultant,
Call or text me on 07700900743

Theodore had got the name and quite a bit of supporting detail from a social networking site. It surprised him just how people would share their private lives and personal details with all and sundry, quite openly. He even thought he could get a copy of Kevin's signature if he ordered Kevin's company's accounts, but that would have cost money and been one more diversion on his road to illegality. He hoped that Kevin Sedgley-Ahern would have suitable alibi if he was interviewed; his concern for Kevin was to lessen in due course. He boarded the bus that was dormant at the terminus and, after a quick scowl at a shopper who had occupied the adjoining seat with a carrier bag full of shopping, struggled past with his own bag of shopping and selected his favourite seat by the emergency exit, where he dumped his bag on the adjacent seat. Shoving his purchases to one side, he delved into the bag, rummaged around for a second or two, pulled out an orange, dug his thumb into it, and removed the peel, leaving it in a continuous strand, which he placed in one of the multitude of pockets in his shorts, possibly to be forgotten until the shorts were next laundered. The bus driver started the engine and engaged a gear, causing the bus to jolt against the brakes; it then proceeded to lurch and yaw him homewards, reminiscent of a sailing ship on high seas. The journey that would take nearly two hours because of the randomly scattered Wessex villages, some picturesque, others not so, that dotted this part of this route. Things were moving apace, well, somewhat anyway.

Theodore had either in his possession, or on order, the components he thought necessary. However, he needed a plan to bind the project together; he sought the comfort of a schedule or procedure to support it. He drew up a checklist on his computer, comprising tasks, dates and times, status, etc. Once he completed his column headings and input as much data as he knew at present, he copied the content of the document to the clipboard and ran an encryption program he'd written a while ago, before pasting the encrypted text back into the document. He also created a batch job to delete it, along with his Internet browsing history, cookies, and any other marketing intrusions that were deposited, nearly always without consent. In addition, the batch job would kick off a little program to overwrite the free space on the computer with randomly generated numbers. This job would run at start-up if the date on the computer exceeded his 'go live' date and would be hidden among the multiple other services at system boot. He didn't want the checklist to fall into anyone else's hand; although he would store the pertinent telephone numbers on his second-hand mobile phone, he felt that were his laptop to be seized, there may be enough circumstantial evidence to support a case against him, assuming the Wessex constabulary had adequate digital forensic capability. He tested the job several times before declaring himself satisfied. As long as he remembered to copy, encrypt, paste, and delete the plain text version, every time he amended the project documentation, he didn't think he would the evidence was easily retrievable, whether he would keep his peace under stress interview techniques, would be another matter.

It probably wouldn't surprise you that it took a little while before Theodore realised his current limited wardrobe didn't contain the array of shirts, suits, and ties of a management consultant. He preferred comfortable trousers, a blazer in spring and summer, for winter precipitation, a khaki gabardine raincoat that kinder members of staff at the laboratory called his 'Columbo' coat, the less kind, his 'flasher mac'. His 'all rounder' coat of choice was his anorak. You need to understand that this was Theodore dressing for work; his casual attire comprised long shorts with many pockets, cheap 'T' shirts or sweatshirts, and white socks with sandals, but since sandals had increased in popularity and consequently price, they had been replaced by cheap training shoes (or daps, in the local parlance). He decided to brave another grey damp Saturday (although hinted at, spring had not yet fully sprung) to see what was available in the High Street for his fuller figure. 'No time like the present,' he thought, and before he set out, he decided to browse what was available online; Well, the weather was miserable, and online shopping meant you didn't have to brush shoulders with the hoi polloi. The top result thrown up from the search engine was a 'Tailor for the Discerning Gentleman, jackets from £985'. Theodore had paid £50 for his summer blazer, and he thought *that* was pricey enough, especially for watching a cricket match. He surfed on and found a popular High Street name that was selling suits from £100 through to £300 but was astounded to see that the waist size stopped at 38 inches. He thought he'd never fasten the buttons; and if he did, it would not be comfortable. To be honest, all the models looked like skinny teenagers, so it wasn't the image he was seeking. He clicked on another selection; this was a site based in the United States, where you could choose from sixty-five fabrics, assorted linings, cut and style, pockets, pleats, price, and delivery options. Totally confused, Theodore closed the browser, took off his cheap reading glasses, shut his computer down, and set out for the charity shop. For occasional items of clothing, a charity shop is always worth consideration. Looking up at the sky, he decided that his anorak would suffice in case a surprise spring shower fell, albeit from nowhere. Two hours later and £20 lighter, a seriously shaken Theodore returned with a suit which wasn't exactly the height of fashion and might require a belt or braces but looked like it would fit the image that he wanted to portray (whether someone with a reasonable dress sense would agree was a moot point and certainly not a high-flying management consultant).

Two hours exceeded Theodore's estimate for the elapsed time by a considerable margin. This was due to being waylaid in a charity shop that provided some funding for cancer care. He was innocently flicking the suits from side to side, looking for the nearest fit, and was causing the hangers to click-clack together, when he was approached by an assistant, obviously attracted by the noise like some cicada. She was approximately Theodore's age and also had approximately applied her lipstick. She sidled close to Theodore, very close, and sought to provide advice on each suit or jacket that Theodore moved, more ill at ease than when he had first started browsing.

'Now there's a good choice for a gentleman of your stature and only £10, a real bargain, considering the material.'

This was said as she reached across him, and a heavy left breast, with a staff name tag attached that spelled 'Pat' (Theodore trusted that this was her name and not an invitation), was pressed against Theodore's right elbow. He turned towards her and tried to look dismissively into her open, frank-looking eyes made up in the startled 1960s and 1970s look, the mascara of which gave the impression of a brace of crows flying full tilt directly into the cliffs of Dover (it's hard to not steal one of Clive James's metaphors, even if you word it slightly differently). Theodore was bossily manoeuvred into a changing room to try the suit jacket on; Pat, the assistant, followed close behind and fussed over his anorak. He held his palm up towards her and drew the curtain huffily closed. After a slight pause, Pat whipped the curtain aside and, after invading his privacy, assisted him by adjusting the lapels and taking the opportunity to be uncomfortably close to him.

'There, I told 'ee that would fit a gentleman. Now, let's see about the trousers.'

After noisily swallowing his rising panic, Theodore said that he only needed the jacket and that he must go, but he would take this jacket if it would be bagged for him. Pat brushed his ruse imperiously aside and stood facing him with a slight frown, legs akimbo, and fists on hips. The scarlet, slightly ragged slash, masquerading as her lips, indicated that she would tolerate no debate.

'I thought you were looking for a suit. Surely you should at least try the trousers? And the price clearly indicated it was a suit. You just stay there, and I'll be back in a jiffy.'

To Theodore's horror, she had found a tape measure and returned to the cubicle; putting her head to one side and her ear against his chest, she whipped the tape measure around his waist. Adding to his concern, he felt a stirring in his underpants as his nether region started to stiffen. Theodore closed his eyes and recited in his mind the stages of growth of various calliphoridae to try and control his reactions, however, as he imagined the squirming and wriggling of the larvae, it made things worse. Anyway, this mantra was cut short by Pat crouching down and running her hand along the inside of his thigh and measuring his inside leg. Theodore gave a mouse-like squeak. She took the measurement three times, each time touching the underside of his scrotum and slightly lifting it and the contents, with the back of her hand. He uttered a further squeak of indignation, fear, and, paradoxically, impotence. The tension was interrupted when a voice penetrated the closet.

'Cooee, shop!'

There was a little old lady holding a book and waiting at the till to pay for it. Pat peered round the edge of the cubicle and told the little old lady she'd be out in a jiffy. Theodore thought, 'Thank you, God!' and then wondered what exactly a 'jiffy' was because Pat certainly had affection for the term. A perverse thought in his head suggested that maybe a jiffy was another name for the outfit that ladies called a 'teddy'. He remembered such an item when pawing and poring over his mother's catalogue. He created a mental film trailer that showed Pat pulling on such an item, tucking in the excess flesh as if stuffing a pale, pink chicken, and then appearing in it with a flourish and with one arm extended above her head coquettishly with the wrist cocked down. It was this distraction that led to an escalation of the whole issue. Pat looked like she was going to leave the cubicle that caused Theodore to step forward with intent on escaping. Unfortunately, Pat stopped dead, causing him to bump against her rump, his swelling making contact with the swelling of her considerable rear end. She also stiffened with a slight gasp, and, reaching behind her, cupped him neatly with her right hand and lightly squeezed. 'Hmmmpf,' grunted Theodore with his eyes started out of his head. Pat left the cubicle and flicked the curtain shut behind her as if she was locking Theodore in his cell.

Theodore stayed in the cubicle long enough to extract the £20 note from his wallet count to ten and, flinging the curtain aside with a swish, made an ungainly leap into the main area like a gawky matador, with two left feet. The little old lady gasped and nearly fainted. Pat merely raised an eyebrow. Theodore galloped towards the exit. He came close to slapping his own buttock as if geeing up a horse, stopping very briefly to place the £20 next to the till with his right hand, his left grasping the scrunched-up suit trousers. When he was safely at the exit, he turned and said, 'This will do nicely. The rest can be a donation.' (There was no comment from his parsimonious internal pal.)

With a sigh of relief, he also left and abandoned his anorak to charity. Fortunately, all his important items such as keys were in the pockets of his knee-length shorts. He ran several knock-kneed steps and turned round, and realising he was not being followed, he slowed to a stroll.

'Well, what was he up to?' said the little old lady, fortunately not the LOL that Theodore assisted occasionally on a Saturday.

'Hmm, I'd guess about seven inches,' replied Pat, but under her breath.

'Well, I never!' added the old lady.

'Neither did I, but I'll keep an eye on 'ee,' replied Pat, this time not sotto voce. The little old lady picked up the book she wanted to buy, *Naked Lunch* by William S Burroughs, paid Pat, and put it in her bag.

'Oh, I do like that cheeky cockney chef, Jamie Oliver.' As she turned towards the exit, she was certainly in for a surprise when she started that bedtime read.

Once at home, a relieved, but also not relieved Theodore stood in front of the mirror and shrugged his shoulders. Even with *his* waist, the trousers were too loose, and if Theodore jumped up and down, they would end up forming a pool, well, more of a lake considering the material involved, around his ankles. He was sure the suit trousers were marked up as being the same size as the last pair of work trousers he'd bought. It would not do to close a meeting after agreeing the purchase of the headsets with his trousers at his feet like a stage comedy farce. A voice in his head said, 'Take them to Pat. I'm sure she'd take them in for you.' Theodore forced the voice from his head and again went looking for his mother's sewing box. It was about half an hour later with the odd puncture wound in his forefinger, as a tailor Theodore wouldn't have lasted long in Saville Row. He stood in front of the mirror, and despite much jumping and contorting, the trousers stayed around his waist. His elementary sewing skills meant the repair wouldn't last long, but he never intended to keep the suit, and he did intend that it would find itself in a charity shop (but definitely a different one) as soon as he had collected the headsets.

The other voice in his head came to life, teasing him like a schoolboy in the playground.

'There is a stirring down below,
There is a stirring down below,
There is a stirring down below,
Down below, in your pants.'

He wouldn't want to encounter Pat again. What had made her decide to come on to him? Was it caveman mentality, from a female point of view? Did she use the charity shop as her lair to leap on unsuspecting middle-aged men, like a funnel web spider? What would have happened if he hadn't made an escape? Too many unanswerable questions because he didn't intend to pursue this train of thought, let alone any further action. Charity shops were to be approached circumspectly. Despite his discomfort at being waylaid and his unanswered self-questioning, it was as he took off the suit and stripped down to his Y-fronts he pondered the fact that he *had* been sexually aroused in the charity shop and also there was a tingle of excitement at being cupped by Pat. Theodore, despite being in his sixth decade, had not had such an experience, commonly called the 'cough treatment' since he had started secondary school. He recalled being a link in a chain of skinny boys queued outside a room, beyond whose door were two middle-aged ladies in nurse's uniform holding court. He was also unmoved by the fact that the boys were clad only in vest, underpants, socks, and shoes (some with the laces done up correctly and others not so); the boy in front was weeping with fear at having to drop his pants in front of a member of the opposite sex who wasn't his mum; he would probably be reluctant in front of his mum too. Some cruel, older lads had been taunting the boys about having a large needle being stuck 'in yer bum, or even worser, it depends dunnit' and to 'watch out for them 'ooks and spikes'. Obviously, these boys were not taking English Language and were shepherded away by a form master. Despite being a good grammar school, although not exempt from enrolling quite a few less-gifted, and this being the early 1970s, Theodore was amazed at the number of boys who wore vests and Y-fronts that were holed; they were clean, but definitely holed, whereas his mother was constantly checking his underwear for faults. Although schoolboys can quite often be cruel, for some reason, there was no teasing because someone's pants had extra holes in them. They shuffled serially forward, occasionally peering round the ear or over the shoulder of the boy in front to discern what may happen to them, with apprehension on the level of a batch of Christians awaiting a one-off wrestling match, no holds barred, against King Leo and his pride (Lions seven, Christians nil; Christians in heaven, lions ill). One by one, they disappeared behind the oak door. No one noticed, nor did the survivors announce their re-emergence from a side door to pick up shirt, short trousers, tie, and blazer. Theodore couldn't remember stripping off down to his underwear, but obviously that had happened because the image of boys queuing in vest and pants was so vivid.

After the ordeal, the boys bonded together like a band of brothers back in the form room.

'It was OK until she told me to drop my kacks and then lifted me cock wiv a lollypop stick and *then* she put her cold hands on me pills an' told me to cough. Cough? I couldn't even breave!'

'Yeah, that was the worse bit, but at least 'er 'ands weren't cold.'

'Garn, she probably warmed 'em 'specially for you, ha!'

The nurses had learned the valuable lesson of warm hands when one of them having run her hands under the cold water tap (there was rarely hot water in the school, except during a *cold* winter) and applied them to a child's scrotum. Before she could utter the word 'cough', the poor boy started to piddle, first in a dribble but gaining force, although not achieving a sufficient jet to catch the nurse. She rose nimbly for a matronly woman and took an aghast step back. After the boy had been comforted and led away, the two had argued whether it was the running of the tap or the temperature of her hands that had caused the reaction.

Back in the classroom all those years ago, it seemed like each boy had his own experience to share.

'I couldn't help it,' wailed Trott (L), 'when she lifted my willy. I was so scared. I farted.'

'Ha ha, maybe she thought it was yer fart lever.'

Chacksfield, although a relatively small and quiet pupil normally, was also drawn out of his shell when he added somewhat to the surprise of the others.

'Yeah, my dad had a fart lever. Only it was his little finger. He'd get us to pull it, and then he'd let one go. It was horrible.'

The conversation paused as all present made different vocal impressions of various categories of flatulence. Some used their lips and tongues, and others cupped a hand under an armpit and flapped the arm up and down. Purcell caused all to turn round a stare at him when, at a timely lull in the raspberries being blown, he proffered, 'Well, I was worried in case mine started to stick up.' He mused, 'Yeah, my mum said if I saw anything really rude, I'd turn to stone—I thought I'd started!'

There was a silence as all digested this confession; being at the age they were, certain physiological changes were starting, and it had not been explained to them why, apart from yarns spread by boys with older brothers or, more worryingly, older sisters. Young boys seldom pause in thought for long.

'Pervo, Purcell, you must be an OMO, ha ha.' It ought to be explained that Persil and OMO were brands of often-advertised washing powder and that colour televisions were becoming prevalent, adding power to the advertiser's sorcery. An OMO was an abbreviation for a homosexual and popular phrase among schoolboys, not known for consideration to other people's feelings. Calling someone an OMO or even a MO was tantamount to a challenge to prove one's masculinity. This school was a state grammar school and *not* a public school.

'Shut it, Phart.' This was shouted at Phillip Hart, and there ensued a schoolboy-type scrap that involved trying to get each other into a headlock. Purcell and Hart wrestled, bumped, and scuffed their uniforms against desks until interrupted by a master who ordered them both to wait under the clock. Waiting 'under the clock' was an expression apparently peculiar to this school; it was because the clock in question, funded by the school's old boys association, was installed high on a wall opposite the head master's office. Under the clock was a bench where the transgressors sat and awaited the head master's appearance. The weary-looking head master would eventually emerge and inquire what offence the boys had committed. His punishment varied and was often suggested to the transgressor to confirm suitability before being dealt.

Hart and Purcell swivelled on the bench and peered out of the window to the front of the school, above which, there was a stained glass pane in commemoration of a fighter pilot from the Second World War. Despite the dirt and dust obscuring the clarity of the glass, they could both identify Wolfie loping round the block, like a home-counties gazelle. The boy Wolfe, D, was born to run, not as a sprinter, nor a track runner, but as a cross-country runner; the cold, damp, mud, and rough terrain were his domain. No Kenyan would match this boy's tolerance of the English winter with the speed that his mighty legs (for a twelve-year-old) generated. 'Run, Wolfie, run,' they muttered under their breath, quite a few years before the *Forrest Gump* movie was released. The former antagonists were now comrades again after their sparring match. They turned back and sagged on the bench with their shoulders hunched in resignation, facing the office and awaiting their fate. Occasionally, just being made to wait under the clock was deemed sufficient as waiting for an unknown punishment was recognised as often *more* uncomfortable than the subsequent event. As anyone who waits in the dentist's chair will know that sometimes, visit is not always wracked with pain. After all, this was not the Victorian or Edwardian Era, where pupils may have been thrashed with a belt or a cane or lashed to heating systems. Hart and Purcell, being born in the 1960s did not experience anything of the sort. They were summarily lectured and dismissed after a brief caution against physical violence on the premises: 'The rugby pitch or the boxing ring was the place to vent one's aggression.' In addition, the lecture comprised the usual moral about the grain of sand that sinks the battleship, which was a favourite analogy of Joe, the headmaster. The boys, despite being considerably chastened, realised that this cloud has a silver lining and that they could miss a mathematics lesson from Speedy Taylor and get an early lunch of smashed monkey (mutton stew, in an orange or red gravy) before football in the inner quadrangle. Sometimes, things work out for the better, if you're a lucky schoolboy.

A grim Theodore had watched the whole prelude, the main event, and the finale where the two combatants were sent under the clock, disappearing down the corridor as silence descended on the form room. He remembered, as usual, being sat on the periphery and wondered what fool said that 'school days were the happiest days of your life' and whether he or she still sported rose-tinted spectacles and *which* school they attended that fostered such nostalgia. Theodore could distinctly recall from his school days the reluctance to use any of the dozen or so 'water closets' that were housed in a dilapidated hut. This 'building' was the haunt of the rougher boys who shared a cheap brand of cigarette and intimidated anyone who encroached on their 'manor'. Also, the closets had a door that was either not present at all or would not shut sufficiently to offer any privacy. The WCs in this block were only ever used for their intended function in the direst of situations. Theodore also remembered how their lack of use pleased the caretaker of the school as it certainly meant a few less tasks that he would have to perform. The caretaker was a miserable and lazy individual, whose mouth sported a sneer and a perpetual roll-up cigarette dangling from it, like an obscene growth (whatever persuaded him that caretaker at a school would be an ideal career choice is hard to fathom). He was easily driven to nastiness to both the boys and young men preparing for university, by the merest of perceived trespasses. He only deferred in typical lickspittle manner, strangely to the deputy headmaster rather than the headmaster. Often to the deputy head, he would even touch the peak of his flat cap. To others, his stock line of address that required no response, nor would tolerate any, was unvaried in wording or tone: 'Get orff the bleedin' premises!' The end of the summer-term show, which was put on by the dramatic society, invariably included a link between sketches or acts consisting of one of the fourth or fifth formers, dressed in flat cap and beige overalls, pushing a broom steadily across the stage. He would stop at the centre of the stage and notice with surprise that there was an audience, and, tilting his head back to show the upper part of his face, after slowly raising his arm, he would then issue the order, 'Get orff the bleedin' premises!', resulting in the uproar of pupils, mild amusement of staff, and total bemusement of any attending parents or guests. The caretaker had departed to his flat long ago and never bothered with events outside his contracted hours; it was possible that he never even knew he was being satirised.

An unlucky pupil of a keen young master was sent to inform the caretaker of a light or switch malfunction. He approached the caretaker's lair and stumbled into the room with the caretaker and a maintenance crony indulging in one of their many tea breaks. The boy peered through the fog from the cigarette smoke and caught the teapot in mid pour, and before he could announce his errand, the crony told, 'Whadda you want? Eff Off,' his thumb indicating exit. The caretaker merely sneered, causing the cigarette to droop at an even more precarious angle. The boy quietly backed from the room and shut the door with a barely audible snick.

With the door safely closed, he stuck two fingers up at the sign. A master strode by, gown fluttering, caught the boy in mid gesture and, apparently agreeing with the sentiment, wafted on to his next class without issuing any punishment. The boy related this story in the inner quadrangle to Theodore and took some time doing so. Theodore even now couldn't recall the boy's real name but to his shame could instantly recall his nickname of 'Wingnut', which was on account of his rather large ears that stuck out at right angles to his head. Theodore wondered if Wingnut had bothered with an operation to have his ears pinned back or whether the nickname was carried into later life. Wingnut announced in a matter-of-fact manner that he and an accomplice-cum-lookout intended to *get* the caretaker and his sidekick. Why he took Theodore into his confidence was unknown, possibly because Theodore was the only boy in his peer group who wasn't scuffing around after one of the many plastic balls pinballing across the rough asphalt. This plastic ball was of a special type that wouldn't retain sufficient kinetic energy to smash a window despite being healthily kicked or smote with a cricket bat. It was pushed through as a compulsory replacement to other types of ball (typically a tennis ball) by the caretaker, the predominant motive being the amount of maintenance it would save him. It didn't stop him entirely from having to replace a smashed pane because the ever-enthusiastic Phart, while endeavouring to hook a wide bouncing ball, let go of the bat at the wrong moment, causing it to sail into room C1 via a shut window. The bat was confiscated. It was a couple of weeks later that Theodore noticed the caretaker supervising his maintenance crony in the installation of a brand new mortise lock on the door to his office. A mortise lock is not susceptible to an accurately inserted steel rule, or more precisely, a steel rule of the sort readily available in the school's metalwork shop. Theodore, although a grim boy, didn't lack powers of deduction. He cornered Wingnut and asked him what he had done to provoke the caretaker into performing the only bit of maintenance Theodore had ever witnessed. 'Peed in his teapot'—then after a short pause—'an' his kettle' was the succinct reply. Wingnut wandered off muttering about wishing the caretaker had left his sandwiches about. Theodore blanched at what this young rogue would have done, had the caretaker's lunch been to hand.

Chapter 4

Theodore hadn't had a properly active sexual life; his interest in sex and his testosterone level were both apparently low. Living alone with his mother during and after puberty and, in addition, going to a single sex school provided little opportunity for curiosity or even experimentation. Certainly having to expose his genitals to middle-aged nurses wasn't going to kick-start matters. Always wanting to be a scientist, he viewed sex as one of the means of acquiring children (and the only means of creating them). The fact that sex could be enjoyable was the incitement to create, not a means in itself. This was where a devout scientist and a devout Roman Catholic would come close to agreeing. However, to contradict that, whilst a teenager, he'd also discovered masturbation, and being a scientist rather than a Roman Catholic, was not overly bothered by any guilt. He had already put some of his semen on to a slide and viewed the 'wrigglers' through a microscope. He had various stimuli that he would use as part of the ritual such as the catalogue which his mother used for occasional browsing and mail-order shopping being first choice; some of the pages featuring ladies underwear and lingerie were particularly creased, particularly pictures where the panties clearly showed a dark triangle nestled beneath the lace. However, the horror when his mother caught him 'in flagrante delicto' put a halt to this practice. She muttered, 'I *wondered* where that had disappeared to', as she whisked the catalogue away, his swift reaction being to turn on his side quickly away from the door and pretend to be taking a nap (his mother was not fooled). Although he had managed to close it, it still looked 'book-marked' where the pages of interest lay. She didn't help matters, a mere couple of weeks later because having recently read Stephen King's book *Dead Zone, she* showed the chapter in the book about acquiring a sexual disease and explaining that it felt like having a clothes peg attached to the end of your (well, you know). Theodore's mother had a sound sense of humour and shared this with him as a means of trying to forge a bond between herself and her only sullen child's adolescent phase. She would never have attached a clothes peg to her son's manhood, but her humour was lost on a seriously grim Theodore. He just didn't appreciate subtlety and would never have chosen to read one of Stephen King's novels (who had never been known to write about cricket). However, the sharing of the paragraph had a profound effect on Theodore, causing him to cease the practice (unknown to his mother, she simply thought he'd become more discreet). His mother would have also been horrified to learn that he had actually tried attaching the clothes peg and had experienced the excruciating pain it entailed. Theodore would never forget doing so and never remember why he did; he would never, ever forget that when he looked down at his throbbing organ, he was quite surprised that it wasn't red and pulsing as if in a *Tom and Jerry* cartoon.

Theodore's mother, having done well at every examination she had taken at school, until having to leave, had been one of the early recruits of Female International (FI Group). This organisation existed prior to, but blossomed with, the expansion of home computing and the modem. The company realised that you didn't have to be in an office to write computer programs and that you could be sent a specification and have it converted into code that was sent back to be translated into punched card. The pay being determined by the lines of code completed, magnanimously, the company also treated comment lines as eligible for payment, the rationale being the better the commentary, the easier to maintain the program, rather than rewarding extra waffle. This role was perfect for educated women, who had the requirement to work coupled with the need to be available for their offspring. It was pretty good for the company too as there was no need to provide accommodation, heating, pensions, etc. for their employees. Theodore's mother had been a classics student, and her fondness for the old languages seemed to pave the way naturally into the logic of COBOL, ALGOL, FORTRAN, and their ilk. Theodore had watched his mother fill out the forms; she put lines through the numerics zero and five to ensure they weren't confused with the characters 'O' and 'S', and a little triangle denoted where a space was required. She had also realised that a lot of programs tended to be bracketed within similar boundaries. She named these procedures as CRUD (Create, Read, Update and Delete) and started using reusable routines that meant that lots of repetitive coding could be saved. The company was delighted and arranged for the compilation of common routines to be written by Theodore's mother to be catalogued in order that they could be loaded by other programmers' code. She had demanded an increase in rate because of this and the fact that now her specifications were delivered by courier and was surprised when the company (note the change as the original altruistic motive had been replaced by shareholders, accountants, and a hefty management layer) readily acceded. This meant that after the departure of Theodore's feckless father and with him any financial support he provided, the bills and mortgage were met with a little to spare by Theodore's mother, not enough to encourage profligacy, but enough to exceed the modest budget. It also meant that Theodore's mother could add to her stock of books, which was increased by careful monitoring of second-hand bookstores and book sales for charity.

Theodore's father departed as Theodore was leaving for secondary school. Although they had no real issues between them, they hadn't been very close. His father was a happy-go-lucky, bohemian type of man with long curly hair, dark brown eyes, and an earring worn as if he were a gypsy. He was often given to go walkabout, and his easy-going attitude probably attracted Theodore's mother to him. He called his only son (in wedlock) 'the German' for his stern countenance and apparent lack of humour; his nickname for Theodore's mother was 'half an ounce of Old Holborn', and it took Theodore an awful long time to decipher that one (he was quite embarrassed once he realised). It was this penchant for nicknaming that Theodore possibly got from his father, or more likely from school, where the pupils would often introduce words peculiar to that school. Theodore never found out what his father did for a living. He never asked, and his father never volunteered. As mentioned, Theodore's father departed early September, before apprising Theodore of the 'cough treatment'. He also hadn't tried the 'pull my little finger trick' on him for about a year or so. He set out with his battered acoustic guitar and harmonica whistling Canned Heat's 'On the Road Again' through his teeth, possibly for some Southern Californian free love commune. No one knew the reason for his departure, although both Theodore and his mother speculated. Theodore's mother was distraught, but unsurprised. She had been abandoned at twenty-eight by a thirty-year-old teenager but wasn't to marry again. She had a few dates, but nothing was serious nor was allowed to become so, partly because of the look of disapproval from a scowling Theodore at any male visitors. It was years later before she started speaking about Theodore's father as feckless (not an ounce of feck in him, then feck, feck, feckity, feck), sometimes this litany ended in tears and sometimes a sigh. Theodore swore that no one would call him feckless.

Chapter 5

Theodore didn't bother owning a car, and even though he had a current licence to drive, he hadn't operated a motor vehicle by himself for twenty years and was reluctant to sit behind the wheel again. This gave him a bit of a problem if he were to pose as a management consultant. Who'd ever heard of a management consultant who didn't drive his own German-built 'macht wagen' and could recite all the available optional extras for each model from memory? He chose the pretence of his own vehicle being off the road at short notice and decided that a private hire company would be engaged, one that operated with more upmarket vehicles, but *not* a chauffeur service with a Rolls Royce, which would be far too ostentatious and may involve another party, thus increasing the possibility of being traced *and* adding to a budget that was starting to burgeon. There again, he would use the same false name and invent a reason why his normal vehicle would be off the road, but where to get picked up and dropped off? He wouldn't want to use his home address and certainly not his place of work. Yet more complications that would require plausible explanations! In addition, credit cards were required if you needed to transact online, and these would always leave an audit trail. Theodore's risks listed against his project plan increased, causing an incipient headache. He decided that he was probably inventing more problems than would happen in normal circumstances, and maybe, there wasn't an army of police officers waiting for him to transgress, so he simply selected a private hire company on line and arranged everything via email, including agreement to settle in cash. After he had returned home, the headache disappeared. It seems like cash still maintains its attraction. Theodore reminded himself not to be overgenerous or too miserly in case he would be easily recalled (though grumpiness was the most memorable thing about Theodore's character). He didn't want to try a disguise, like dying his hair. He was sure if he dyed his hair, he would look like a clown because quite rightly, it would look ridiculous and the sly comments on his return to work ('fancy a cocoa, CoCo? Ha, ha') would require him to invent a story. He was not a good story teller. Explaining himself to others made Theodore irritable and even more sullen. He decided to wash his hair and brush it straight back and realised that he could just about make a short ponytail at the back. He could revert to his normal look for work without comment.

The private hire driver turned up on time in a large Mercedes at the rendezvous. Theodore had simply chosen to sit in a window seat in the cafe on the High Street, sipping tea. When he noticed the Mercedes halt, he put down his tea cup, left the cafe, crossed the road, confirmed with the driver that he was the customer, opened one of the rear doors, sat down, and fastened his safety belt. After a cursory glance in the rear-view mirror at Theodore and another in the door mirror looking for a gap in the traffic, the driver glided the Mercedes silently away from the kerb.

'Hatch End, sir, wasn't it?'

'Yes, please, the meeting should only take an hour, and if you would meet me at the gates again, that would be kind.'

Theodore noticed how well the car drove and was tempted to comment but realised that he knew very little about modern cars or even which model this particular Mercedes was. He could envisage the driver rolling out technical details and then saying, 'What do you think of the new Dynarod, Electrolux, and Draper 14.4v?' and Theodore being absolutely flummoxed. There was a time when he was about five or six that his father bought him a pocket car encyclopaedia which had some of the models of all car manufacturers in the world. Theodore devoured the book and carried it wherever he went for almost a year, until he realised he no longer needed to reference it and could identify cars by the rear lights alone (the Ford Cortina Mark 1 had circular rear lights segmented like a pie chart, a bit like an inverted Mercedes badge). Probably the reason Theodore recognised that it was a Mercedes was because of the brand consistency and it was one of the few manufacturers that hadn't gone done the jelly mould school of design. In addition, the Koreans, Malaysians, and Chinese had now added their own designs into the melting pot. Whilst he sat in the rear of the Mercedes, he cast his mind back to his pocket car encyclopaedia and the thought, which he had whilst poring through it, that if he owned a luxury car, he would never be driven. What's the point in owning a flash car if someone else drove it for you? His time travel ended when the car pulled up outside the gates at Hatch End ('How appropriate!' he thought)

'See you in an hour,' he ordered as he pushed the door closed with a satisfying clunk, strolled through the gates, waited until the Mercedes was out of site, and then walked up the road to the electronics store.

A bell chimed as he pushed his way through the door, and a friendly assistant beamed at him and asked if she could help.

'Sedgley-Ahern for Mr Greatrex,' he announced in what he thought was a management-consultant-type way, i.e. not paying too much notice to the minions, while looking around the office as if he were a surveyor assessing the value. He lightly nodded his head with the business card held between his fore and middle finger and pointedly ignored the assistant.

'Certainly, you prig,' thought the assistant, her beam extinguished by his trite manner, but instead sniffed, 'I'll let him know you're here.' She tossed her head back and left the counter to go through to the back office, thinking that a man who conversed like that should have a decent hairstyle, not a pathetic little ponytail.

'Brian, I think I've got a sales weasel for you, or something that's acting like a sales weasel. He's very musteline.'

'Ah, that'll be Kevin Sedgley-Ahern, a bit of a nice chap who's trying to be someone from the eighties, a sort of Del Boy without the charisma. He's here to collect the custom headsets he ordered for a hush-hush project, but I fear he's a bit of a sad case of self-importance. I'll deal with him. Would you collect the parcel from the store and play along? He's paying well and in cash.'

'Yes, of course, Brian.' She turned away the back again. 'Cash? That's unusual! Normally, this is the sort of person who flashes the platinum cards about.'

'True, Shirley, by the way,'

'Yes?'

'Please don't call him a stuck-up wanker or something similar, even if it may be true, and don't comment on the size of his mobile phone or anything. I've heard that one before from you.'

'Yes, boss,' she huffed.

Shirley called Brian 'boss' when she wanted to let him know he'd said something she disagreed with. She hadn't called anyone a wanker for at least a week, nor that their mobile phone suited them as that was as thick as a brick too. Brian sometimes called her Surly Shirley when she huffed and pouted. They had a good working relationship and sparred frequently like a married couple, but without barbed and spitefully spat comments, nor long periods of not speaking.

Shirley returned with the package as the one called Kevin Sedgley-Ahern was counting out the notes in a curious, suspicious, card sharp sort of manner, but far more clumsily. Because Theodore was so miserly, he had little experience of counting significant amounts of bank notes. To boot, he looked guiltily at Shirley as if she'd interrupted something more intimate.

'Looks like you've had a bit of practice at that, Mr Sedgley-Ahern,' she twittered, causing Brian to close his eyes and slowly shake his head. She dropped the package between the two of them and flounced off.

An apologetic Brian shook hands with Theodore and exchanged niceties. When Brian asked if Theodore swung a club, Theodore just looked back blankly but picked up with a promise to 'pick up again, old boy' and maybe 'do lunch'.

Brian returned to the counter shaking his head at a consultant who didn't play golf. He found Shirley smirking. 'Shall I count it out,' she said and then produced an admirable impression of Theodore's gauche-card-dealing manner, with an exaggerated flick of the wrist.

'He shot off a bit quick I thought.' Brian knew better than to retort and left to deposit the cash in the safe. What a pain dealing with cash was! It was for this reason and his poor play-acting, together with his pathetic ponytail that Brian would remember Kevin Sedgley Ahern. In addition, why would he collect in person when postage and packaging were built into the price? He ought to take up golf. That would sort his priorities out!

Theodore strolled down the road and, outside the gates of Hatch End, looked at his watch. 'Oh dear, there is still half an hour before the driver is scheduled to return,' he mused. He considered going to a local 'greasy spoon' cafe, but fearing he might be tempted to go for a full English breakfast (well, he couldn't possibly think of ordering a fresh salad in a 'greasy spoon'), he decided to wait by the road and play the word game he had invented for long, boring journeys to occupy the brain and time void. The game involved deciding on a word and spelling it out using the letters from car registrations; he'd started this when he was about six or seven, after he got bored with recognising all the cars that flashed past and the first word he used was his own name. A car with a 'T' in the registration would cross the first letter off mentally, then spotting a car with an 'H', etc. He added new rules and jargon to the game as it developed through the years and tried to merge it into a cricket type of game, with certain car models scoring one (Ford), two (Vauxhall), three (Austin, Morris), four (Rover, Jaguar), or six (for a Rolls-Royce). A taxi would be an appeal, and if the subsequent car had an 'O', a 'U', or a 'T', you lost a wicket. However, because of the added complexity, this needed paper, pen, and of course a companion, which Theodore rarely had, so it remained on the drawing board in his mind. He hadn't told anyone else about the games, nor had he thought up a name. Probably his father would have played, but he hated being distracted from driving or commenting on the driving of his fellow road users. Such comments were in the form of favoured expressions as 'Come on, you could get a tank through that gap' if a driver was shy about passing a parked car with traffic flowing in the opposite direction, or 'Wassamatter, haven't they got a colour you like?' if someone dallied too long at the traffic lights. The expression 'Garn, I might have guessed, a bloody woman' often resulted in a slap from Theodore's mother. For a good-humoured happy-go-lucky sort of man, Theodore's father grew horns when he grasped a steering wheel, although this is not a unique occurrence in the male of the specie (and sometimes not limited to just the male).

Theodore had completed the words 'Cochlea', 'Tympanum', and 'Stapes' and was looking for the 'S' in Eustachian when the Mercedes cruised to a halt beside him. The driver had noticed Theodore from a distance where he was waiting in a lay-by and was curious about the reason why Theodore's head flicked from side to side, studying each car as it flashed past as if he was watching a tennis match. What does he find so interesting in passing cars? The driver thought that he was definitely a bit strange, still, as long as he pays and didn't do a runner that was fine by him.

'All done, sir?' Theodore slightly jumped as the car cruised silently in front of him with the front passenger window lowered. He opened the rear door and once inside issued praise.

'Yes, thank you, and thank you also for being on time. I finished early but declined to call you as I didn't want to cause any distraction if you were driving your car.'

'Thank you, sir.'

Although there was something very artificial about this punter, Theodore went up in the driver's estimation as possibly a bit of an 'OK hatstand' because of his politeness and consideration (the driver had hands-free mobile installed in the Mercedes, but the driver appreciated Theodore's point). Anyway, this was easier money than picking up the drunks on a Saturday night and trying to remove the smell and other detritus on a Sunday morning.

The return journey completed, Theodore counted out the agreed fee and then placed an additional £20 into the driver's hand, thanking him for his prompt service and promising to contact him again for his services, subject to his own car being available, of course. The driver would not be able to identify Kevin Sedgley-Ahern, apart from the stupid little ponytail.

Theodore watched the Mercedes disappear gracefully into the distance and, shading his eyes against the sun, which seemed to be quite a constant recently and increase in intensity as the summer approached, turned towards his home. Once inside the house, he placed the package down (fifty headsets did not weigh much, and even with the packaging, it wasn't a sizeable item). The LED that signalled a voicemail message had been left was quietly flashing on his telephone station. Theodore felt a cold stab of concern hit the pit of his stomach. This was ominous; he hadn't had a message left on the telephone since he had bought it some time ago. Theodore ripped the elastic band from his ponytail, together with a few wispy hairs, and went off to find the instructions on how to retrieve a voicemail message, being a bit of a 'completer-finisher' (management-speak for a pernickety person or merely meticulous). He kept all instructions and quite often the packaging for his purchases. Theodore followed the 'How to retrieve your voicemails' section and was greeted by a computer-synthesised voice: 'Hello, this is a message from the tax-avoiding, irresponsible lending, ridiculous bonus paying bank, a large percentage of which is owned by the taxpayer (possibly the introduction wasn't quite like that). 'Our systems indicate an unusual pattern of spending has taken place on your account. Please contact your local branch to confirm whether these transactions are according to your wishes. The number for your local branch is . . .' Theodore placed the telephone back on the stand and ran upstairs, where he was copiously sick in the toilet, simultaneously easing his nerves. They couldn't be on to him *that* quickly. He went downstairs and called his bank. Apparently, the transaction analysis engine on the fraud detection system had flagged Theodore's recent cash withdrawals was indicative of losing one's card and being exploited by someone who knew the personal identity number (PIN). This is occasionally perpetrated by the customer who pretends the card has been lost but doesn't report it immediately to the bank, hoping to get some free money. Theodore was curt to the polite customer service expert called Kylie and just said, 'This is correct. I have needed cash on my person recently, but thank you for your concern,' and promptly ended the conversation. Theodore hadn't predicted this complication. He never suspected that the bank would spend money on systems to protect their clients' assets, when it could contribute to executive bonus payments. Given such a trivial issue, and Theodore's reaction to it, he ought really to call it a day. His nature, however, forced him to try and finish anything he started (both parents used to preach this, so it's unsurprising he didn't give up).

Chapter 6

Working later than usual, it was one of his own strange principles that Theodore seldom worked more than his contracted hours, or if he did, he insisted on taking time in lieu, unless, of course, there was some form of crisis. This being a Friday, the laboratory had rapidly emptied, so no one would observe his actions. He carefully selected an egg from the clutch using a very fine paintbrush; he wore a special pair of magnifying glasses, which were of far superior quality and were an awfully lot more expensive than the reading glasses he had bought. Because of the viscous layer that coated the surface of the egg, it would cling to the bristles of a paintbrush, was making it the best (and cheapest) instrument for the purpose, without damaging the egg itself. He placed it on a lint-free, gauze, padded dressing in a small pill box. The pillbox went into a wallet with a cool block in one of the sleeves. The wallet went into his jacket pocket, where wallets normally go. With a thundering heart, Theodore approached security tentatively. He rarely acknowledged and never spoke to the security staff. Some other members were over-familiar with them from Theodore's perspective, so he felt that his anxiety would be obvious and that they would delight in searching him. Security were permitted to search other members of staff with consent, but any member of staff not giving consent would be dismissed for breach of contract, so that sorted the human rights issue succinctly. Well, that's all right then.

'Just a minute, sir.'

Why oh why had he not rehearsed this possibility as well as he'd planned his act for collecting the headsets?

Lovejoy, the security guard, tilted his head back to peer at Theodore from beneath his low-slung peak. He jutted out his jaw in Mussolini style, but for some reason, there was a twinkle in his eye. For the second time since a toddler, Theodore again came close to filling his pants.

'Yes, what is it?' Theodore nervously stuttered as he squeezed his buttocks and looked nervously back towards the staff area.

'Enjoy your weekend!' the guard said with a stoic look.

'Yes, of course, you too!'

Theodore would never hear the stories told in the guard's restroom of how Lovejoy got old grumpy to talk. Neither would Lovejoy have known that the fear in Theodore's eyes was due to the fact that his ruse might be discovered rather than awe at a finely ironed services uniform topped by low-peaked cap, bottomed by highly polished shoes.

On his journey home, Theodore sat on the bus concentrating on his disturbed digestion. He really should have used the toilets at work. This was not made easy as the bus that turned up was an ancient affair (surprise), which rattled and jolted as if the clutch was slipping and alternately sticking and the shockers shot, so every bump reverberated through the aluminium biscuit box that was the passenger cabin. He sat stoically still until he alighted at the bus stop and then walked stiff legged to his front door, where he hurriedly unlocked the door, threw off his jacket, scuttled upstairs, flung himself into the toilet, and, once seated, found that the urgency had departed. He stayed there until he'd eventually eased his bowels, head in his hands, but definitely relieved. What was that security guard playing at? Perhaps he had given something away? This was only the third time in ten years that his bowels had been less regular as clockwork, and the first occurrence was due to a gastrointestinal rebellion, which was incurred after being invited to a fruit juice tasting event that turned out to be a bit more than a tasting and a little more potent than fruit juice. One beverage was a refreshing pear juice which had been fermented and attained an alcohol by volume reading of 7.5 per cent but tasted remarkably sweet and innocent with a slight fizz that resulted in disastrous consequences. After a few glasses, he'd whispered endearments to a female member of staff, confiding how much he missed his mother and dissolving gradually into tears on her shoulder: *I loved my mum and now she's gone.* Having vented a lot of past tension, his mood swung to a more boisterous one when he boasted of the cricket matches he remembered that included events such as Botham's Ashes (Bob Willis played a huge part too) and Brian Johnston's renowned commentaries. His mood swung again when he realised he'd never be able to bowl a maiden over. As the afternoon faded and night drew in, everything became hazy, and Theodore never remembered who had poured him into the taxi or how he had managed to give the taxi driver his address or how he had paid the fare. He spent the whole of the Saturday trying to recover his equilibrium, and his delicate constitution meant that he was unable to stray too far from the toilet. He handed in his resignation letter on the Monday and barely spoke to the staff members of that organisation until he'd served his notice (minus leave due), despite entreaties such as 'C'mon, Ted, it's perfectly human to let your hair down out of the laboratory', but under the breath, 'but that's assuming Ted is human, of course, and he could let that mess on his head could be loosely labelled hair.' Theodore decided that his socialising days were over. Everyone else could go out and have fun, but Theodore's fun would be watching cricket with possibly a cup of tea from a flask if he was watching at a cricket ground or from the teapot if not. He would be content with that.

Theodore changed into more casual attire and went downstairs into his meticulously organised garage-cum-workshop. He vowed that there would never be a car in his garage, even if there were sufficient room. He placed the dummy head on his workbench and positioned it on where an ear should be. He held it steady by using an old inner tube from a bicycle. Using a medium drill, he made a hole approximately where the right ear would have been, about an inch in depth. He pushed some semi-thawed minced meat into the hole and, for realism, daubed a bit of ear wax from a cotton bud on the meat. Theodore opened the package containing the headphones and placed the right arm that held the ear piece into a vice after protecting it from damage by wrapping it with a piece of another bicycle inner tube. Bicycle inner tubes are fantastically versatile clamps that seldom damage the object being clamped. He gently adjusted the vice until it was held and using a piece of tape kept the left earpiece from obstructing access to the right. He left the workshop, locked the door, and went into his lounge, where he started up his computer to see if any cricket was being played on a Friday evening (or whatever time of day) around the world. He found that the West Indies were hosting a one-day tournament, and he watched with pleasure the game, the weather, and the sun sparkling off the ocean, which could be seen when the camera panned out. If ever there was a heaven that would be Theodore's choice, it was there in front of him; even the languid accent of the commentators was transporting. While the cricket was played in the background, Theodore inserted one of his mother's compact discs (Springsteen's Nebraska) and ripped it into mp3 format which could be copied to a flash card and inserted into the second-hand mobile phone or just transferred via a cable. He followed Springsteen with Hendrix, Thin Lizzy, and Pink Floyd. When the ripping had finished, he connected the phone to his laptop via a USB connection and copied the files over. In the break between the innings, he returned to his garage, where he went to the small refrigerator. Taking the pot from the refrigerator and selecting an egg with a fine paintbrush, he teased it into the hole of the earpiece and, peering into it, was satisfied to notice the egg attached to the side, like a small grain of rice. Theodore removed his glasses (the reading glasses, the quality magnifiers stay at work), set the head upright, and placed the headset on to the dummy head. He then plugged the jack into the headphone socket in the mobile phone, selected the mp3 feature, and adjusted the volume until he could hear the hiss. Now, his whole project depended on the hatching, which should occur within a day, nature permitting. He closed the garage door on his experiment and went back to the cricket in the Caribbean sun.

The next day saw Theodore awake early, and after drawing shampoo from his super-saver half gallon container, he took his weekly shower. He towelled himself dry, styled his hair using his fingers to move the hair to cover where his scalp was appearing, shaved with a disposable razor that he'd used several times already, dressed, and went downstairs to the kitchen, where he breakfasted on tea and toast, followed by plain yoghurt to which he added some pieces of orange. After washing the mug and plate, Theodore completed his housekeeping chores with the running of an old vacuum cleaner, bequeathed by his mother, across the tired old carpet, similarly left to him, along with the house. Theodore had customised the vacuum cleaner to make it more efficient, which included designing and manufacturing the paper dust catching bags, so although old, it did an admirable job. Whilst Theodore's miserly nature meant that he seldom replaced furniture or fittings, he wouldn't disgrace his mother's memory by letting the house gather too much dust, nor would he take breakfast until he had made his bed and dumped his discarded clothes into the relevant laundry basket (one for dark colours, the other for light). Actually, his surly, miserly character aside, Theodore would make someone a steady husband.

All housekeeping completed for another week, Theodore went into his workshop and turned on the fluorescent lights. He approached the head, which, although eyeless, seemed to be looking at him, and he turned off the mp3 player feature on the mobile phone and removed the earphones. Nestled in the cavity among the remnants of the meat writhed a larva of Cochliomyia hominivorax; the vibrations or acoustic frequency had expedited the hatching process to less than twelve hours. He momentarily clenched his fist in victory and mentally ticked another box on his project's progress. He had the means of delivering retribution to the inconsiderate; he would present them with a replacement headset, and within one day, they would have their eardrum neatly punctured. (*This should be the point where it ought to occur to him that if the workings of the ear were interfered with, surely, the owner would be inclined to turn the volume up?*) Theodore turned the head and shook the larva on to the workbench where he collected the larva and placed it into the pillbox. The pillbox was taken to the freezer, where the larva would be humanely killed. It may have made a tasty snack for a bird or a fish, but Theodore wanted to make sure this larva did not become a viable fly. As Theodore passed the mirror on his way to the freezer, he caught a glimpse of himself. Was that a slight twist to his mouth that was the beginning of a smile? Was this the start of a smile of a lunatic scientist? He placed the pillbox into the freezer and thought of 'the Mantis' munching on her snack while inside her ear a larva munched its way through its own snack. It was beginning to dawn on Theodore how serious this project was becoming. But how do you persuade the target to adopt a headphone set loaded with a fly's egg? Admittedly, they wouldn't know there was an egg in the ear piece.

Theodore's plan was for the hominivorax egg to be stimulated into hatching by the warmth and vibration and the larva to make its way down the natural path until it was forced to eat its way through the tympanum (eardrum). Once through, he hoped it would be drawn by gravity down the Eustachian tube into the sinus where the need to equalise the pressure loss would stimulate the swallow reaction. The larva would be swallowed by the victim into the stomach where the digestive acids would destroy the evidence. He imagined that if one of the larvae survived and was identified correctly, it wouldn't take the modern-day equivalent of Sherlock Holmes very long to put two and two together and then knock on the facility's door. Guess who would be the prime suspect? He also didn't know the level of discomfort the larva would cause as it punctured the eardrum and made its way down the Eustachian tube. The earache he'd experienced as a child was extremely painful because of the build-up of pus and pressure. Theodore thought the larva should pierce the eardrum without the pressure pain of earache. But would the larva squeeze down the Eustachian tube, or would it climb into the cochlea? How could he test this? Should he issue the headsets after the egg had been in place for five or six hours, or even more? Could he find a way of suspending the hatch, so there would be an amount of control on when the larva emerged? He thought that this would be achievable using the chill control on his refrigerator. He would test this on his return to work; it would take a bit of time and logging of temperature versus hatch speed.

After much Internet browsing, Theodore was about to order an anatomical model of the human ear when he realised that this would leave another clue to piece together Theodore's culpability (on top of that, it cost nearly £100). How could he acquire an anatomical model anonymously? Was he getting paranoid about the trail of evidence? Could he copy the image of the model and, using image processing software, enlarge it sufficiently to make his own model? Would he find another issue that would cause delay to the project? How many eggs should he smuggle out? Theodore was asking more questions to himself during one Saturday at home than he was asked during one *week* at the laboratory. He decided to take a break from the project, started his computer, and donned his reading glasses to surf around the world in search of a cricket fix.

Monday evening return journey home was eventful. The emergency exit seat was occupied by a youth bearing a sleeve of tattoos, his mouth noisily squelching a wad of chewing gum and his dirty, scruffy boots plonked on the seat opposite. The squelching was only occasionally audible between tracks of the noise that issued from the earpieces. It was the sound of guitars and drums being thrashed within an inch of their unfortunate and abused existence. This was an 'A' grade offender. The din emanating from the youth drowned Theodore's exhalations of disapproval from the seat behind. After a short while, a wiry man of a height who wouldn't qualify for the Coldstream Guards and an age between fifty and seventy stood up and approached the lounging youth who plucked an earpiece, with a sneer and a mimed 'Wot?', in order to hear what this old man was about to say.

'Would you mind turning your music down? Some of us are trying to travel here.'

A pretty reasonable request elicited a response that offended all passengers in earshot with its obscenity, age-related abuse, and a challenge along the lines of 'who would make me, you old fart?' Only Theodore saw the man's eyes light up like two electric blue LEDs. What followed was a flash of violence that rendered the bus silent with shock. Holding the youth back in the seat with his left hand, he drew his right arm back level with his shoulder and landed a punch that travelled about eight inches into the centre of the youth's face. There was a distinct scrunch of the bone in the nose being smashed mixed in together with the splat of flesh on flesh. The man turned, rang the bell, and, without looking back, alighted at the next stop. The youth was frozen in shock and awe; he slumped, sobbing and snuffling in the seat, his face a mess of snot, blood, and tears. At the stop for the hospital, he sought no one's eyes, and all avoided his. He got off, pushing past the nurses and administration staff waiting to board, with his hand covering the mess that was his nose. Some of the fluid was caught, and some was dribbling down his chin. Theodore wondered.

(a) whether the youth would confess at triage that the person who caused his injury was a pensioner and

(b) just who was the wiry man who had been stung into such a response and how much power was behind that punch.

Theodore never recalled seeing the man or the youth again, but he would never forget that incident. He pondered in his head a short summary of the whole event in a script with the punchline delivered, by the electric-blue-eyed pensioner as he turned to exit, in a Churchillian sort of lisp, 'I have nothing to offer you but blood, snot, and tears.'

Chapter 7

The ensuing week yielded one further surprise for Theodore: Sitting in reception was an older version of the student with whom Theodore had studied some thirty years previously. She was an American by birth and still retained an endearing accent. She had certainly changed since university, where she had looked like a coltish young woman like a typically brainy, but non-cheerleader teenager material, as if she were a stereotype for the swotty or bookworm character in a children's cartoon program. At university, it was the first time that Theodore had seen anyone older than seven wearing a full set of braces that made her mouth look like a portcullis. Theodore thought that she was marvellous. The woman who was in reception was somehow taller (she couldn't be, surely?) and classically dressed in a suit, the skirt of which finished mid-patella. Theodore knew that there was a vacancy, but what a coincidence it would be if they were to work together again after all this time and especially after both being disciplined by the head of the college. She hadn't noticed Theodore breeze past her and the security guard, using his security pass to gain access to the inner reaches of the facility. He went to his locker, and after donning his laboratory white coat, he closed the door, turned around, and reminisced. Because of her intensity with him, he would always remember her first name: Natalie.

Theodore remembered how Natalie would sneak up and try to pin him down while he would jump and run around the college laboratory like a shorter but no less awkward version of John Cleese. ('Maybe,' thought Theodore, 'this was his appeal.') They were soulmates in their interest in the more uglier and distasteful of God's creatures. Theodore never plucked up the courage to ask Natalie out for a date to see a picture (or movie) until eventually she asked him, and with linked arms, they walked all of 400 yards to the college's film society showing of *American Graffiti* (to be fair it had been out for some years but was popular viewing). The film confused

Theodore immensely (he'd never seen it, or even a trailer before), but Natalie enjoyed the whole movie to a similar level. To be honest, although the climax of the film was a drag race and a lot of activity revolved around motor vehicles and of course Theodore had no understanding of American youth culture, he thought it was quite a touching finale. He thought his mother would have enjoyed accompanying them (but possibly Natalie may not have appreciated it). They stopped in the students' bar for a drink and a post-mortem of the film, including reciting the funnier lines. Natalie had quite an advantage because she'd managed to see the movie when it was released in America because of her age, with connivance from an older sibling. Theodore was unsure what to drink and plumped for a bourbon. He told Natalie that he should ask for a shot of Old Harpers as one of the youths in the film requested (she was impressed at his memory). Theodore drank the bourbon and followed it with a couple more until he felt quite as sick and disorientated as 'Toad' in the film. Natalie was delighted (she thought he was making it up!). Even when they parted, Theodore made some inane promises that Natalie interpreted as 'chivalrous English'. He didn't kiss her goodbye or anything; he just bumbled off down an alleyway with a wave and a lurch. She was enchanted; he was an arse.

Thirty minutes later saw Theodore making a drunken call to his mother, from a telephone kiosk near the houses of residence.

'Mum, I need a tenner, becorsh. I've just been wiv a girl.'

He couldn't think of anything more to say, so he hung up. Theodore's mother thought she knew her son, but there was a certain amount of trepidation associated with this call. She had hoped he would spread his wings, but more in a romantic sort of way; this sounded like a belly full of beer and a visit to a massage parlour. The university was only 40 miles from where he lived, but such a distance was the equivalent of intercontinental travel to Theodore at that age. Luckily, his mother was more geographically aware. She knew that a friend of her husband occasionally visited the university town and would be happy to drop a small envelope at the porter's lodge for her. This friend also had a long-standing crush on Theodore's mother. She called him that same night, and he turned up like a superhero within an hour. She gave him £20, plus a £5 for petrol, to deliver it to Theodore's halls of residence. To be honest, he would have done the favour for her for nothing; however, he made no trite protestations by trying to press the money back on her. He had maturely accepted the fact that his affection would never be returned, they would never be an item, but this was friendship, and that required certain obligations. He had grown up and decided that if he couldn't be with her, her friendship was next best. Ironically, he wasn't afraid of telling Theodore's father of his affection (being 6 ft 6 in and 18 stone), but he was a man of old-fashioned honour and wouldn't interfere with other people's affairs, no matter how it impinged on his emotions. Even when Theodore's mother became single, their relationship remained platonic. Some of the potential suitors for her were dissuaded from pressing suit or even asking her out if they heard that Peter Mack was her friend.

The porter at the college was a little bit taken aback when Theodore's minder (or so he thought) turned up in a large, dark Jaguar and said he wanted to leave an envelope in Theodore's pigeonhole. What looked like a postage stamp in the minder's hand was an A4 envelope in the porter's. After thanking the minder, the porter thought he would give Theodore a little more consideration than he had done recently. Besides being a massive gentleman, Jaguar owner, and a downright good egg, Peter Mack had a sixth sense for being about when there was trouble brewing for his friends. Peter's presence had dissolved many a difficult situation when Theodore's father had stepped over the line in a bar, a late night event or a restaurant. Peter could persuade someone to turn the volume down on their personal stereo simply by raising one eyebrow. He'd also taken a blow across the legs from a baseball bat when Theodore's father had decided to 'do a runner' from an Italian trattoria; he looked at the owner's son who'd swung the bat and smiled as he took out his wallet to pay. Gino, the restaurant owner, berated his son, pressed Peter's wallet closed, and bade him sit down while he called for coffee, grappa, and ice wrapped in a towel for Peter. They both knew that Theodore's father would turn up and pay next day when his guilt bit him. It was the fun of doing something illicit and being a bit of a rogue that appealed to Theodore's father. He would be at a loss of why Peter Mack had taken a blow on his behalf. Mack would just smile at him.

Theodore sprung awake next morning after dreaming he'd wet himself (he hadn't), but he struggled to the toilet and relieved himself mightily. He then realised that he'd abandoned a female friend (the only one he'd ever known apart from his mother) at night (OK, a university town, not the Bronx) and had no means of apologising or asking if she was still alive and had not been sexually assaulted. Hurriedly throwing on some clothes, he galloped down to the porter's lodge, flapping like a fledgling seagull. On his arrival, the porter who'd been manning the lodge throughout the night and collected the parcel from Mack beckoned him. ('Oh no,' thought Theodore, 'what now?')

He walked up to the porter and collected the envelope and realised what the contents were. How did his mother get the cash to him so quickly?

'You have got some big acquaintances, Master Grouchier.' The porter was aware that Theodore's father wasn't in the picture so to speak and, given the size and demeanour of Peter Mack, suspected that Theodore was the offspring of a Mafioso. The porter devoured crime stories and was quite concerned about criminals being allowed in the hallowed halls. It was of course all right if students left the university to join parliament to then become shadier. It didn't help that Theodore called Peter Mack a friend of the *family*. Immediately, *cosa nostra*, *omerta*, and *sleeping with the fishes* went through the porter's mind, and there was that female student whom the porter had seen close to Master Grouchier with the American accent in the student bar last night while he supped his half pint of 'Bitter and Twisted' (a real ale produced in Scotland). At the university Theodore attended, porters were allowed a free half pint everyday on behalf of the student's union. This was a custom dating back some 100 years when part of the porter's job was to report any student returning to the college after midnight. The student's union got together and agreed this approach as a smarter solution and a reduction in unnecessary waste of everybody's time. The students would deliberately stay out at the pub, inn, hotel, or a party just so they could be back after midnight and indulge in hide and seek with reluctant porters (sometimes called scouts or beagles, depending on the fashion) who thought students were a pain. To top it all, the college tutors didn't really want to hold disciplinary meetings just for staying out late. It was a waste of time that could be spent in producing better-rounded individuals (hah!). The porter would chew the cud with one of his colleagues over his next free half pint and share his half-baked findings.

'Hi, TG, how's it, man?'

Theodore was disturbed from his reminiscences by the facility's computer technician, a cocky undergraduate with the open university battling his way through computer studies and digital forensics, rejoicing in the name of Stephen Stiff. He'd been known to introduce himself to girls with the line, 'I'm Steve Stiff and with you as my companion I'll change my first name to' (pause) for effect 'Always'. Some responded to this corny introduction that he ought to be called 'Bored Stiff' as that's the effect you have on me. He was called Stiffy by most of the laboratory and marketing research employees, with the exception of Theodore, who, of course, called him Stephen. Steve Stiff hated being called by his first name in full and bleated that his mother always called him that when she was vexed at him ('Stephen, look what a mess you've made of the shower, and *why* do you want to dye your hair *that* colour?'). Stephen loved recalling stories about his mother, on whom he obviously doted. He also would relate (quite often) about how his mother always insisted that he wore clean pants before he went to a doctor's appointment. ('Why, Mum? The doctor doesn't inspect the patient's underpants, and I'm sure even if he did, he wouldn't accuse you of being lax in the laundering department.'). The other story he liked to share was about when he insisted on going out to play football with friends in the winter snow, she called after him, 'If you fall over and break your leg, don't come running to me!' All Steve Stiff's friends thought his mum was 'wicked' (meaning really good in pre-teenage speak at that time).

He also wore his white laboratory coat as much as possible, chiefly to hold a set of screw drivers in case he had to replace a disc drive, but his role didn't really require him to do so at all. As with all people who've worked with computers, he had his own jargon. He referred to outdated technology with the same romanticism as a train enthusiast would talk about steam locomotives, like the inventors of the Small Computer System Interface, who wanted the acronym to be pronounced Sexy, but despite their contrivance with the name, it would be forever known as Scuzzy. Theodore also held a similar romanticism in that he reminisced about the days when emergency vehicles made a noise more like 'Uh-oh, Uh-oh', which sounds a lot less serious than the modern shrill shrieks and howling counterpointed with lower pitched wails, followed by the odd stuttering whoop. He remembered once, when very young, watching a television program called *No Hiding Place* where the introductory music sounded dynamic and serious, but the police cars had twee little bells on the front. Who had ever thought that a tinkling *bell* (if heard) would be enough to clear traffic out of the way? Theodore expected that the amount of traffic that a 1950s police car needed to warn wouldn't be of the density of these days.

'What's with the health kick? Is there a lady in the offing?'

'Hello, Stephen, and no, there isn't a lady in the offing as you so endearingly put it. I'm sure 'offing' is not in the Oxford English Dictionary.'

'There's a smart lady in reception. You should have a crack at that.'

'One does not have a crack at a lady.'

'Oh sorry, TG, I meant a pop.'

Theodore rolled his eyes and decided he wouldn't evoke any more inane or sexist comments by responding. Theodore wondered what made a young man with healthy hair change the colour so that it looked like a toupee. Well, at least he hadn't styled it like someone or something had sat on his head with very large bare buttocks and, on standing up, had clenched those mighty buttocks together that left a greasy peak of hair making the wearer look like he was a face in a teardrop. Worse still, who came up with that as an idea for a hairstyle? *and* then once decided that it would be the latest thing in coiffeur, *how* did they convince people that this was all the rage and that this is the way cool people *should* wear their hair? With that thought in his head, Theodore left Steve Stiff to start his day's work.

Theodore was hunched over the workbench with his trusty paintbrush poised when the door to the laboratory opened, and there was Natalie being shown round by the director of the research company.

'I'd like you to meet our chief scientist, Theodore. This is Natalie who is seeking to join the company.'

He had taken off his glasses, but before Theodore could close his dropped jaw, Natalie answered that they'd had the privilege of studying together before, holding out a slender hand. Theodore was struck dumb and just shook hands with shaking right hand while he closed his jaw with a click. He didn't recall peeling off his surgical glove. She turned her steel grey eyes back to the director.

'Madam, if you go around paralysing members of staff, just by looking at them, I'll have to reconsider the offer just made.'

Theodore recovered his composure and spoke in favour of Natalie.

'Natalie is a very good scientist, with a similar interest and dedication as me but with far better qualifications.' He tried not to look too hard at Natalie's figure, especially the knee-length skirt that clung to her hips as if it had been sprayed on. The saliva drained from inside his mouth like a bucket of seawater thrown on a beach when he looked into her steel grey eyes.

'Theodore, that was quite a speech for you and quite a recommendation for you too. Natalie, our terse chief scientist is not overindulgent in compliments.'

Leading Natalie away and closing the door behind them, the director left Theodore at the workbench. He couldn't put his discarded surgical glove back on using his still shaking hands and had trouble positioning his magnifying glasses. He decided it was time for a tea break. Alone in the small canteen, his memory skipped back thirty years.

She bent him backwards until the gas taps were close to his right ear, now she had him at her mercy. She hoisted her white coat and coat above her knees and crawled over him like the determined predator she was.

'I'm like a spider, and you are my prey. I have you in my web, and I shall devour you.'

There was no clothing removed and no overt sexual activity, but the head of college burst into the laboratory and made a quick summary of the scene and said, 'You two, my office in fifteen minutes.'

He then retreated, shutting the door firmly behind him. Fifteen minutes later, they were given a severe dressing down, professionalism, health and safety, messing around in a laboratory, in parentis loco, sent down, et al. Red faced and somewhat shocked, they left the office and never repeated their playful activity in the university. Even after graduation, they were still subdued and didn't speak much at the graduation ball. Thus, it seemed, was Theodore's love life destined.

Steve Stiff breezed in for a coffee and for the second time disturbed his reverie.

'Yo, TG! How's it hanging?'

Steve bashed the vending machine, obtaining a free coffee, whilst subconsciously nodding his head to a tune only he could hear.

Theodore drained his mug of tea and went to the sink to rinse the empty vessel.

'Never mind, Stephen, perhaps you'll possibly mature with age.'

'The boss said you were the epitome of me when he introduced the new chick to you.'

'What, twenty or so years old with a strange hair colour and passing knowledge of the Queen's English?'

'Ha ha, dude, this health kick is doing wonders for your badinage. Next thing, you'll be buying new threads for your trimmer physique!'

Theodore left the canteen after placing his mug on the draining board, went to his locker, grabbed a banana, and peeled it while thinking, 'What is happening to me, having conversations with juniors, not correcting that little oik Stephen, also not insisting that he call me Theodore or Mr Grouchier, and, worst of all, being distracted? What did he mean trimmer physique? This is taking my mind off the project. I must concentrate more.'

Back at his workbench, he forced himself to concentrate on his task with the little creatures in his care. The director walked into to the laboratory and standing close to a now-intense Theodore said, 'You may have to say goodbye to those evil little critters as I'm afraid the funding has been pulled out. I have just taken the phone call immediately after Natalie agreed to take the position. God bless our government for promising to extend overseas aid and within two months performing yet another "U" turn.'

The director wrongly interpreted the worry in Theodore's eyes.

'Don't panic, Theodore. There's plenty of other useful work for you to do We have other projects,' he lied because he didn't have at the moment, but there was an idea germinating. The director patted Theodore gently on the shoulder and turned to leave the laboratory and wondering what sort, or more importantly, how long a contract he should offer his new recruit.

'How long do I have left?'

'I told you there's plenty of work here. That's why I'm recruiting,' he lied again.

'No, I mean before we stop the sterilisation program with hominivorax.'

'Well. There's no reason why you can't wrap up this last batch and get ready to work on something new.'

The director left Theodore with a problem. He had just received an issue to his project, and as issues went, this one was large with a large red light on the top that flashed the word ISSUE. He needed to work out some options. He had also forgotten to spend time testing whether he could control the hatching by using the chiller and monitoring the hatch speed versus temperature. He was no longer in full control (a bit worrying for a completer-finisher).

Chapter 8

The director of the facility was an appositely named Andrew Goode, who'd had the fortune to win the National Lottery. Out of altruistic spirit, he tried to improve the lot of the less fortunate by deed rather than by donation. He left as financial director from an insurance company, after deleting the spreadsheet that monitored the outcome of each lottery result (it was no longer required, anyway), to pursue his vocation and to escape the office politics and back-stabbing. Andrew Goode got promoted to director because he was, so to speak, very good at his job. He bought the establishment, which was an equipped testing facility, from a company that was rather unscrupulous with the manner it treated the animals that it used for the trial of experimental drugs. In its previous guise, its walls had been sprayed and daubed with fake blood many times by animal rights activists, who, in this case, had a pretty valid reason. He got the facility at a bargain price. Being a qualified accountant, he knew there was no goodwill at all that could be included in the deal and was able to drive through to include all equipment. Goode was able to retain the existing security staff and tried to employ the more disadvantaged members of the local community where possible. He'd given over one car park of the grounds as a vegetable garden and recruited a head gardener, who, as well as deciding which plants to cultivate, could employ casual labour—this being anyone who fancied honest toil for cash. The building had not had an ad hoc paint job since. Andrew Goode was not making a lot of money from his venture; his wife had left him as soon as she realised the win was not going to result in a life of luxury on the Costa Dorado. The divorce was prolonged and acrimonious, but Goode came out of it all, if not unscarred, the wounds were not of serious depth, resulting in more lines on his face and additional grey hairs and an earmarked pension. He occasionally thought of his wife and was not bitter even when her affairs were revealed to him, possibly out of spite or jealousy, by a neighbour, not an immediate one, but definitely a nosey one. Goode's spoilt children, both having just left their teens, just acted, well, spoiled. They berated Goode whenever they had chance to speak, in a whine more associated with teenage behaviour. Goode loved his children but did not like them. Losing the funding for the sterilisation was an additional headache; he needed to seek research funding to keep his business turning a profit, and salaries would be draining his reserves, but where was a business with synergy? The marketing research section that arranged opinion polls or just recorded people's scores on an assortment of products was a steady, but a cut-throat business, where the supply would dry up for no apparent reason. He refused to sell the details garnered from interviews to other third parties. If, as a result of prolonged loss of income, he were to choose to do this for money, there'd be a considerable outlay in getting his marketing research literature changed. His marketing research team comprised a balance of disadvantaged members of the community and so-called marketing professionals. It seemed to Goode that the professionals learned more about life from the other team members than they did from their marketing qualifications and experience. He was looking forward to a couple of pints in his local and a heart-to-heart with his old friend Brian Greatrex, who was also a good egg when it came to entrepreneurial activity. As well as enjoying his companionship, he'd pump him for ideas, it may also require a round of golf, which Brian tended to win far more often than not.

While Goode mulled over ideas in his office, Theodore wondered whether to steal a batch of eggs that very afternoon but didn't want to act in haste. Should he just tell Mr Goode that he'd destroyed all the eggs, larvae, and pupae? This would buy him time. He also wondered what was the next project he would work on, given the economic climate. Theodore was surprised at Mr Goode's nonchalance. Just how did his employer make any money? The salary portion of the budget alone must be £500 k per annum, and there were other embedded costs. Theodore didn't really need the money that his salary brought in; unlike Mr Goode, his costs were low, and he had plenty of money saved. Well, he *was* a bit of a skinflint. He had also invested £30 k in premium bonds that gave the odd chunky win as a pleasant surprise. Theodore thought he might ask for a sabbatical, but if the truth be told, with the thought of Natalie being at the laboratory, work had an additional attraction. Had Natalie married? Was she still married? By golly, she was still attractive. His project had acquired another issue. Being unable to concentrate, Theodore left for home early, not acknowledging the cheery au revoir from the security guard or even the 'ciao' from Steve Stiff. Still lost in thought, Theodore mounted the bus and slumped in the nearest available seat. The rear of the bus was fully stocked with vociferous and scruffy school children, who, when they weren't arguing, swearing, or singing, were feverishly typing text messages, probably to each other. Even with the environment and the concerns that he had, the sun pouring through the window and the gentle rolling of the bus had a soporific effect on Theodore; with his head supported by his right hand and the elbow on the windowsill, Theodore dozed off.

The sun sparkled through the hospital ward window that was surprisingly clean, on to his mother's tired and drawn face. She smiled at Theodore, being pleased with (and somewhat surprised by) the flowers that her son had brought in.

'Hello, Son, how are you?'

Theodore's throat was so constricted he couldn't speak and just let the tears course down his face.

The surgeon had removed his mother's womb and the accompanying tumour. He was optimistic about the cancer being contained and not metastasising; he would arrange for chemotherapy to further increase the period of remission.

'I think I've been kicked in the belly by a very large and angry Boxer, who has discovered Napoleon's treachery,' *whispered his mother into the back of Theodore's neck as he whimpered and dampened her prim nightdress (she meant the cart horse from Orwell's novel,* Animal Farm, *that lay open and face down, by her left hand).*

'Come on, stop it now, or you'll get me started.' *They both reached for the box of tissues and after selecting a couple each snuffled into them.*

Theodore hadn't realised his mother was unwell, let alone ravaged by an aggressive and personal tumour. She had hidden the illness well, assuming it was just 'women's trouble'. Menses were not discussed in the Grouchier's household. Both were uncomfortable with advertisements about tampons and sanitary towels, especially the one where the tampon grows to fill an entire glass was horrifying in a B-movie sort of way. Then there were several alternative comedians who had a routine about menstruation, which was also not in the best possible taste—something like I can't go out with you because I'm on my menstrual cycle. It's OK, I've got a Suzuki myself. He was astonished that his mother was nearly taken away from him; she was only forty.

It was ten years later that Theodore's mother was in a return visit to the very same hospital to have a relative of the first tumour removed from her brain, leaving a curved and deep scar on her head. 'Fucking Boxer kicked me again, sooner he's burgers and glue, the better' *was her comment this time. A distraught but still grumpy Theodore nearly upbraided her for swearing but, given her recent tribulations, kept his mouth shut, pleased she had retained her memory. Two years later, the X-ray revealed a blizzard of white snowflakes throughout her upper body, which was to be the last visit to that particular hospice.* 'It looks like a 1960s television reception' *was his mother's comment.*

She passed away one afternoon under palliative care at the local charity-supported hospice. She just stopped breathing, her spirit left an empty husk sunken into the bedclothes, and her jaw dropped as if in surprise.

'Mother!' *he wailed, then loudly,* 'Oh, Mum.'

He woke with a start, with a string of drool connecting the corner of his mouth to his upper arm like a pedicle fashioned by Archie McIndoe. Some people stared, and some looked deliberately away. His dream had fitted the journey time to perfection; he alighted in the late afternoon sunshine and wandered home, downhearted. Even the impending dawn of another home cricket season didn't lighten his spirit. He closed the front door, tossed his anorak on to the coat tree, wandered into the kitchen, and selected a banana from the fruit dish. Banana consumed and its biodegradable wrapper placed in the 'green' box, he changed into shorts and switched the laptop on. After finding there was no live cricket being played (which was reported on his favourite cricket site), he decided to look on a social networking site to see what his alter ego was up to.

'Yo, got a tweet from some anonymous Doris calling me a w*nker,' Kevin Sedgley-Ahern announced on his page a couple of weeks back. Fortunately, Kevin didn't display a photograph of himself. He used an image of a rooster with sporting a T-shirt with a large 'S' on its proud chest, while flexing its wing biceps in an impressive manner. Beneath the image was a scroll emblazoned 'SuperCock'. There were several additional comments from his friends, alternatively agreeing and generally being 'laddish', in common with Theodore, girls didn't seem overly attracted to his character.

It was probably lucky that Kevin didn't post a real picture of himself as Shirley might have worked out that the visitor to pick up that stock of headphones and pay cash was not same person behind the social network page. Theodore was blissfully unaware what Shirley thought of him and didn't realise how close his ruse had come to being questioned. Shirley just wanted the satisfaction of letting someone know what she thought of them. (She wasn't far off the mark with Kevin.)

'Taking the Scoobie out at the weekend for a blast, probably have to sponge the seats afterwards' was a later comment. 'What is a Scoobie?' thought Theodore (he presumed a car, motorcycle, van, or maybe speedboat). 'Why drive it so fast that you wet yourself?' Theodore and Kevin seemed to belong to two different species.

'You are such a maggot, Kevin' was a response from one friend.

'Better a maggot than a faggot,' Kevin replied.

'Leave us meatballs alone' was from another friend.

The childish banter (which is apparently social networking, to some) was batted to and fro for another page or two before Theodore got bored. Mind you, Theodore thought this type of application wasn't *too* bad. You could just disappear from a conversation without appearing impolite. It was acquaintanceship (not friendship) without responsibility so you would poke a friend because poking an *acquaintance* was probably too posh for the Internet, where properly constructed sentences were at a premium, simply because of the lack of editorship. The other thing that appealed was that he could sit on the sidelines, as he'd always had difficulty with people trying to drag him into contributing to conversations (with the best possible intent) when he was quite content listening or just *hearing*.

Theodore closed the application, a little bemused, but in a better frame of mind. He went into his workshop and looking at the violated head decided he should arrange for its disposal; however, the hole in the right ear would be puzzling to anyone who decided to make use of it. Theodore took down his drill and after fitting a 12-mm drill bit drilled through the head from ear to ear. 'Nothing like overkill,' he thought. He selected a couple of his mother's more romantic novels and placed them on top of the head so that if it did have eyes (which could see), it wouldn't look up at him in accusation, from the bottom of the sturdy carrier bag. Patting the pocket that held his house keys, he left the house, pulled the front door shut, and strolled up the road to the High Street. Studiously avoiding the charity shop, where Pat worked (and it was just about closing time), Theodore placed his carrier alongside other donors in form of the cancer care charity shop; he was tempted to reorganise the bags, when a voice said with the unmistakable accent of Natalie, 'Ah, donating to charity, how noble!' Theodore started and stared like a dumbstruck fool at the youthful-looking fifty-plus-year-old standing there with a grin, pulling at one side of her mouth. She was leaning to one side, a hand on her hip, and she looked like a film actress. The way she had positioned one foot in front of the other looked as if she had been frozen mid-catwalk, as if posing for his mother's mail-order catalogue.

'Come, take me for a coffee. It's the fly season,' she ordered the open-mouthed, but speechless Theodore. Possibly the choice of fly season may have had influence too.

'I suppose I'll have to order because you seem to have lost the power of speech.'

The coffee shop stayed open later than most of the surrounding businesses. This meant that the workers leaving for the evening who wouldn't go into a pub could have a wind down. Even at this time of the evening, the staff were busy behind the gurgling and hissing espresso machines. Natalie chose a frothy concoction named after a monk. Theodore had a pot of breakfast tea and was relieved that he had put his wallet in his shorts, paid. Their conversation was dominated by Natalie, her hands fluttering like doves and her steel grey eyes flashing. Theodore thought his life was too boring to share and the only exciting project on his mind needed to be kept secret; anyway, she had just enchanted him totally. They paused in their one-sided play, only to order another drink. Natalie had returned to the States and married a serviceman whose career meant postings at various bases dotted around Europe. After the divorce, their children having completed college, he had returned 'Stateside', but Natalie preferred Europe. She stayed in touch with her two married daughters via email. Her ex-husband had not remarried; being married to the air force seemed to be sufficient. Their divorce had not been acrimonious, but it was fated. They stayed together as acquaintances for continuity of parenthood. The way Natalie spoke of Clint, her husband, roused a spark of jealousy in Theodore. Why had they got divorced if she was happy to keep talking about him? She said they had just realised they hadn't been in love and had just wandered different ways in the boundary of their own home still held on a leash by a marriage contract.

'We kinda grew out of love and affection but didn't want to harm each other merely out of spite,' she drawled.

'Well, I've never found the right person' was Theodore's response, as he stared at his hands folded held between his thighs; to be honest. He hadn't bothered looking, his main outing being cricket matches, where the only women you were likely to meet were interested in bedding the players or were in the company of their husbands. You didn't have much chance of striking up a meaningful relationship in a queue for a takeaway meal, an occasional dash round a supermarket, or working as a scientist. Theodore quite rightly thought it would look too ridiculous if he tried too hard to pick up a partner and was concerned about using the Internet because he knew it was a haven for unsavoury characters. He hated the idea of posting a picture of himself for other people to view because he hated how he looked in a mirror.

Natalie, to Theodore's astonishment, asked if he was gay. She thought it was quite funny when Theodore responded that he was thought of more as a bit grumpy than blithe and gay.

'Naw, not that gay, I mean homosexual.' Once again she had caused his jaw to drop.

'Eh?'

'Heyyyy, don't get offended. Things have moved on.' She gently patted his forearm. Theodore came very close to covering her hand with his and just holding her there, but by the time it had occurred to him and he'd plucked the courage to do so, she had withdrawn it.

'But I've never even thought of having sex with a man!' he squeaked, a bit louder and more falsetto that he intended. Only a few heads turned. (Theodore didn't think about having sex with *anybody* that much, except for recently when it popped into his head, only a *lot* more frequently and with females, he thought self-righteously.)

They parted outside the coffee shop, Theodore clumsily offering to shake hands, but Natalie just stepped inside his outstretched hand and gave him a US-style hug and lovely pat on his back like she was burping a small child. The proximity of the hug caused another stirring below his waist; he arched his pelvis away as if suddenly struck by cramp in the back.

Invite her . . . back for coffee . . . no, you fool . . . she's had plenty of coffee already . . . well then, a drink . . . what of tea?

He was about to utter or splutter an invite, but she had already released him and was striding back to where she had parked her car (Theodore assumed she had driven). She turned around and gave him a cheery wave; he swore he saw her eyes sparkle. Theodore's heart lurched. He stood rooted on the pavement as she disappeared up a side road, the clicking of her heels gradually decreasing in volume. It was a minute or so before he dragged his feet into motion and trudged back home, berating himself for cowardice, but perversely congratulating himself for not allowing her to laugh at his offer to come back home with him, if, of course, he had made the offer. Night drawing in added to his personal gloom.

Inside the house, the gathering twilight caused him to switch on the lights. He looked at the ancient television that hadn't been switched on for many a year because he had the urge to listen to a human voice and that definitely ruled out the radio, especially the pop music channels. Reaching behind the television, he plugged it into the wall (realising he hadn't dusted or vacuumed behind the television for some time). He pressed the power-on switch and waited while it warmed up and then slumped on the sofa with the remote control in his right hand. After it occurred to him that because of lack of use, the battery inside the remote was totally useless, he got up, went into his orderly workshop, where he had a drawer devoted to batteries, and put a new one in, and once he had replaced it (he was relieved to note that the terminals hadn't corroded), he flicked through the few channels that were available (these would soon be gone too because of the analogue transmission going off air). It took him twenty minutes to realise that the infantile game shows, peeping tom reality shows, and other dross reminded him how pointless television was becoming or probably had become. There was no chance of cricket being broadcast by anything other than satellite channels. The television was switched off and unplugged. If it were to be switched on again, there would be nothing to watch, not even a test card.

It was a waste of a battery. He sat down, defeated, and the remote controls hung limply from his right hand.

'Flobbaddob de bop weeeed.'

'Weeeed.'

'Ahhh flobbbabdobdob de bop weeed.'

'Weeeeed.'

Theodore was sitting cross-legged in grey shorts, held together by a snake-clasped belt, in front of the television, trying to understand the language that was being spoken on the Watch with Mother program. His mother was humming as she was running an iron across various items of clothing, which strangely included socks and things that Theodore would never consider wasting electricity on some thirty years hence.

'Here comes Mummy Woodentop going to the fair.'

Three petrified-looking furry animals were puttering down a river in a small boat, sniffing or sniffling over the gunwales (obviously not voles or lemmings, who surely would have swum for it), while a guitar was being plucked melodiously in the background.

'Here we go, Looby Loo, here we go, Looby Ly, here we go, Looby Loo, all on a Saturday night.'

Theodore didn't budge from the start to the end, whatever was on at the time. Some were better than others, and he thought he liked the one with the live animals the best. It was certainly better than the gobbled-gook spoken by the Flowerpot Men. It was many years later that Theodore drew a connection between the availability of psychedelic drugs and the writers of children's television programs.

This was the second time in one day that Theodore had dozed off; maybe he had picked up some sort of narcolepsy. He got up and groggily went into the kitchen to boil the kettle for a mug of tea. There was no point in having an early night. He didn't think he would fall asleep for some time; maybe he would thumb through some of his mother's books and see if one might act as a soporific should he be unable to sleep. Taking his tea back into the lounge, he flipped open his laptop. He was sorely tempted to scan for Natalie in the social network sites or a search engine, but this felt a bit like stalking, and he didn't know her surname because of her marriage. He couldn't remember her maiden name from college, and he couldn't even recall asking her at the time. Natalie was enough; there would only ever be one Natalie for him, so there was no need to add a qualifier. He'd had enough of Kevin Sedgley-Ahern for a while and wasn't particularly interested in what information, fact or fiction, he was exchanging with his virtual friends.

His day of gloom was compounded by the announcement at the dedicated cricket information site that players of several nations had been banned because of the attempted fixing of parts of the game because of the new online craze of spot betting. Theodore was unsure of how to place a bet beyond the obvious one, i.e. bet who wins, so he was really confused as to how you could win money, or who would offer odds, on passages of play in a cricket match that had far more outcomes than a litter of Schrodinger's cats. He had always held cricketers as akin to mortal gods, who played to win with honour and lose with grace (no pun) at all times, and now, there were individuals who would sully the game he loved for filthy lucre. Given the recent economic climate, the gambling industry was performing extremely well by the number of advertisements that 'popped-up' on his laptop's screen, offering free bets. Using a search engine combined with an online encyclopaedia, he discovered that in England, gambling on cricket matches had been going on since the early seventeenth century and was between gentlemen, who settled the bet on a win. The methods of 'fixing' the match was by arranging how long the game lasted or who played for whose team; good cricket players were paid to play for one side or the other, and gentleman players were not paid at all.

Nowadays, and this is what depressed Theodore and most true cricket supporters the most, was that it appeared to be the amount of money gambled was disproportionate to the general wealth of the nations. In the subcontinent, it was endemic, but being judged by the number of pop-ups on the Internet, it was surely of epidemic proportions. Theodore hated gambling on cricket, and general gambling with a vengeance was personal because the thought of him losing a pound far exceeded the anticipated joy he would get from winning a hundred. Gambling to Theodore included vehicles like national lotteries, which seemed to raise money for good causes, which, given the prize money, still left a sizeable portion as profit. The depression made him fancy a strong drink, as more tea didn't seem to be an option, especially on top of the recent mug, he'd got through two pots in the coffee shop with Natalie. Theodore had drunk spirits maybe only three times. The middle occasion was after the date with Natalie when they had watched the film. The first was one Christmas evening with his mother, after she'd been given a bottle of Glenmorangie as a 'Secret Santa' (one suspected by mistake) and she had forbidden him to put anything in the whisky when he tasted it. He thought it was like drinking smoke, but his mother seemed to enjoy the flavour (albeit with a wistful look in her eye, suspiciously attributable to her memories of Theodore's father). The third time was when they finished the bottle on New Year's Eve, just before the start of the year when she was first diagnosed with cancer. This was enough to sour the desire for spirits in Theodore's mind. He was at a loss what to do (Oh how he wished he had Natalie's company, or even Steve Stiff's!). For the first time in an extremely long time, he found his own company inadequate.

He took one of his mother's books to bed and read most of it through the night. The book was a compilation of short novels by John Steinbeck, namely, *Of Mice and Men* and *Cannery Row*. He chose this because of the thickness. It was alongside *The Moon Is Down*, but *Of Mice and Men* had a more appealing title. The descriptiveness, dialogue, and characters grabbed him within the first chapter, and later on, he almost burst with satisfaction at the construction of the scene that led to Lenny crushing Curly's fist. He couldn't put the book down and at the end felt the pain in the back of his throat from restricting a sob, when George shoots Lenny. He carried on straight into *Cannery Row* and had digested most of it when he looked at his clock and realised the alarm was about to sound and that it was nearly time to get up. This caused him to immediately feel very sleepy, and he was sorely tempted to call in and feign sickness. Instead, he fell out of bed and stumbled upright in a fog of fatigue and went through his ablutions and dressed. Approximately twenty minutes later (a banana and an orange hastily thrust into his blazer pocket), he left the house and joined the queue for the first bus. It wasn't a real queue, more a scattering of a few individuals who knew that there would be no problem getting on the bus that had plenty of empty seats to choose from. Theodore managed to get the seat by the emergency door and leaned against the window, noting that although it was now spring and surprisingly warm for England, the heating of the bus was set to a temperature that would start glaciers calving in the Antarctic. This was allegedly due to the heating only being allowed to be set by a qualified mechanic in the bus depot. Theodore was quite sure the driver could finely tune the temperature in his vicinity without consulting anyone else. The Uvula and the Mantis got on at the same stop, and with one plonked in front and the other behind, they managed to prevent Theodore dropping off to sleep. The Uvula should not really hold conversations about medical conditions on a phone in a public place, although it didn't put the Mantis off an early breakfast. A young man in his twenties boarded and commenced twitching and the ejaculated the odd expletive complete with a body spasm. Theodore had seen him before and had also spoken to him (he was testing the man's avowal that he had Tourette's syndrome and thought that whatever his symptoms were, they weren't Munchausen's). After a spasm, he would apologise to all present profusely. Theodore was too tired to engage in conversation with the man or listen to his apologies; he slunk down in his seat and pretended to sleep. He must have dozed off for a second because there was a signal change in the atmosphere on the bus. The Uvula was threatening the Tourette's man for swearing while he was discussing personal details on the phone.

'I have a lady on the phone here!' yelled the Uvula, holding his phone away from his ear and pointing at it with his left forefinger.

The Tourette's man being what he was swore spectacularly and told the Uvula where to put his medical condition in juxtaposition with his lady's medical condition. Theodore disliked confrontation, but this, because he knew this would not escalate beyond words, pulled the corner of his mouth into a slight smile. A young African lady, who had a child in a push chair at the front of the bus, attempted the diplomatic approach and was racially abused by both antagonists. Theodore leapt to his feet (quite tricky given the swaying bus and his fatigue) and ordered Tourette's man to the front, where he apologised contritely to the African lady and explained his condition. Tersely, Theodore told the Uvula to sit down and turn his phone off. The Mantis selected another snack, blinked a couple of times, and crunched on it, the music hissing from the vicinity of her ears. Theodore alighted to thumbs-up from Tourette's man, gratitude from the driver, a beaming smile from the African lady, and a chuckle from her charmingly chocolate-coloured child.

Theodore entered work, strangely satisfied and somewhat puzzled. Here he was, the most morose man since Victorian times feeling out of character and frankly to him, quite alien. An event like he had experienced would have left him unnerved and trembling from the adrenaline, historically because he'd somehow unintentionally managed to offend somebody, thus diverting everyone else's wrath against him. This time it was different; he'd actually come out the hero, rather than the villain-cum-scapegoat. He remembered slightly smiling at the onset of the contretemps that he could see unfurling. Theodore suspected that he was having a reverse puberty, puberty meaning the conversion of happy and garrulous children into sullen and selfish teenagers, owing, partly or conveniently, to hormonal surges. Again, his thoughts were interrupted.

'Yo, Kofi . . . Mr Annan, can I have your autograph?'

Theodore hadn't noticed, possibly because he was so tired, that Steve Stiff had been on the bus and, having alighted shortly after, closely followed him through security. Another possibility was that he hadn't noticed him because of his smug satisfaction in dealing with the dispute; anyway, if Stiff had been a bus regular, surely he would have christened him with a nickname? He turned to the smirking youth and tried to transfix him with a withering stare, but seeing it was ineffective, he turned back with a slight shake of his head and proceeded to the locker room to get changed. He wondered what Steve Stiff's nickname should be? Wiggo1, possibly?

'Man, you sorted out those stroppy dudes set on aggro and standing up against racism . . . cool.'

Theodore opened his mouth to explain and then decided that discretion might be better than total honesty and also save a lot of time. He just grunted. This would add to the legend that circulated around the office before lunch, being embellished at each retelling. He thrust his hand into the jacket pocket and realised he'd crushed the banana against the bus seat, and the contents that had oozed from the burst skin was clinging slimily to his fingers. He shut the locker door, transferring banana flesh to his keys, and he decided that he needed to clean up the mess. He held his hands away from his body, holding a bunch of keys clogged with sugary stickiness, and putting his fingers into his mouth, he realised that the copper from the keys had contaminated the sugar already. He went to wash off the residue. After this distraction, he buttoned his white coat and thought how many hominivorax eggs he should smuggle out of the laboratory. He decided that he would just take four or five enough to establish a colony in his workshop; he would need to escape proof cages that he daren't ask whether he could buy from work. Using this strategy would mean that he could ease the pressure on his project (assuming the flies would breed in his workshop and he could get hold of a suitable incubator or cage). He would bring the pillbox in tomorrow and start his own colony. He felt as smug as a politician who'd had his expenses signed off, without any scrutiny. Steve Stiff did not lose time sharing his observations. He'd managed to buttonhole the director and also Natalie, and by break time, he'd managed to inform nearly everyone in the laboratory of the exploits of the in-house hero, exaggerating the forearms of the Uvula and the latent violence of the Tourette's youth. When Theodore went for a mid-morning tea break, he found that Mr Goode, Natalie, Steve Stiff, and others were already there waiting for him. Theodore scowled at Steve Stiff, while Andrew Goode and Natalie beamed at his discomfort. Theodore bemoaned Steve Stiff's exaggeration, and this added credence to Steve's story.

Chapter 9

Andrew Goode declared that the day being a Friday (also having loss of funding), all would repair to the local hostelry ('No exceptions, Mr Chief Scientist') for lunch and not return to work. This effectively scuppered Theodore's plan for smuggling eggs from the laboratory today; he would have stern words with Mr Stiff at lunch. The time between tea break and lunch was spent with tidying things up for the weekend; some drove to the pub, offering lifts. In the pub, clasping a half pint of bitter, Theodore rounded on Steve Stiff, wagging a finger and accusing Stiff of arranging the whole thing to scrounge a half-day. Steve Stiff looked offended, and then Natalie stepped in and acted as peacekeeper.

'How could you be cruel to this young man? Why? He's just a teddy bear.'

Both echoed in disbelief, 'Eh?'

Theodore thought Steve Stiff was an impudent youth and not a teddy bear at all.

Steve Stiff thought he was a bit more dangerous to girls' virginity than a stuffed toy, although stuffed toys have a much better chance of being taken into a lady's bed, for an additional reason is that they don't pinch all the duvet and then snore.

Natalie was overjoyed at their confusion and explained, 'Richard Steiff is the German father of teddy bears. They are quite collectable, you know.'

Steve Stiff was distraught; not only had he been compared with a teddy bear, he was now a German! He had always been a keen supporter of England's football team despite the lack of success considering the salaries the players' enjoyed, some salaries that were paid via a Jersey loan scheme that resulted in serious tax economies. Although Stiff never travelled to watch England play, because there was still an aftertaste from the soccer hooligan phase. He never would want to be associated with hooliganism, aspiring computer geeks being football yobs is a rare combination.

Theodore just stayed grumpy, but only for a moment. He and Steve Stiff formed an alliance against Natalie, questioning why she would wish to butt in on a private debate, turning their backs on her huffily (of course, they were only teasing and wanted her company). Natalie made a peace offering of a round of drinks. Andrew Goode came over and overruled Natalie buying the drinks, complimented them on their bonhomie, and saying there were good things coming. Theodore raised an eyebrow and said he would take another half of bitter. Andrew returned with the drinks, and the four sat at a table in the bay of the old pub, where the sun streamed through the window, bringing a hint of a promising summer season. The landlord came over, bringing a plate of sandwiches, a bowl of crisps, and also some side salad. After talking about sport for about half an hour (Theodore—cricket, Steve Stiff—football, Andrew Goode—golf) and then a further round of drinks, Steve Stiff announced that the men had been hogging the conversation and asked Natalie whether she had a sport.

'Well, at university, there was a bit of sport,' she said, looking slyly at an increasingly red-faced Theodore.

'Oh Really?' Steve Smith asked and leant forward in a conspiratorial manner, sensing Theodore's discomfort.

'You must tell us more.'

Theodore leapt up and looked for the Gents, nodded, and set off across the lounge.

On his return, they looked up from the table, and all three were smiling.

'What have you told them?' demanded Theodore.

'I was just explaining our little shared secret.'

'Eh? What secret?' screeched Theodore, seriously concerned.

'Nothing, just about the obstacle race that used to take place around the inner quadrangle.'

'Oh yes, I remember, we used to alternate slow motion and then old-movie-style scrambling . . .' The tension drained from him like he was emptying another bladder.

'Yes, we used to whistle the *Chariots of Fire* theme tune while running in slow motion and running along benches and over chairs. Well, we thought it was funny at the time.'

'Wow, you were at university at the time of that old film!' blurted Steve Stiff.

'Why, you cheeky tyke!' Natalie playfully cuffed the youth.

'Oh, I didn't realise it was released in the eighties. I thought it was before the Second World War!'

Had Natalie forgotten about their tryst and the close shave they'd had at university? Had she also forgotten that they had once shared the cost of a film and a few drinks? She was a very confounding woman. Theodore looked sadly into his beer and felt a little upset.

'Would anyone like another drink?' he asked, trying to force a little joviality into his demeanour (ignoring the skinflint side's '*What!?!*').

'Another St Clement's for me. I'm driving.'

Noting Theodore's puzzlement, she explained that a St Clement's was an orange juice mixed with bitter lemon ('oranges and lemons, say the bells of St Clement's'). Theodore asked how a colonial knew English nursery rhymes and was in danger of being cuffed himself. Andrew and Stiff had another pint. 'This Natalie is really something else,' he thought cheerily as he went to the bar and decided to get himself a full pint this time. Taking the drinks back to the table, he looked pleased with himself.

'I see you sexist wouldn't let me buy *you* a pint!'

'But, but, I didn't want a pint before,' stammered Theodore. Andrew Goode and Steve Stiff sniggered as they picked up their pints. Goode was also smiling at Theodore's obvious relief that his unknown secret remained exactly that.

Their bonhomie was interrupted when a middle-aged couple calmly walked in, carrying drinks, and selected a seat close to where the four were seated. They had just about got settled when there was a commotion. A woman in her late thirties, wearing a clinging peach dress, marched determinedly into the lounge with a couple of children trailing snottily and confusedly behind her. Her march continued up to the table where the couple were looking puzzled at her arrival; she came smartly to attention and promptly tossed a drink into the face of the man in front of his escort, but the assailant's words were addressed to his companion.

'You just ask him where he's been last weekend. Go on, just ask 'im.' She nodded once in his direction.

There was a pause while she waited to see whether the woman, who was staring stonily face straight ahead, would respond.

'Well, I can tell you.' She paused for dramatic effect and to draw breath for her revelation. 'He's been dabbling . . . He's been dabblin' with me . . . He's been dabblin' with me in Dublin. That's right, a dirty weekend dabblin' in Dublin with me!'

Chris Robbins, the landlord, had observed the contretemps and came round the front of the bar, just as the woman was reaching for the drink of her recent travelling companion-cum-traitor, with a view to hurling it into his face. The man grabbed hold of the glass; simultaneously as the woman, the landlord was only a split second behind. The three of them stood and looked at each other in a bizarre tug-of-war stand-off. This lasted for a minute or so until at a glance and a nod from Chris, the woman decided enough was enough and waited calmly for an escort to show her from the pub. This was to be done by one of the staff, wearing the new natty uniform that came as a deal from one of the beer suppliers. She threw a valedictory comment more at the man's companion.

'I'd watch 'im. Mind, he's a born dabbler. Keep clear of 'im, 'specially if 'e asks you to go to Dublin. 'e does a lot of 'is dabblin' in Dublin.'

The man dripping with drink and embarrassment (none of the drink she'd thrown had missed him) sat there, his salvaged drink still locked in his fist. Chris calmly picked up the menu and set it upright on the table asking, 'Is sir ready to order now?'

Natalie guffawed into a handkerchief. 'Aw, you English!'

'I think he's Irish, Natalie,' Andrew Goode whispered behind the back of his hand. This caused Natalie to whoop, nearly loud enough for a true American. The woman who had accompanied the alleged philanderer sat rigidly upright as a poker with a poker face not betraying any emotion, possibly because of shock.

'Shee yit, I can see why they called this pub The Folly,' muttered Natalie. Theodore, who hadn't really been paying as much attention as the other three, took a little while to understand her comment.

The woman and her children had turned in formation accompanied by a coltish junior waitress and were heading towards the exit of the pub. Steve Stiff was hypnotised by the woman's peach clad buttocks, which were bisected by the white G-string that could be easily discerned through the fabric less than a foot from Stiff's face.

'My God, I love peaches,' he mumbled.

The older of the two children tugged at her mother's dress and whined loudly, 'But I don't think uncle Danny looks like a fish when he's drinking.' The woman flounced away with her two children in close 'v' formation.

Andrew Goode noted without comment that the clingy fabric also highlighted the cellulite that gave the dimpled appearance of orange peel rather than the soft smooth surface of a peach. There was also a chocolate stain shaped in a child's hand below the left buttock, where the material had been granted a bit more slack. He wondered what the mother had done with the children while she was on her illicit weekend. However, he could also empathise with Stiff's lust because when Goode was Steve Stiff's age, he had spent a lot of energy attempting to satisfy a divorcee who was several years older than himself. She was also comfortably built and lived close to the golf course, which added to Goode's incentive to play the game. So when it came to that sort of attraction, Goode understood. Steve Stiff nearly fell off his chair, following the route the woman's backside took from the pub.

Natalie wondered if Stiffy was familiar with a band called the Stranglers. Theodore glanced to and fro for a second like a spectator at a tennis match. Stiff was also puzzled. Natalie clicked her fingers and hummed the rhythm line and finally quoted the lyrics 'Walking on the beaches, looking at the peaches'.

'Wow,' said Stiff. 'That was before I was born!'

Both Goode and Natalie responded that there hadn't been much originality in the music world since.

Andrew Goode rose, and after being reminded of his youthful detour to the golf course, he said he would see if he could get a sneaky round of golf in with a chum and looked pointedly at Steve Stiff. Steve Stiff paused for a minute as if something was prohibiting him from standing, finally got up in slow motion in a crouching fashion, and said he was off out tonight to paint the town red with a couple of mates, so he needed to get himself equipped to fight off the ladies.

'Don't forget to take plenty of cream for those peaches, Stiffy!' was Natalie's au revoir to a reddening Stiffy.

Andrew Goode chuckled at the youth's discomfort. *He* wouldn't like to have a verbal confrontation with a sharp-humoured Natalie.

Above the reciprocal 'see yous', 'cheers', and 'have a good weekends', a pointed voice was heard coming from the woman who was sat with the damp dirty weekender in Dublin.

'You said you were visiting relatives, not having relations.'

'But I've never seen that woman before in my life!'

'Well, one of her brats knew your name, Uncle Danny indeed.'

Natalie couldn't wait to share the alliteration with Theodore, Goode, and Stiffy (Danny, the Dublin Dabbler); however, as Goode and Stiff had departed and the couple were still behind, it could wait. The two were left alone with the last couple of sandwiches and a few crisp crumbs, she smirking with amusement, he looking a bit perplexed but happy with having Natalie to himself. Natalie opened one of the sandwiches and sprinkled crisps on the filling and munched away happily. Theodore thanked her for not revealing their 'secret'. He was relieved that it was Steve Stiff who had ended up being embarrassed rather than himself.

They left the pub an hour later with Theodore feeling a little woozy from the beer, especially when they stepped out into the bright sunshine. Natalie opened the car door for him. He couldn't remember her offering him a lift, but he shrugged and slipped into the bucket seat of the small sports car. Natalie started the car, and the engine roared and then settled down to a growl. It was then Theodore noticed that it was a TVR sprayed a deep burgundy and heavily lacquered to give depth to the colour (he'd remembered the marque from his childhood book). Natalie blipped the throttle, and the torque caused the car to twitch. Depressing the clutch with a shapely leg, she engaged first and left the car park. The burble of the big V8 caused heads to turn as they made their way back to the High Street.

'Do you like the roar of my beast?'

Theodore was in a quandary; he was an advocate of public transport, fuel efficiency, and anti-pollution, but he didn't like to step on to the soap box. He knew he'd have to respond quickly; she would take his silence as disapproval. He settled for a side-step and explained how TVR had been in his childhood book, although British Racing Green might have been a more suitable colour for a British sports car.

'British car, US-designed engine,' she grinned, noticing Theodore's frown.

The Theodore had an inspiration. Casting his mind back to the film they had seen at university (*American Graffiti*), he said in a pretty poor imitation of an American accent, 'Wotcha got in there?'

Natalie quickly caught on. 'More than you can handle!'

They laughed.

The car burbled up to the front of Theodore's house. Natalie had insisted on driving him home, and Theodore found that his mouth had suddenly gone dry. He looked guiltily at his hands in his lap, guilty for his cowardice, guilty for his lack of planning, and guilty at not knowing what to do.

'C'mon, invite me in . . . you *do* stock coffee, don't you?'

'I'm sorry, I don't buy coffee.'

Natalie looked a bit taken aback, thinking she was being pushed away. A surprise (and rare) moment of inspiration caused Theodore to blurt.

'But I have plenty of good tea!' She raised an eyebrow and then smiled, especially when he said that she ought to park her beast in the drive to a) keep it off the road and out of the way of envious people who carried keys and had a nasty tic that caused the keys to be dragged along the bodywork and b) give the neighbours good reason to twitch their curtains. This latter option was made a certainty when Natalie blipped the throttle, causing the five litres to grumble just short of a roar before she finally cut the engine. After a final snort, the engine ticked like a benevolent time bomb as their eyes engaged. Theodore's brown caved in before the steel grey and broke the look first. He opened the car door and fumbled for his house keys. As he opened his house door, various fears of potential embarrassment gripped him. Had he got sufficient toilet paper? If so, was it of suitable quality or had he just bought the cheap stuff? (Theodore preferred to take advantage of the toilet facilities at work, as his parsimonious side urged him to do.) Was the toilet seat down? (He knew, admittedly from Steve Stiff, that leaving the toilet seat up was something that women hated.) He hadn't purchased any chemical air freshener since his mother had died; he didn't approve of the way she spent money on them. She would spray the ozone-attacking aerosols around as if she was performing a gymnastic display, or she had possibly picked it up from hearing about what happened before a plane was allowed to disembark passengers at an Australian airport. For a hippy, Theodore's mother didn't seem to hold all the green attributes of a true 'friend of the earth'; air freshener, anti-perspirant, and hair sprays were her Achilles heel. Showing Natalie into the lounge hoping to get a head start on inspecting the kitchen before she could observe was not successful. She just followed him into the kitchen as if on a lead, and then for the second time in one day, Theodore took control and shooed her from the kitchen on pretence of it being cramped and that in the kitchen he was the dictator. She backed off into the lounge with a slight laugh. This bought Theodore some time in getting rid of the dust from the china tea set, teapot, and so on. He even poured some milk into a jug. Putting milk into a jug had been carried over from his mother (some forty-five years or so ago), who begged him not to say to a childhood friend who'd invited him to tea that at Theodore's home the milk bottle was allowed to be placed on the table. Being a grim and somewhat boring child, Theodore never questioned the rationale, nor did he let the secret out to his friend; he also never even commented when he noticed that his friend's mother had no qualms about putting a fresh bottle of milk on the kitchen table. This, of course, was in the era when giving children as much milk as they could consume was de rigueur, more so when compared with carbonated brown-sugared water. When Theodore was at junior school, milk was provided to children free of charge.

The boiling of the kettle interrupted him, and he unsteadily carried the tray, which rattled in rhythm to his nerves, into the lounge. Gratefully and without any spillage, he placed the tray down on the table. Natalie was unselfconsciously thumbing her way through the large book case. She was totally engrossed, and it wasn't until Theodore cleared his throat that she turned around.

'Wow, there's so much stuff here that I'd like to read and quite a few that I'd like to reread. I didn't realise you had a fondness for novels and classics.'

'Well, once you read those, then you qualify for Wisden and cricket biographies! Please note the lower shelves!' Theodore couldn't believe he had just spouted something semi-witty. It must have been the beer! 'Well, actually, the classy stuff was my mother's. She would devour books of all sorts and then kept the ones she thought most important.' Theodore's mother definitely had catholic taste in books. She could happily read Aristophanes and Shakespeare's plays and poetry, Churchill's histories, Leslie Thomas's humour and pathos, Henry Miller's raw artistic sexuality, Nietsche's arrogance, Clive James's descriptive brilliance and counterpointed humour,

James Joyce's stream of conscious thought, and John Irving's sculptured characters, together with lots of other writers' output.

'Your mother certainly kept a rounded library of books that makes you want to just keep dipping into. I don't wish to pry, but she obviously isn't around here anymore.' Natalie turned towards Theodore just in time to catch him closing his eyes and inhaling deeply.

'No, she has been gathered unto God some ten years ago.'

'Crikey,' Theodore thought, 'where did I pluck that phrase from, being a scientist? It seemed to fit the moment.'

'Ah, but what taste.'

Theodore addressed himself to the tea. 'Shall I be Mother?' he announced and then paused with the significance of his utterance. His eyes welled as he looked at Natalie, for the first time for many a year. He swore, 'Oh Feck', and then remembering his mother's litany, he just let the tears roll down his face. Natalie just remained looking at the book collection and didn't notice Theodore's condition. He put the teapot down and went into the kitchen and tore off a sheet of paper towel and composed himself. He walked back into the lounge with the milk jug and the scrunched-up paper towel protruding from his trouser pocket.

They addressed themselves to the nicety of afternoon tea. Theodore couldn't offer a sandwich or a biscuit because he'd simply stopped buying biscuits and when he bought bread, it went mouldy before he could finish the loaf.

'I'm sorry, I'm not much of a host, and I don't have many visitors. Actually, I'm lying. I don't have any visitors.'

'Not exactly a lie, Theodore, just an extra letter.' She paused and then continued, 'You know many, any!' (She had to explain as Theodore looked a bit puzzled.)

'Just to whom were you married? Colonel North?'

The mood had rapidly changed within five minutes, and Natalie's fruity laughter echoed round the lounge.

'Now the neighbours are really going to gossip,' Theodore accused but found he didn't really care. The mother was probably picking up her sole child from school for which she needed a highly polished four-wheel-drive jeep (known in these parts as a Chelsea Tractor, even though Chelsea was over a hundred miles to the east.), while the father was working late hours at the bank to pay for both the jeep and the child's independent education. It was this late working that caused the neighbour to make the local paper, and possibly the management at the bank should have caught on quicker when they realised they had one employee who worked extra unpaid hours and was reluctant to take holidays. His research and development activity was uncovered by data analytics when they started monitoring dormant accounts that would suddenly become active, make a payment, and then become dormant again. The research was researching into the dormant accounts, and the development was developing a method of leeching money from them. The bank was particularly ruthless in dealing with its oversight of its overseeing. It forfeited the neighbour's accrued pension and slapped a charge on the house, whilst keeping him as a customer, so it could deduct compensation from any earnings he credited through the account. He wouldn't be accepted as a customer by any other bank. Additional irony came in the subsequent fine of the bank by the regulator for having inadequate fraud controls to prevent financial crime, and of course, the fine exceeded the amount stolen by a factor of three. This was to come to light a couple of weeks in the future when unfortunate circumstances would lead Theodore to come face to face with his neighbour, Andrew Dipper.

'I must use your rest room. Where is it?'

'Rest room? *Rest room?* Ah, she means toilet. Oh no, I hope it's clean, and the seat's down,' thought Theodore, optimistically. If one of these turned out to be true, he would have been relieved.

Seeing the concerned look on his face, Natalie promised him that she wouldn't write on the walls. This only caused a grimace to appear on his face. He was about to follow her in order to hear any comment she would make about his housekeeping, but if she were to see him listening at the bottom of the stairs, what would she think? Theodore sat in the lounge, hands dangling between his knees, and hoped miserably but pessimistically that things were spotless and no telltale dribbles on the twee carpet that was fashioned to hug the base of the bowl, another legacy from his mother. The flush crashed and gurgled loudly, and the plumbing moaned, which it had done for the last five years, but this was the first time it had penetrated Theodore's conscious thought. The loose floorboard creaked, which was echoed in chorus by the staircase, and then Natalie rejoined a doleful-looking Theodore in the lounge. He came very close to asking how everything was but bit his tongue just in time. She sat next to him on the old sofa and linked her arm through his elbow.

'C'mon, give me the guided tour.'

'Natalie, you know I'm a bachelor. You know it will look like a bear's cave. Do you really want to see how a lonely old man lives?'

'*Yes*, just take me round,' she bossily demanded. 'This isn't one of those crass TV programs where they score each other's homes. I want to see the whole of your personality.'

'Well, it shouldn't take long,' Thought Theodore, 'the house tour or seeing the whole of *my* personality.'

'Bear my ass,' exclaimed Natalie when she saw his workshop. Again her fruity laughter echoed round 13 Acacia Avenue as she realised her double entendre. Theodore was extremely glad he'd disposed of the head with its telltale hole drilled in the right ear that would have sponsored some intriguing questions, no doubt. She wandered around the brightly lit workshop, with everything racked or filed in meticulous order, clucking approval, not noticing the incongruous package of headphones in the corner. Theodore locked the workshop with a sigh of relief. To him, the package of headphones stood out like a lighthouse. They went into the kitchen to make a salad (fruit and vegetables were not scarce).

'You really ought to reinforce that garage door. If someone realised the extent of your toolkit, they would open that door in next to no time,' said Natalie.

'That's women for you,' muttered the skinflint inside Theodore's ear, 'always thinking of ways for you to part with money, although. Give her the benefit of the doubt. She wants you to spend it on you.'

She continued opening various kitchen cabinets, looking for olive oil and balsamic vinegar and then turning round to see Theodore meekly holding a bottle of salad cream. 'Please don't tell me you're going to dress a salad with that!'

'Well, I'll dress my half with it, and you can find something else,' huffed Theodore. 'Oh yes, I have a gallon can of vegetable oil for cooking. We could use that.'

Natalie pretended not to hear and kept on looking, and eventually from the back of cabinet after extracting some well out-of-date cook-in-sauces and powdered items such as cup-a-soups, although no olive oil was located on this search, she joyfully held aloft an unopened bottle of rapeseed oil.

They ate a massive bowl of salad dressed with the rapeseed oil and then cleared the dishes away. With the kettle on, Natalie asked what this game of cricket that seemed so peculiarly English was all about. She couldn't resist asking if it was true that a game could last for five days and still be a draw.

'Not only that,' he replied. 'It could last five days and still be a tie!'

Theodore explained that for a cricket match to be tied, the aggregate runs must be the same, plus the number of wickets taken in the last innings is ten. The last tied test match was Australia versus India in 1986. There have only ever been two tied test matches.

The kettle boiled, and more tea was poured. Theodore picked up the thread and explained that there were many formats of the game and opened his laptop to show her and was rewarded by a twenty-over match of one innings per side.

'T20 they call it,' he explained, 'but I call it pyjama cricket.'

Natalie noted him squinting his eyes and trying to make out the text where it was in a smaller font.

'Oh for goodness sake, Theodore, put your glasses on!'

Theodore reluctantly found the tatty case and cleaned his reading glasses with a none-too-clean cloth and then perched them on his nose.

The match was between Australia and Pakistan with Pakistan batting in pursuit of Australia's score. A towering six had been struck by one of the batsmen.

'Did he just say, "Oh My God"?' Natalie enquired. 'Isn't that a bit offensive to Allah or something, Pakistan being an Islamic nation?'

'Pardon,' said Theodore. Just then, another similar shot soared into the night through the beam of the floodlight before landing among the spectators, some trying to avoid the missile and some seeking to catch it.

'Oh my God, he's on fire.' Theodore came close to laughing. The Indian commentator was gushing, his accent adding credence to Natalie's interpretation, and when has an Indian ever been less than enthusiastic about cricket? At the time, India was the number one cricket nation in the world, which ensured ongoing worship for the game in the subcontinent.

'Natalie, the batsman's name is Umar Gul. The commentator was saying that Umar Gul—he's on fire!'

Henceforth, Umar Gul would be pronounced in a slight cockney accent, courtesy of a Charlie Drake impersonation to sound similar to Oh My Gawd, particularly among the section of travelling England supporters who call themselves the '*Barmy Army*'.

Theodore was truly upset when Natalie pronounced it a reasonable imitation of baseball. He caught her slight smile out of the corner of his eye. He would take her to a cricket match for a short while, if she would consent, but he didn't want to spoil things by seeming too keen to convert her.

It was some time later that Theodore showed Natalie to the door, where she kissed him on the cheek and whispered in his ear that they should do it again when he'd stocked up on olive oil, chilli oil, balsamic, and oh of course, a mixed selection of good wine. She counted the shopping list on her fingers. Theodore cheerily waggled his fingers at her when she fired up the big v8 and thundered off into the humidity of the gathering gloom.

Chapter 10

Saturday morning saw Theodore on the bus to work. After Natalie had departed, he decided it was time to press the accelerator on the project before it became too late. He would acquire a batch of eggs today. To be honest, he was losing interest in the project in proportion to the interest he was gaining in Natalie, and like a true completer-finisher, he didn't want to abandon one project in order to start another. As he sat on the bus, even the hiss of a personal stereo emanating from the young girl with multiple piercings didn't penetrate his thoughts. This should have been a big enough hint to convince him that just maybe he didn't really need to pursue his project at all.

Theodore marched through security; the look on his face brooked no challenge from the guards. He donned his coat and went straight to the refrigerator. He quickly transferred a clutch of eggs into his wallet with the cooler block. He didn't bother counting, but it looked like at least twenty. The rest he placed into the freezer to kill before disposal, which he would do on Monday. Having nothing left to delay him, he went back to the locker room and stripped off his white coat. Already the cooler block was chilling his thigh as it rested in his pocket, and also the weight was starting to call his trousers to slip down his backside. He should have worn a belt. He closed the door to the locker room and was walking through the security area when he noticed out of the corner of his eye that Senor Mussolini was the other guard on duty and was walking purposefully to block his exit.

'Yes, yes, very good. Have a good weekend too.' Theodore attempted to finesse the guard's patter. Now there is nothing an officious jobsworth hates more than being palmed off as if his role was unimportant. The wafting of Theodore's hand was a red rag to a bull.

'Sir, I do not dress like this to be casual in the execution of my duty.'

Theodore rolled his eyes and offered his pass for inspection.

'Very good, sir. That appears to be in order, but as you're outside of working hours, would you mind turning out your pockets.'

'Well, actually I do mind,' retorted Theodore, thrusting out his jaw and bottom lip, Churchill style in confrontation with the jutting jaw of Mussolini.

'In that case, I must remind you of your contract of employment and that I have the right to search you,'

Theodore's brain was working quickly, fuelled by the adrenaline of his panic.

'But only in the presence of either the director or an independent person,' responded Theodore, uncertain of his grounds, but seemingly correct, as it is well known that officious people read every scrap of pertinent regulations that they can hide their real character behind.

'Very well, sir, I must ask you not to leave while I contact the director as per the Raid Procedure.'

Actually, the raid procedure was more to cover the unexpected arrivals of officials, such as bailiffs or police officers, but it had been adapted to cover other security processes as well. Andrew Goode was not into producing pages and pages of procedural documents that cost money for little return.

'The Raid Procedure? I'm not raiding anything!' Theodore almost squeaked in indignation. ('Theodore, actually you are,' said a sneaky toad-like voice in his ear.)

'Sir, please wait while I contact the director.' Lovejoy was at his most officious. He was sure that Mr Goode would support his opinion.

Theodore thought about running, but he felt that he could convince Andrew Goode that he was doing anything malicious (he was, though). He wondered what he could do if Andrew didn't answer his phone and whether he should empty his pockets. What would the guard make of a wallet with a cooler block and a pillbox with insect eggs? 'Actually, it's the remainder of a rice salad, but you can finish it if you want.' A better choice would have been white caviar, but it didn't occur to Theodore what caviar looked like. Theodore gleefully imagined the guard swallowing a teaspoon full of flies' eggs.

The guard was behind the desk, phone to his ear, waiting for Andrew to answer his mobile. Theodore saw him speaking into the mouthpiece and then looked at Theodore (Andrew had obviously answered). The guard beckoned Theodore over to speak to Goode. He didn't allow Theodore into the inner sanctum of the security desk; therefore, the handset was passed over the protective screen.

'Theodore, what are you playing at? I'm having a most enjoyable round of golf and then you come in on a Saturday, I suspect, because you felt guilty about leaving early yesterday, and interrupt my paradise.'

Actually, it wasn't quite paradise. Goode was losing to Brian Greatrex *again*.

'Well, Mr Goode, I'm only wearing trousers and a shirt, it's not as if I could conceal anything significant, yet this, this . . . guard wants to pat me down as if he wanted to feel my backside.'

'Theodore, he's only doing his job.'

'Well, it seems to me that his job is also his hobby!' spluttered Theodore. The security guard glared at Theodore.

'Theodore, please do not borrow lines from *Blackadder*.'

'Who or what is *Blackadder*?' responded Theodore, genuinely ignorant.

'Theodore, oh, Theodore, what the heck am I to do with you?' (you can imagine the patient Andrew Goode shaking his head while having to endure this farce) 'Will you swear you are not walking off with the gold bars that I have hidden in the safe?'

'Mr Andrew Goode, I swear that I do not know the existence of any gold bars, nor the location of any safe within these premises, although I must caution that despite the over-fastidiousness of the security you have, it isn't sufficient for high-value items.'

Again, the guard found reason to glare at Theodore.

'Oh my Gawd, please put Mr Lovejoy back on the phone.'

'Umar Gul?' I didn't know you followed cricket.

'Eh?'

Theodore handed the phone back to a frowning Lovejoy, who took it with a cursory nod. Theodore overheard a few 'buts' and then turned away. When Lovejoy placed the handset back on its cradle, he picked up a folder and requested that Theodore sign off a security waiver in the Raid Procedure. Without further ado, he signed it and spun the folder back towards Lovejoy for countersigning. Now that all the bureaucracy was complete, Lovejoy's frostiness thawed. Theodore apologised for causing a scene, explaining he was upset at the loss of funding for a project and didn't really wish for Mr Goode to be disturbed. Lovejoy responded in kind, saying it wouldn't do for security to be seen to be lax, and then expressed concern regarding the funding loss and whether the laboratory was a still profitable.

'Well, I think this is the only place around that pays security professionals an appropriate salary. I expect you know the old moral about peanuts . . .' Theodore agreed and warmed to Lovejoy somewhat, especially as he'd deceived him. For a short while, he considered returning to the laboratory on the pretext of having forgotten something and disposing of his contraband. For the second time, he missed a signal and was to regret not following this whim.

Theodore boarded the bus that was almost full, and the predominant number of passengers were pensioners, who enjoyed free travel outside peak hours ('God's waiting room', Steve Stiff would have commented, but the pensioners would probably have said it first and also many years previously, like sex, youth thinks it also invented wit and humour.) His thigh was now numb; the heat of the bus was oppressive. The sun was blinding, and tabloid newspapers were sporting onomatopoeias like Phew, Cor, and sCORchio. The more staid broadsheets were predicting something about 'could be the hottest/sunniest/driest since records began, hosepipe ban to stay until Christmas' and so forth. Theodore had just finished scanning the various newspapers that were being shaken and folded when a warning horn sounded in the driver's cab. At the next stop, the driver killed the engine, which sighed and juddered to a halt and then emitted a plume of steam from the engine cover. He opened his door, which doubled as a counter, and announced to his passengers that the bus was in need of an ambulance. Theodore was genuinely shocked at the number of pensioners who pulled out mobile phones to report in (to whoever) this exciting or exasperating piece of news. The engine ticked like a bomb on countdown and transferred its heat into the cabin as all fans and any air-conditioning were now inoperative, and all the windows were sealed units. A bead of sweat trickled down Theodore's face, and he could feel a similar bead of moisture trickle down his thigh and sneak around his right buttock. He wished he had worn his shorts, but he would never wear shorts to work, even out of hours. A susurrus of grumbles and 'what's happenings' rose, steadily gathering volume. The bus driver was off the bus, talking into his phone. A couple of busybodies had also got off and surrounded him, spouting questions for which he was probably trying to acquire the answers, anyway. On board the bus, people were using newspapers and magazines as fans to try and cool themselves. Theodore imagined a similar scene in the days of the Raj and smiled secretly to himself. It was while he caught himself smiling that he realised it would have been less than a year ago he would been in the forefront of the complainants, voicing things like, 'It's just not good enough, I am a season ticket holder, and I demand to know what you are going to do about it!' He wondered what had changed in him recently. It was as if his hormones had finally settled down after a prolonged puberty. However, he was also starting to get concerned with the rise in temperature. The eggs might start the process of hatching. The bus lurched slightly on its springs as the driver and accompanying busybodies got onboard again.

'Ladies and Gentlemen, I apologise on behalf of the bus company, but this bus needs towing to the depot. There will be a replacement for this service, but it won't reach here for another twenty-five minutes.'

This prompted various mutterings, which were probably rhetorical, although no one alighted to seek an alternative means to complete their journey. After about three minutes of internal debate, Theodore arose and left the bus, deciding he might as well walk.

It took him an hour to walk home, but that included a stop for shopping and a refreshing orange drink. He dumped his shopping in the kitchen and quickly changed. He would charge all the headsets with eggs today and transfer them to the refrigerator to be deployed this week. How he would deploy them had not been finalised. Somehow his change of character had also interfered with his meticulous planning process. To an outsider with his type of cricketing bent, he was risking dropping a catch or spoiling an immaculate innings with a rash shot or even worse, running himself out.

Theodore's mind raced with the delivery method; he couldn't just hand them out willy-nilly on the bus to people with some banter like 'Try these for size. They're much better quality than the ones that are producing the noise you're listening to.' Similarly, just leaving them at random wouldn't target the right (or wrong) people. He wouldn't want to recruit someone to deliver on his behalf because that would involve a co-conspirator whom he couldn't trust and they might just drop the headsets in the nearest rubbish bin (and to whom could he complain?), let alone the time and costs associated with recruitment. A small voice in his head whispered to just freeze the eggs and call it quits (which is probably how Natalie would have put it), another signal that he ignored. Theodore decided that he needed to get out of the house to think. He also decided to buy some wine, which he hadn't included in his shopping list. He hadn't a clue about what was a good wine and what was not, but he would simply go into the local wine merchant and ask. He also thought about calling Natalie for more information, and he wouldn't want to use the Kevin Sedgley-Ahern 'phone (which he should dump sooner rather than later) and hadn't dialled out from his home phone for some time because he had an inbred reluctance to dial someone else. This reluctance was inherited from his mother, who was particularly miserly because of the historical cost of outbound telephone calls. Anyway, he didn't have a number for her, so with the eggs safely in the fridge in the workshop, a much older version than the one in the kitchen, Theodore grabbed a rucksack and strode from the house, thinking that he might buy two or three bottles and the rucksack would be used as a convenient way to transport them home.

Chapter 11

Theodore arrived at the wine merchant (there was only one) and put his nose against the window and tried to ascertain which wine proved to be the best value. The labels were multifarious and bemusing; he was surprised that one wasn't called 'Drink Me' (it surely would have been New World and highly likely to have been Australian), there was a whole old and new world of countries producing wine. Theodore was confused and intrigued. He pushed open the door, and a bell softly chimed. The manager or proprietor smiled and looked pleased to see a new customer, or possibly just a customer. He also looked pleased because this person did not seem like an armed robber. This had happened before, only once admittedly, but this was enough to disturb the man from his idyll of providing fine or at least good wine to the Wessex region. This person looked like the perfect innocent, whom he could convert to the finer points of the palate.

'Dear Person, how may I assist you?' Well, how else would somebody who wore half-moon glasses, large, spotted bow tie, and a boating blazer speak? He was definitely the proprietor.

Theodore succinctly explained his difficulty around being told to get some decent wine in and not having a clue what a decent wine was.

'Commendable honesty, my dear chap! A lot of people show their ignorance by their choice or asking if I had any red wine in the chiller, ha-ha. Now where shall we start? Well, why not at this fruity red?'

The proprietor was the sort of person who held conversations that could also be soliloquies. He deftly whipped the cork from the bottle and poured a small measure into two glasses that appeared as if by magic.

'One swirls the wine around the glass, noting the corona as it resumes its place according to the laws of gravity.'

Sure enough a crown could be discerned. Like most, if not all, scientists, Theodore loved expertise.

'Now one puts ones nose into the glass and inhales the bouquet. Just tell me what you can smell, and don't say wine!'

'Er, OK, flowers and plums?'

'Good, I agree, now you may taste, taking in air as well as wine. It is acceptable nay de rigueur, to slurp! Thinking of what you just told me, do you get similar flavours? You must forgive me, but I must spit out the wine. It wouldn't do to have one stumbling about, before closing time.'

Theodore slurped and decided to buy a case. He then requested that dear person select a suitable white of a similar price range. Delivery was arranged for a small charge. There was no way a dozen bottles of wine would fit in his rucksack. However, a litre of orange would. 'Dear person' gladly sold good-quality orange (not from concentrate) at a premium. After a hot walk home, the second of the day, Theodore was looking forward to a second refreshing drink of orange to boot.

Less than half an hour later, a sweating Theodore opened his front door. He went straight to the kitchen, took a glass from a cupboard, tore open the carton of orange, and poured a measure. Pausing for a second and determined to savour the experience, he sipped the drink slowly, allowing the citric acid and fructose to sparkle around his taste buds. The carton was placed in the fridge with a vow to purchase a couple more to act as company. This was worth the premium price. He took his drink out of the French windows and placed it on to the patio that could have been done with a scrub or power-hosing. He righted a chair on the patio's set that had not been sat in for some ten years but, being galvanised, had not rusted, although it wasn't too clean. The patio furniture would need a scrubbing, too. He used his foot to position one of the other patio chairs into position as a suitable footrest and tilted his head back under an azure sky. Surely, this wasn't England? He was about to peel off his shirt when the thought of exposing his white body made him demure. The neighbours might be peering from behind the net curtains. He ought to start priming the headsets, but his languor and the weather got the better of him. The doorbell and loud knocking penetrated his doze; he creakily lowered his legs and stood.

'Dear person' stood at the door with the wine on a sack truck, which had triple wheels on each side, which made getting the wine over the threshold a piece of cake.

'Dear person, where is one's wine rack? Ah, OK not the best place for it, and one needs another couple. Luckily, I have two in the jalopy. I can let one have it for a discount price, deal?'

Theodore agreed it would be a deal.

'Ah yes, I see one has already sampled the jus d'orange. I have taken the liberty, given the weather, of loading a couple of cartons, c'est bon?'

Theodore nodded assent, and whilst 'dear person' operated his business as a labour of love, it looked like he would still be in business until he chose to close. The extras were wheeled in, and the wine stacked. Theodore held the door open. After walking down the path and into the road and then making a sweeping bow, 'dear person' closed the door of his 'jalopy' and puttered off back to his shop. He left his business card on the telephone table.

Theodore closed the front door and pondered whether to resume his loafing or get to work with the headsets. The do-it-yourself colony idea had been abandoned in favour of keeping the eggs in suspended animation in his refrigerator. He decided that his work ethic should win out and went into his workshop. He lifted up the box of headsets and arranged them individually on the workbench. It took two hours to apportion an egg to each headset (sometimes, he used the right earpiece and sometimes the left). He had insufficient eggs for all the headsets, but hadn't made a detailed count of how many he had charged. Which for Theodore, was unusual. Something caused a break in his concentration and he left them in their individual re-sealable plastic pouches on the bench. He intended to store the primed headsets in the fridge. Much later, in retrospect, he was sure there was an evil influence at work as this was just totally out of character. He locked the workshop and went into the kitchen and poured a glass of orange. In the lounge, he opened his laptop and found his favourite cricket website. The recent hot weather was starting to take a toll on the outfields as the usual hosepipe ban had been tightened to include sporting arenas. 'How', thought Theodore, 'can a country with as much average rainfall as the UK consider banning hosepipes?' He scrolled through the test scores and the county championship results, noting his county was propping up the second division, again. He noted that the humidity had risen, so he opened the French windows to try and drive a breeze through the house. He thought about scrambling his way into the loft to retrieve a fan that had been purchased during the last heatwave, and at first, he couldn't be bothered, but another thirty stuffy minutes later, the heatwave made him lower the loft ladder and gingerly edge his way upwards. Good old Peter Mack had come round many a year ago to install the loft ladder when he'd seen Theodore teeter perilously on the apices of a step ladder to haul himself upwards and into the loft space to retrieve a suitcase. Peter had also turned up with a van load of wood, and together, they had boarded out the loft, turning it into a pretty useful storage space. Theodore flicked the switch to turn on the fluorescent tubes and waited a second or two until they stopped flickering. He recalled the last heatwave when he had poked his head into the loft and heard the unmistakable angry buzz of wasps indignant at his approach, which resulted in a hasty scramble down the ladder and then an urgent call to a pest control company. Theodore knew from study and experience that you treat wasps with respect before you kill them. He could have disposed of them himself, but that means sealing the nest at night and then introducing a poison. Anyway, it was £20 well spent. He stood up in the loft and had moved the fan close to the hatch, when he looked at an old chest of drawers that held old photograph albums. The next thing that happened was the usual thing that happens when people go into the loft. He went to the chest of drawers and pulled open the top drawer. He located an old chair and flopped down into it with an album on his lap; the sweat coursed down his face. The album held photographs of his mother and father in their courtship phase, laughing and posing on and around an old car (Volkswagen) that Theodore's father had managed to scrape together the money for its purchase. Theodore looked at the photographs and realised that both of them were thirty plus years younger than he was now; somehow, this was really upsetting. There were no photographs (to his knowledge) of his life (or lack of it). He hastily shut the album, gave a fond farewell to the cases of books standing like a silent army, and cautiously descended the ladder after dragging the fan over the hatch edge and seeing it safely deposited on the landing. He closed the loft hatch and decided to shower off the dust and debris that clung to his sweating body. Theodore stripped off and dialled the shower to a tepid setting (he had been forced to replace the shower unit a year or so ago) and allowed the water to refresh him. Theodore only used to shower when he thought he was dirty or when his hair needed a shampoo, but recently he had the sybaritic urge and quite enjoyed stripping off and being massaged by the cascade that spouted from the nozzle. He stepped from the shower and knotted a tatty towel around his waist after a brisk rub-down. Feeling very Roman and imagining a laurel wreath around his head, he marched down the stairs and decided to open a bottle of wine. With the French windows open and still not much air circulating, Theodore selected a bottle of red and poured a glass; he started his laptop and watched the highlights of the England cricket team battling back to parity in a test match. The red wine was very fruity and palatable; the glass was soon replenished. A third refill was then followed by a fourth, and that saw the bottle empty. The lounge had cooled slightly, and he closed the French windows and lazed back on the sofa, occasionally clicking a gadget on his laptop for news and cricket updates. The laptop hibernated five minutes after Theodore dozed off.

A muzzy Theodore was disturbed by a metallic twang, a sound out of tune with the normal harmonics that the house made. He blinked, and slowly, the room came into focus; he could hear shuffling and the odd grunt like a pig was snuffling around. Theodore creakily rose from the sofa, and the towel fell from his loins as if in a poorly choreographed stage farce. He knotted the towel round his waist again, and another sound penetrated his fuzzy mind. Natalie, being fond of John Irving's novels, would have said it was the 'sound of someone trying not to make a sound'. He fumbled the key in the lock of the door to his workshop, opened it, and without thinking poked his head in, and then he heard a loud ringing noise, which sounded like 'DANGGG'. The noise was inside his head, and before he could say 'what's that?' he crumpled on to the floor thoroughly unconscious with blood trickling down his neck and dripping on to the floor in a wine dark pool. 'επι οινιπα ποντον' Theodore's mother would have said either in the vein of Homer or James Joyce.

When he awoke, he was sitting on an old wooden chair that he used as a step to reach things from the higher shelves in his workshop. There were no other noises than the ones he made by breathing or swallowing. He was bound to the chair with his own packing tape, from the same roll they had gagged him. There had definitely been two in the gang; additionally, they had taped headphones to his head. He guessed whose headphones they were. Why he was gagged, he could understand. Why they had blocked his hearing was something he didn't understand at all. Did they think he would recognise their *voices*? If he had put the headsets in his fridge, would they have muffled his ears with something else? Whoever had broken into his house had not attached a personal stereo to the jack, so the hatching would take longer than if there were vibrations disturbing the egg (he fervently hoped). They might have picked a set that didn't contain an egg! But Theodore knew his own luck. His throat was parched from dehydration after all the sweating and the wine that he had consumed; he tried to swallow as if in practice for the arrival of the larva, which shouldn't arrive for at least another twelve hours. He hoped he would be discovered and released before then. The tape used on the headphone partially obscured his vision, but he could see that the burglars had left the overhead fluorescent tubes on *(weren't burglars supposed to have torches and masks?)*. If he tilted his head back, he could make out the workshop layout, and whilst they had taped his arms to his side, they had left his hands with some ability to manipulate things if he could get within reach, although if he moved his hands, the hairs on his arms were painfully tugged. Sunday is probably the worst day of the week to be taped to a chair (is there a *good* day?) and unable to call for help. Theodore had few callers on normal working days, but on a Sunday, he expected none (Oh for a nosey neighbour!). However, he did have experience of being patient, even as a teenager! He remembered going to Trent Bridge for an England versus Australia test match around his eighteenth birthday, and seeing the Australian openers Marsh and Taylor bat all day, he watched England's mighty new fast bowler Malcolm being blunted by the flat pitch and stubborn, solid bats of the Australian pair.

He recalled not being upset because he had been an opening batsman; he sympathised with their cause. In addition, when the boot was on the other foot, opening batsmen often had to put up with the occasional ball that whistled past the ear in excess of 90 mph as well as juicy green wickets that caused the new ball to jag off the pitch, making one look like a fool. He daydreamed of being at the crease and setting himself in for a long stay. But being passive wouldn't assist in acquiring his freedom; he decided to think and see if he could come up with a plan to release himself. He wished he'd watched more James Bond, Jason Bourne, or any other adventure film whose lead character was initialled JB, which surely would yield an idea for a heroic escape. The first course of action would be surveillance. Theodore could rock the chair backwards so he could see his position relative to the layout of his workshop. He could make out the position of the cupboards and drawers. Ideally, he would like to be close to the drawer where he stored his assortment of craft knives. Even as he thought about it, he knew that the drawer would be too high for him to be able to open it by hand, but he wouldn't give up, he may have been caught out in his first innings, but he would try some adventurous shots for this one.

Chapter 12

Natalie awoke in a hot bed and wished that the owners of the flat she rented had invested in air conditioning. Living in a garden flat, she would not have wanted to leave a window open and possibly get a surprise visitor. Shortly after she had risen, the church bells started tolling as if to celebrate another hot sunny day. This was a day for getting the beast out for a cruise, a bit of lunch in a pub, and then a burble home. Now where should she go? 'God bless computers and Google,' she thought and fired up her tablet and using the maps feature did a virtual tour based on a 75-mile radius from the flat.

Natalie had decided to meander to the south and south-west of the country and just tick along, away from the urgent families with packed estate cars or towing caravans that were starting to congest the motorways at this time of year. There are some remarkably good, quiet roads in this neck of the woods and some interesting off-the-beaten-track routes that connect relatively significant towns. Natalie set off to pick up the first part of an 'A' road that caused her to pass Theodore's house, where she paused for a short while, and was curious why the garage door seemed slightly ajar. She halted in the middle of the road and pondered; the v8 of TVR mumbled to itself as if pondering too. After a while and thinking it would be too forward to stop and ask him out for a ride, she heard a honk of a horn behind her. Irritated, Natalie looked into the rear-view mirror and depressed the throttle, and the TVR grumbled away.

Inside the workshop, Theodore heard the burble of the big V8, and for a minute or so, his hopes soared. Depression soon clouded over him when the horn of an impatient, selfish, supercilious prat caused the TVR to growl and then sulkily rumble away. Theodore paused and choked back a sob; it was back to getting his own plan together for setting himself free. He rocked back on the chair and, still surveying, spotted the instrument that had been used to break into his garage as well as poleaxe him when he unwittingly poked his head into the workshop. A garden spade is a useful burglar's tool for popping open windows or garage doors and has an innocuous appearance even when blatantly hefted about. Theodore was thankful that when he was struck, they used the flat of the spade rather than the edge. Although the edge would have done some serious damage to his head, he knew that it wasn't sharp enough to cut the tape that bound him.

Kevin Sedgley-Ahern wiped an invisible speck of dust from his car, a Subaru Impreza, with a cherished plate of R16 KSA. The car was sprayed to look like a packet of cigarettes. Kevin thinking was that he was cool, and a rickshaw was a coolie-operated vehicle. He slotted himself into the driver's seat and buckled up his racing harness, ran his hand over the steering wheel, adjusted his baseball cap neatly above his sunglasses whilst grinning inanely, and then gunned the car out of his drive with a rasping snarl. He aimed the 'Scoobie' to the ring road where he knew that there were no speed cameras and looked for suitable 'victims'. Victims normally comprised young drivers of small cars with the odd enhancement made to the wheel trims or exhaust fittings. Kevin would spot one pootling up the road in the overtaking lane, zoom up behind, flick on all the lights, and roar past when the car was sheepishly pulled over, looking over with one hand on the steering wheel as he delivered the coup de grace. Kevin and his car chuckled off along the country roads, with its air scoop snootily mounted like a gunner's turret in front, whilst he enjoyed the wheel in his grasp and noted that he had a tank full of fuel to turn into pollution.

Natalie had cruised the TVR along the Dorset 'B' roads along the charming villages with the somewhat earthy names of Piddletrenthide and such. It was so tickling that Natalie had to stop for a break in the Piddle Inn (there is a river called the piddle, so this is not schoolboy stuff, but it does raise a snicker). An apocryphal attempt was made to rename the river, villages, and valley to puddle; in deference to royalty, but for the sake of posterity, this didn't stick. Natalie parked the TVR away from the pub and strolled back down the sleepy village. She ducked under the low lintel into a shady bar; the reaction from the locals was friendly but without any hint of intrusion. She sat down with an orange juice and a ploughman's lunch and drew a book, a notepad, and a pen from her handbag. This was all subterfuge and a barrier against unwanted conversation. The book on this occasion was a collection of Aristophanes's plays, with original text and English translation on a facing page, which was enough of a rampart, but also provided amusing reading, although she had to be wary of the odd or not so odd classical scholar, one of whom reprimanded her for reading such coarse works. She beckoned the man closer with a crooked finger and whispered *Ορχεις* into his ear, causing him to retreat with a huff (*Ορχεις* translates as testicles). Theodore's mother would have embraced her as a kindred spirit as Theodore's mother had translated Aristophanes's *The Frogs* from the classical Greek as part of an examination some fifty years previously and would have laughed at her rebuttal of the stuck-up old Φαλλος. That particular memory was recalled and filed; Natalie took her empty glass, plate, and cutlery back to the bar to the nods of approval from the regulars, who mumbled, 'You can come again, my love.' She exited into a pleasant English summer afternoon and crossed the lane to where she'd left the TVR.

Kevin normally kept to the main roads and navigated by choosing towns he'd previously heard of, or that looked of suitable size, towns of a size that would have young girls who might be impressed by a prat in a fast car that looks like a packet of cigarettes. He avoided the narrow lanes because he could get stuck behind a chugging tractor, and being a bit of a boy racer meant that if he would have to pull out and overtake, he would come face to face with his nemesis, namely another souped-up GT/Saloon, Coupe, or Convertible, the driver of which would probably be wearing a similar cloth-badged rally jacket, despite the weather (Coming face to face with a Volvo or a truck couldn't be ruled out.) Occasionally, a girl may have the temerity or stupidity to accept a cruise with Kevin behind the wheel. (Kevin thought it was arousal of a sexual nature, not fear, that caused the girl to squirm in the bucket seat.) On Kevin's social networking page, this 'conquest' would be grossly exaggerated with inappropriate postings like 'Need the sponge for the front seat, again.' This was probably his most serious offence (apart from raising the possibility of an imminent and premature death in them); he didn't make a pass at them and would throw a hollow-sounding 'Perhaps we could go out sometime?' as her shoes clicked a tattoo of retreat on the paving stones. Although no one could possibly have had less sexual congress than Theodore, Kevin didn't exceed Theodore's experience by that much.

Having spotted the deep Burgundy TVR ahead that had halted at one of the few sets of traffic lights on one of the wider sections of the A37, Kevin swept the Subaru superciliously alongside Natalie and blips the throttle, causing the dump valve to make the engine gasp. He tilted his head forward and peered at Natalie, only his baseball cap caught on the visor causing it to sit askew on his head as if he was doing a Norman Wisdom impersonation. He angrily pushed in back on his head and adjusted his driving gloves. Again, he impatiently blipped the throttle on his 'Scoobie-Doo'. 'Oh my gosh', shushed the Subaru. In the TVR, Natalie thought, 'this guy thinks he's Harrison Ford' (from American Graffiti that she'd watched with Theodore all those years ago). 'I may have to educate him'. (Natalie didn't mean she wanted to see Kevin's car flaming in a ditch, as per the final few sequences in the film. She just wanted to out-accelerate him and thus teach him a lesson.)

On the dashboard of Natalie's TVR, there was a switch that had a simple label of NO! This is part humour and part fact; flicking this switch caused the progressive delivery system to operate that discharged nitrous oxide into the manifold of the TVR. The system had been installed a couple of years ago by the USAAF at a local base, not as part of a NATO agreement, but one of the crew chiefs was a keen drag racing enthusiast and had performed the necessary examination of the TVR's engine to permit the system to be installed safely. Being an honest citizen, Natalie had declared the customisation to the insurance company, who were classic sports car insurance specialists. The company was bemused by the fact that anyone would want to boost the power of a TVR, but being specialist, TVR insurers couldn't reject cover although the premium was boosted by a higher percentage than the percentage of additional power supplied. Given this advantage, Natalie wouldn't just beat Kevin Sedgley-Ahern's vehicle, but she could also leave it standing if she wished. A Subaru was pretty good in a straight line, but it was more of a rally car. Natalie's TVR was just a beast. She tightened her headscarf and turned her head towards the Subaru and smiled coquettishly as if she didn't really know what would happen next. Natalie did not blip the throttle; the TVR grumbled at tick-over. The lights changed to amber at the crossroads, and both drivers concentrated, in the true spirit of fair play. Neither Kevin nor Natalie anticipated the lights to get an advantage. When the lights turned green, they still waited for the other to start proceedings, so much so that a grumpy old man with a hat on his head and a Volvo seat under his bum honked his horn from the centre of the steering wheel over which he could just about peer (of course neither paid attention nor had even spotted the Volvo's arrival at the lights). Neither did they bother to glance in the rear-view mirror to show concern at the impatient driver's arrival. Kevin lost his nerve first and dropped the clutch on his Scoobie; seeing out of the corner of her eye, the twitch of her opponent's car was enough to goad Natalie into slipping the clutch and stepping on the accelerator, using a delicate touch, as she did not want to spin the rear wheels, nor cause the car to leap slightly (as Kevin did), but she gave enough pressure needed to keep the Subaru within a car's length. As Kevin stamped on the clutch and slapped the Subaru into second, he couldn't help glancing to the left at the same time. Natalie flicked the NO! Switch. The TVR exceeded a hundred as Natalie shifted into third and stopped accelerating. There was also a bend approaching, and it was time for serious concentration. She flipped off the switch (the bottle hadn't fully discharged) and used the throttle, brakes, and steering wheel to manage the roaring beast in and out of a couple of bends; the dry roads made this far safer. Kevin had already slowed, even having four-wheeled drive and better traction, knew that he was outclassed. He sought, and quickly located a side road which he swung his car down. (He was not travelling slowly. The Subaru blatted its exhaust call through the little village as if it was loudly sulking.) He hit the call button on his hands-free kit and made a call to a friend to complain about his tuning of the Subaru.

'Beaten by a girl, beaten by a girl, beaten by a girl.' He drummed on the wheel. 'Get an electric car or better still a smart car, arf arf,' echoed a malicious alter ego in his head. However, Kevin was of a character that bounced back from adversity extremely quickly. A harsher critic would have called him shallow. A few minutes later, he was his old self again and had glossed over the incident within a couple of minutes by blaming everything else. He didn't bear grudges, which was made easier by his short attention span. Like a lot of us, he conveniently forgot or dismissed his failings. Kevin's entry on his social network page was pretty good fable. 'Stonking smoke out in the Scoobie, cool bitch in a classic tried it on, but I pratted a gear change and for safety's sake let her through. All I'm saying, babe, is next time.' (You could picture Kevin clicking his tongue and blowing smoke from an imaginary revolver.) It didn't help matters when Kevin's mechanic friend butted in on the page (if one could possibly butt in on a system owned by an corporation) and announced that KSA's vehicle was tuned to perfection without spending an awful lot of money, but it would be a waste as he'd probably prat up the gear change again anyway (hey, hey). It didn't help matters when his friend asked for a description of a registration of the classic car that had 'done him up like a kipper, or was it simply a skill?' When Kevin couldn't provide much detail, apart from being deep red like 'you know a Beaujolais or something', there was the equivalent of hoots of derision via messages in the tone of 'you didn't even get that close, lol . . . Kevin, just face it, you're a boy.' Given the support on his so-called friends, Kevin thought that he ought to give up being a petrol head and seriously think about going green. There were some pretty sexy racing cycles being touted around town, including an Italian job with a Columbus frame and the Ferrari logo (a snip at just over £4 k), with the sunglasses and aero-helmet. This was the new Adonis to whom Kevin aspired. He could ditch the Subaru, buy the Ferrari, and still be quids in (he hadn't thought how he could chat up girls and offer them a lift though, as yet, unless they built a tandem or he bought a matching pair). There again, his Subaru hadn't been a convincing factor (possibly a factor of zero) in adding to his sexual conquests.

Natalie eased the TVR around a couple of bends, decelerating to legal limits, and looked for Subarus and police cars in her mirrors. She knew that some people didn't like being taught a lesson and that the excessive speed she deployed was not, and should not be, tolerated on a public road. The adrenalin coursing through her body caused her to be a little nauseous, and she just let the TVR guide her home, its engine growling playfully in tune and smugly cocky. She wondered where she had put the telephone number of the guy who could arrange to get a top-up for the nitrous oxide bottle.

She drove slowly around without anyone appearing to follow her, and thirty minutes after the race, Natalie approached Theodore's house. She slowed the car to a crawl and noticed that the garage door was still slightly raised. She halted the car; the engine sound of the TVR rumbling and snorting caused Theodore to fervently pray to God he would believe in until his death, if only she would turn into his drive and turn off the engine, or better still lever the door open and rescue him. Natalie noticed that the light in the garage was on when it wasn't really necessary, but being a scientist, she knew that light having adequate light is paramount, so she didn't bother getting out of the car. 'OK,' she sniffed, 'I'll get the TVR to beckon him, and if he doesn't react or ignores it, well, that's that.' Natalie poked the throttle, just over a thousand rpm, for a second, and watched the house. No response. She crossly stepped on the throttle, taking it up past the three on the rev counter and held it for a couple more seconds. (The TVR burped in annoyance). No reaction at all from number 13 Acacia avenue. She was sorely tempted to up the ante and stuff the neighbours, but maybe, Theodore wasn't interested. She thought he was probably preparing for work, and the thunder-music of the TVR didn't penetrate his concentration.

'Hmmpfh, Hmmpfh, Hmmpfh,' a muffled Theodore screamed behind his gag, tears streaking his dirty face. In his desperation, he managed to cause the chair to jump a few inches. Desperation turned to depression as he heard the TVR grumble sorrowfully away, while the towel around his waist sopped up the small amount of urine that he had leaked in the crisis without realising it. Theodore sagged into his bindings and hoped to sleep (possibly for a long time). However, within about an hour, he noticed that something had eased. The moisture had got to the adhesive and allowed better freedom of movement and also made the adhesive cease to try and pluck the hairs from his arms. 'At last,' he thought, 'one for the good chaps, we're off the mark with a four.' He started gentle movements with the aim of not causing the tape to roll into a strong thread. He needed reach and flexibility if he wanted to cut the ties that bound.

Theodore had lost track of time for a while, and therefore, he didn't know how long he had been parcelled up nor when he could expect the arrival of hominivorax. He knew that unless something miraculous happened, he would soon have first-hand knowledge of the route the larva would take after it had perforated his eardrum. For many years, he would have dreaded the thought of swallowing a larva (what's worse than finding a maggot in your apple? Half a maggot!), but now he really hoped he would have to as the thought of the little beast burrowing its way at random into other parts of his head did not bear consideration. Surprisingly, he dozed off.

Natalie locked the garage with the TVR inside, ticking away in apparent satisfaction as it cooled. She walked the short distance to her flat, and after letting herself in, she sulkily removed sunglasses and scarf. Something seemed to have affected her mood after what should have been a pretty satisfying day. After a shower, which did little to lower her temperature or raise her spirits, she slumped down on her couch with a towel binding her hair turban-style and switched on her tablet. She would see whether she could find a phone number to give Theodore a call. Something was not quite right; she thought that she should have been bolder and marched up to the door, but maybe a phone call wouldn't seem so forward. She would also remind him that his workshop door was not properly closed. What was bugging her was that she remembered recommending Theodore reinforce the garage door out. Had she predicted something? She used an online map with satellite images as an option to locate Theodore's house and then located a website that had Postal Address File, Electoral Roll data, and consented telephone numbers. She needed the two applications in tandem because she didn't know that where Theodore lived was called Acacia Avenue, nor did she know the number. With the two, possibly she could get a result. The satellite images were some three years out of date, but Theodore's house hadn't changed much. The trees had matured, but the front door was still the same colour. Natalie managed to get the street name and found a house that had the number beside the front door, so she was able to work out the number of Theodore's house. She was surprised that there was a number thirteen, in a lot of roads, and this number was omitted (Natalie or Theodore's mother would have called this omission triskaidekaphobia—τρισκαιδεκαφοβια). She switched to the address directory website, which listed the names associated with the addresses. At number thirteen, there were several names, all mixed spellings of either Theodore or Grouchier. This is a result of using cheap off-shore data input either human or machine. She managed to find a consented number that was ex-directory in a normal phone book (gathered and sold by marketing research, but not of course Andrew Goode's department). This is one outcome of using, for example, cost comparison websites sharing the details of people seeking the best deal for holidays, insurance, or other online sales. The number was flagged as live and available. Natalie keyed the number and heard the sound that indicated it was ringing at 13, Acacia Avenue. Eventually, the answering machine kicked in with a pleasant female voice (the default voice on the machine). Natalie left a message and a number to call her: 'Tonight would be good even if a little late!' She ended with a cheery 'hope you had a good weekend!' She turned off her phone and left it on the sideboard, almost expecting it to ring immediately.

Inside the workshop, Theodore was awoken by the phone ringing and went into his 'Hmmpfh, Hmmpfh, Hmmpfh' routine because he suspected that it was Natalie because no one else would call him apart from Asian call centres, and this wasn't their preferred time (they always liked to get you as you're sitting down to eat). The TVR burbling previously was perhaps a bit of a giveaway. There was a brief silence when the answering machine clicked in. Obviously Theodore couldn't hear what message was being left, but he knew with deepening gloom that it meant she wouldn't be round to assist his escape. He was galvanised into action as if frustration had built up a store of kinetic energy. He jumped forward and, at the same time, pulled the chair and realised he could get it to move away from its starting position. He paused, and then getting his legs and upper body in synchronisation, he jerked upwards and slightly to the right. He moved about two inches. He rested and repeated the effort, another two inches. He leaned by and saw that the drawer that held his craft knives was only two feet away, just twelve more jerks (he nearly smiled when he thought of what Natalie would make of twelve jerks in his workshop. Natalie had explained what the alternative definition of jerk was in USA, after calling Steve Stiff one). For the first time in several hours, he was feeling upbeat. He rested and jerked another two inches. Once he was close, he could then think of the really tricky bit of how to open the drawer, retrieve a suitable blade, and slice through his bindings. Three more efforts, whilst moving him another six inches, caused the sweat to start from his forehead and the need for further rest. His muscles ached, but the sweat was loosening the adhesive, and during his rest period, he could manipulate his hands and arms, developing more range for his hands. The effort caused his head to boom in rhythm to his heart rate and then ease the pressure by starting to cause the warm blood to trickle down his cheek again. He ought to rest more between each exertion.

Natalie finally realised that Theodore had not received the message (it may not have been his number, sometimes people are not totally truthful when they use online applications) or that he had chosen not to call back. Sunday night television did not give her much hope of entertainment, especially not test match highlights *(how can you have highlights of a game that lasts five days on day four?)*. To be fair, only an Englishman (or possibly a Welshman) would want to see the England cricket team dragging themselves gradually from ignominy to parity. Natalie thought she should have taken the opportunity to borrow a book or two from Theodore's bookcase. OK, she thought, it was time to see what was available online for passing the time until she was relaxed enough to contemplate bed;

her adrenalin levels were still high after the day's excitement and then uncertainty. Natalie went to bed with a John Updike book at about the same time. Theodore still had eight inches to go until he thought he would be in range of his drawer. He was also tiring more with each bout and could only manage a two-inch shuffle before he needed to rest for ten minutes or so, while his body recovered. A fitter, younger man would have undoubtedly made the journey without difficulty but possibly may have not been on the receiving end in the first place. The only improvement Theodore had made to his fitness was his change of diet; a lifetime of exercise deficit meant this was not a sprint or even a middle-distance event. This was an innings required of Geoff Boycott or Mike Atherton, being the collection of runs, concentration and the use of minimum effort. 'Just survive each ball as it is bowled,' he thought. The next rest period told Theodore that night had fallen, the sweat he raised as a result of a two-inch shuffle, cooled rapidly on his forehead. Cold and darkness raised their primordial fears. Theodore leaned back in the chair and realised, as he had estimated before, that he couldn't reach the drawer with his hands. He had to tilt himself back and hope to hook the handle with his foot and try to extract the drawer. With a bit of luck, he hoped to pull the drawer out completely and spill the contents within range, trusting one of his more sharp knives wouldn't pirouette and drop into an eyeball. Suddenly, Theodore was grateful that they had taped over his eyes, albeit partially. He still needed to gather his strength, and whilst he was doing so, fatigue engulfed him, head slumping forward. A brief grunt of a snore echoed in his throat.

Chapter 13

A tickling sensation in his left ear, followed by a short, but audible scratch, startled Theodore awake. In his soporific state he wondered a) where he was and b) what was happening. Both questions were answered rapidly. The hatching had occurred, and hominivorax was stretching its non-existent arms, metaphysically yawning and stirring from its own slumber and seeking to get up close and personal. Theodore gathered his strength, which was now enhanced by a serious dose of adrenaline. Two more efforts and Theodore judged that he was within range; he needed to throw himself backwards and extend his right foot to hook the drawer handle. If successful, he might halt his fall and hopefully plan how to get the drawer contents on to the floor within reach. If unsuccessful, he might fail and break his collarbone as a bonus.

He rested again and waited. Sure enough, another scratch echoed in his ear. Theodore did his best to calm himself and keep control. With a count of three, he threw himself back and was pleased when his right foot lodged into the drawer handle. He was stuck at an angle, finely poised and hoping the chair wouldn't slip, or if it did, he would extract the drawer. Theodore stayed in equilibrium until another scratching sound meant that he must act. A swift one, two, three in his head, followed by what would have been a backward somersault by a gymnast, resulted in the chair slipping and twisting to the left. This caused the drawer to move, and as Theodore's head hit the workshop floor, the stored momentum wrenched the drawer free, and the contents scattered at random (the most serious craft knife missing Theodore's eyeball by some distance). Theodore heard a different noise on his head before being knocked unconscious for the second time in twenty-four hours. The wound from the spade was extended by another inch. Hominivorax was also dislodged and contracted, like a penis in very cold water, as a result of a self-defence mechanism. Theodore was not unconscious for long and was able to see from his position the success of his endeavours. It took several attempts to get the chair and himself on to their respective backs. He managed to get hold of a knife and, with a lot of manipulation, got it into a position to start the first attempt to slice the packing tape. The first success was greeted by a tickle in his left ear. From his school days, Theodore seldom won a race against the clock. Time pressure caused him to make mistakes; even in a game of chess, he was hypnotised by the clock into making a wrong move. Holding tightly to the knife, he rolled on his left side. He was going to make the little bugger crawl uphill. The thought of bashing his head on the floor to dislodge the larva was not an option. The movement worked, and the itching stopped. Theodore managed to get a decent slice in with the craft knife, but he couldn't risk checking his progress in case he dropped the knife. It took hominivorax at least five minutes to establish its bearings and decide where the food source lay; using the hooks that could cut through flesh as grappling hooks, it started upwards towards the warmth. Theodore cut through another strand but still could not release a hand; a hair in his ear was plucked like a harp string as the larva followed its instinct. It would stop as if sniffing the lie of the land. Theodore could imagine it raising its eyeless head, wondering next steps; it wasn't galloping straight to the end game. Another hack with his knife and his left hand was moving a bit more freely, no response from hominivorax. *Just stay where you are,* thought Theodore and tried to move the blade upwards. He hadn't broken his collar bone.

Chapter 14

Monday morning saw yet another sunny day, meaning that the hosepipe bans would stay in force for some time. The weather forecast did not predict any rain for the next week. The first bus of the day saw the usual travellers on board with the exception of Theodore. Even the bus driver was surprised because even though the drivers rotated routes and shifts, he recognised Theodore as one of the 'regulars' and this was not the start of the normal holiday period and the driver knew Theodore was a man of fixed routines. A hung-over Steve Stiff boarded the bus and also noted that 'TG' was not scowling in his usual seat. Neither he nor Theodore ever sat alongside each other; they both preferred to have a window seat. Stiff slumped down and breathed stale alcohol against the window, his personal stereo transporting Adele's full voice directly into his brain, and regretfully recalled the previous evening. He started off witty and elevated; a couple of girls were chatting merrily with him, intrigued with his science and mathematics background. A couple of 'friends' interrupted him and dragged him off for some serious beers, announcing that chatting up the girls could wait. Stiff mouthed something like 'See you later' but saw the girls look at him with resignation. Steve Stiff joined his 'friends' and drank copiously, which ended in drunken acrimony between him and his friends. The girls had long since left. 'Pretty unsatisfactory stuff,' breathed an aching and sweating Stiff against an uncaring window. The bus jolted and awoke him from a haze just in time to alight. He stumbled away from the bus stop and through the gates into the facility. He thought he'd forgotten his security pass and then discovered it in his hand. Several inaccurate swipes caused Lovejoy to peer suspiciously at him from behind the bullet-proof screen. An animated Natalie was awaiting him, and when she got close, she waved her hand in front of her face to waft away the stale booze fumes emanating from Steve Stiff.

'Phew, Stiffy, did you come in with Theodore?'

Steve Stiff's eyes swam into focus despite his head thundering and sparks flashing behind his eyes like steelworks in full production. The image caused him to sweat even more profusely. *Eh?* was all he could manage, but he politely turned his head to one side because his mouth tasted like a gorilla's armpit, and he had gathered from Natalie's actions that it probably smelled similar or worse.

Natalie steered him towards the canteen and, once there, bashed the machine as if she could get a free vend, much to his chagrin. She thrust the hot coffee into his shaking hand and defied him to spill any.

'Have you seen Theodore, *today*?'

'Eh?'

Natalie came close to slapping the youth and betraying her anxiety. Somewhere a penny dropped.

'No, why? I thought he may have had a lie-in.' (as I wish I could have done)

Natalie merely raised a grey eye at Stiff, who had the temerity to even consider that a man like Theodore would laze in bed until mid-morning, like a teenager. She explained that she had a concern that had insinuated itself into her conscience, about something happening because she thought his workshop security wasn't adequate.

'Ah ha, I wonder how you have assessed his security and know where he lives! Nudge, nudge.'

Steve Stiff lazily closed one eye and raised his right hand with a pointed index finger at a strange angle between the two, which caused him to be distracted, and he swayed and almost stumbled. Natalie raised her hand, and Stiff cringed.

'You and me, at lunch break, will take a trip out there and see what's happened, assuming Theodore doesn't turn up in the meantime.'

Steve Stiff nodded and decided to get a breakfast comprising more coffee and a bottle of water. While this was happening, Natalie went off and explained to Andrew Goode that she and Stiff would go out at lunchtime and see what had happened to Theodore. Whilst this was a request, Andrew Goode knew that it was going to happen whether he demurred or not. He was also surprised at Theodore's no-show and a tad concerned himself. Theodore was as predictable as a normal UK wet summer (this year was of course an exception) and as reliable as a German long-case clock. There was no way that Andrew Goode would *not* be part of it. He looked at the accounts pack that had been left by the administrator and wondered how long he could keep the facade up without additional funding from somewhere. It could all be over by Christmas, he thought grimly, unless he threw himself into nagging as many contacts as he could. Maybe he could force his way into the forensic scene, with the closure of the government-funded forensic services. He needed a police contact. Steve Stiff needed a paracetamol or four.

The sultry morning dragged until 12.30 when the two car convoy departed.

While the conversation between Natalie and a delicate Steve Stiff was going on, Theodore had managed to clear his left hand (and sliced his arm in a couple of places). He had also hit his head deliberately on the floor twice in the last two hours or so to dislodge the larva back to its starting place at the earpiece. Each bang of the head caused dizziness after a ringing pain, but he didn't like the idea of the larva getting the better of him by achieving the penetration of his inner ear. A desperate, overambitious hack caused the craft knife to stick in the tape and ping of a few inches out of reach. He nearly had his left hand free, just a little more, and he might be able to rip the tape from his head. Hominivorax started off again, and the tingle in Theodore's ear caused him to whimper behind his gag. He didn't have the inclination to smack his head against the floor anymore. The pain was too much, and he flopped down, allowing the packing tape to support his defeated carcase. As if scenting victory, the larva in an undulating crawl forged steadily on.

Natalie swung the TVR into the drive, hit the brakes, hauled up the handbrake, killed the engine, and leapt from the car in one sleek movement. Andrew Goode with a dopey Steve Stiff parked on the road and noticed that the slightly ajar garage door boded ill. Steve Stiff barely recognised that there was a garage door. They had left the car as Natalie hoisted the garage door and screamed, *Oh My God!* Theodore closed his eyes, squeezing tears out as if from a sponge. Andrew Goode had already punched the emergency number into his mobile. Natalie hugged Theodore's head and nursed him for a while, mumbling 'Who did this to you?' repetitively. Only Theodore heard his left eardrum pop. Everybody heard Steve Stiff stumble over the spade, seeking the kitchen for a glass of water for Theodore and one for himself. The shock of the carnage in the workshop had driven his hangover into a corner. Andrew Goode pried Natalie's arms from Theodore's head and cut the tape from Theodore's mouth away from his head, sensibly keeping the contamination of the crime scene to a minimum. Goode noticed the little red LED flashing on the answerphone, and when Stiff returned with the water, he pointed it out to Stiff, telling him to not to touch, but point it out to the police on their arrival. Stiff was still too hung-over numb to be offended.

There was a selection of chequered vehicles in Acacia Avenue, one of which was an ambulance driven by one of two youthful paramedics who dashed into number 13, carrying a heavy bag between them. Within five minutes, the paramedics 'topped and toed' Theodore and carefully positioned a stretcher underneath him. He hadn't uttered a word and just blinked his eyes when the paramedic asked if Theodore could hear him. Theodore just mumbled something about 'I should have bought the bloody EMP' then just stayed silent.

Gawpers and Gapers nosily crowded around the drive and peered into the garage, where the chair and strips of packing tape were easily discernible.

'It's all that bondage stuff. I knew there was something creepy about *'im.'*

'Yeah, I can't see what pleasure they get from M&S. My 'Arold wouldn't dare. I'd beat 'im within an inch of 'is bleedin' life if I knew 'e was into that.'

The police had cordoned off the area with blue and white tape, marking crime scene.

'Well, bugger me, I didn't know M&S was a crime.'

They had just stowed Theodore into the back of the ambulance when the ambulance came out in sympathy with the bus of a few days prior. The steam and a pungent smoke billowed from the engine compartment as the paramedic swore and then grabbed the radio. All complained of the heat, but not in such a dramatic fashion as the ambulance. The paramedics feared having to deal with a multiple pile-up on the motorway with the depleted resource at their disposal. Fortunately, being the summer holidays, the motorway was nose to tail; therefore, any collision would be a minor shunt unlikely to cause any injury worse than a loss of temper, which in the current heatwave was easily done. Natalie sat in the back of the stifling ambulance with a catatonic Theodore and held his hand that drooped from under the blue blanket like a dead fish. The analogy was reinforced by the line that had been swiftly put in by the paramedic and connected to a saline drip. Andrew Goode and Steve Stiff were talking to a police officer, who made notes. Goode was unashamedly ensuring that the police officer made note of the fact that Theodore worked as a chief scientist specialising in entomology for an independent research facility, of which he (Goode) was the director. Steve Stiff would often play the fool, but he wasn't one. He guessed quite quickly what Mr Goode was up to and ensured that he blatantly put his occupation (computer technician and digital forensics) and current place of work down. He made sure that the officer knew about the LED flashing on the answerphone, which resulted in the machine being unplugged and dumped in a tagged evidence bag. If someone's business needed a bit of free marketing, Goode's certainly deserved it. There was one young, bubbly female local journalist taking notes and fluttering eyelids, which professed innocence, enquiring what had happened.

Chapter 15

The second ambulance had arrived and to save exchanging patient notes simply swapped vehicles, leaving the second pair of paramedics to await the rescue of the stricken ambulance. In triage, they quickly assessed Theodore and feared he might have experienced a stroke, although he reacted to stimuli in each limb. He just stared into the middle distance, immune to Natalie whispering in his ear. After about thirty minutes, the porters whisked him away to neurology, where there was a bed available. Natalie, bleary-eyed from the stress, wandered into the waiting room of Accident and Emergency and seeing Goode and Stiff start to rise from their seats lurched over to them. A three-way hug in front of an embarrassed police constable lasted some while. The three left the PC who went to neurology armed with a virgin notebook to await Theodore's recovery. He changed shift several times before being taken off that particular job.

In his own world within neurology, a sedated and catheterised Theodore experienced a dream that was to repeat itself several times. In his dream, a giant Cochliomyia hominivorax larva is lurching down a corridor towards him. He is standing upright although paralysed, and for a bizarre reason, he is holding an old cricket bat. He can hear in his head the mumbling from larva as if he were a bowler inciting himself to concentrate on the delivery. 'Here comes baby Woodentop, going to the fair,' comes the voice. The voice that Theodore can sense is not that of a child; it is far more sinister. It is the gruff voice of an adult, one who would quite unfeelingly beat a child. The larva closes in (it has gone way past the stumps at the bowler's end), and as it rears up, brandishing its barbed mouth as if to devour him, the larva skin peels in the manner of a banana, and a clown wearing beige overalls and a flat cap perched peculiarly on the mop of hair (strangely, not the usual clown's attire, but the face was heavily made up in the style) leaps out from what was a padded costume, holding a spade. He raises it above his head and clouts Theodore. 'Get Orff,' he says and then punctuates with a DANGGG, 'the bleedin' (DANGGG), 'premises, hee—hee', (DANGGG). In the dream Theodore was not wearing a cricket helmet and blacks out in relief.

'Second Spade Assault in a Month' blazed the headline of the local newspaper. A known drug addict had been located in a car park apparently having been poleaxed with a spade that was found placed next to the unconscious body. Police, while allegedly 'not speculating', suggested that it looked like a dealer had exacted a punishment for non-payment. Police said they would like to speak to a large well-dressed man in his fifties or possibly sixties who was seen in the vicinity and might have witnessed the assault. Peter Mack quietly closed the paper and placed it on the table in the hospital waiting room with his seventy-plus-year-old right hand. It was the same right hand that held the spade as if it were a toy. Mack could bench press 300 lb at the gym, where he kept in shape (pretty good at seventy plus) having reduced from 400 lb when he was in his prime. It was at this gym that Mack had overheard about the druggie (known as Skel because of the scrawniness, as much meat on him as a skeleton, a former accomplice had commented) from another member who purchased steroids and was offered, out of the blue, some workshop tools. Seeing his best friend's son lying withered and staring blankly into space had pushed Peter Mack beyond his normal peace-loving, laissez-faire character. It was easy to establish where the scum lurked. If Peter Mack had found it was outside a school, he would have killed him. Peter Mack had not put his full force behind the blow; a glancing cuff was enough to put Skel unconscious. Having spent less than twenty-four hours under observation, Skel scarpered from hospital next day for pastures new, before being interviewed. He thought that this was a turf warning and that he had got off lightly; he didn't fancy meeting that particular brick outhouse in daylight again, let alone a dark alleyway. He wouldn't let his partner-in-crime from that Saturday night in on what had happened. He could fend for himself. All this partner had done was whinge about getting out, and lashing Theodore to the chair was *too over the top, man*. It was when he started mentioning names that Skel put the headphones on Theodore in case he'd overhear what the fool was crying about. Skel needed him because he could drive the old van they'd picked up for cash at the auctions. After dropping Skel off with the contraband, his partner had enough of his initiation into crime and drove the van that morning to the Cornish coast. He slept for a couple of hours in a car park overlooking the crashing surf and then abandoned the van. There had been just enough fuel to get him there. The smell of the ocean would draw him back as soon as he had collected some clothes, money, a tent, and a sleeping bag. By the time he returned, the van had been taken away to be scrapped by the local authority. He didn't care. The same local authority employed him as a road sweeper out of season and a lifeguard in season; it was to be a low-stress life, with the odd rescue or the odd finding of various paraphernalia in litter bins. Thus, he started on his career as a full-time beach bum never to be suitable husband material, more casual entertainment for bored wives or beach bum dalliances with holiday-making teenagers. It took several years before his guilt over his involvement in the aggravated burglary was expunged from his conscience. He accrued a small but adequate pension assured by the local authority. He made more friends as a lifeguard, but better friends as a road sweeper.

The local police had not missed the significance of the spade being left at both crime scenes. They were just too late in getting back to the hospital. They shouldered aside a young female scribbling into a notepad.

'The scrote has scarpered,' grumbled the uniformed Sergeant to his young, blonde and attractive female partner.

'I wonder why?' she replied. He must surely be able to give some clues as to the relationship between him and the first victim, the post-traumatic stress disorder scientist, both clobbered by spades that were left at the crime scene. Sergeant Dawkins thought that this particular 'scrote' was given a warning with a capita 'W', possibly because of other dealings, and it was made to look as if he was responsible for the aggravated burglary at Acacia Avenue. The description of the character given by the nurse seemed to fit a character known to Dawkins. If this character left the area, there would be a dramatic reduction in petty crime and burglaries. Dawkins would be pleased to let another constabulary deal with this 'scrote', although his enthusiastic partner (Angie please, not Angela) wanted to comb the streets to see if they could spot him and take him in for questioning. Dawkins didn't fancy a chase on foot with this particular suspect whose weight compared with his own would grant the suspect a useful handicap. The information on the admittance form was false. Skel had no difficulty with deceit as he had a Ph.D. in fabrication. Dawkins's partner wouldn't let things go; she wanted to know who partnered the 'scrote' (she didn't like the word but wanted to learn to be a good copper and that, possibly, meant keeping in with the old guard).

'But, *Sarge*, someone must have helped him. He wouldn't have the strength to lift his own shadow, and we know he doesn't drive.'

'Yep, you're right, but we wouldn't get him to talk without squeezing his goolies, and he'd still tell porkies.'

'Goolies, Sarge?'

'Balls, woman, balls.'

'Porkies, Sarge, and woman, Sarge?'

'Pork pies, lies, WPC Dickens, lies.'

'Woman means woman, woman.'

Angie shut up and wondered whether Dawkins had used physical torture to get information. She suspected not, but he definitely had an edge to him, when crossed. Times had changed since Dawkins had signed up from school. He would soon collect his pension and had no thoughts nor desire for promotion. There was no reason to adopt the softly, softly approach, despite it being a police series when he joined.

Skel scurried back to his lock-up to dispose of the remaining bounty from Acacia Avenue. He abandoned Theodore's laptop to its own fate because it was a bit too bulky. He scrabbled together and stuffed the headsets into the rucksack, not noticing the wriggling larvae that were trying to break through the clear plastic bags, eventually succeeding as one by one they dropped into a corner or discovered a hole. The rucksack didn't provide much in the way of release for them as they clustered around each other, awaiting a food source. He went back to his digs and collected his stash of drugs and roll of money. He took one note from the roll and put it in a pocket; the rest went into the zipped compartment. Pausing to take his trusty polystyrene cup (he was headed for the city for a bit of begging), he left without leaving any money for his contribution to the rent. He was only there to make it look like the cannabis factory was a normal household and to keep an eye on the hydroponics (and to be arrested if the house was raided). Skel didn't really give a damn for anything, apart from his own hide, which the bloke who crowned him with the spade vowed he would strip from him just before he sunk into oblivion. This voice he would remember and, if heard again, give serious consideration what advice it offered. Skel was relieved when he woke in hospital that his only injury was the contusion on the side of his head.

Natalie, Andrew Goode, and Steve Stiff visited Theodore in hospital everyday during the ensuing week and saw no real improvement in his condition. He was changing position, and his eyes were open when he was awake. He was just not acknowledging anything. Even when Steve Stiff managed to catch the bag at the end of Theodore's catheter sufficiently hard enough to move the blankets, and make Goode's eyes water, Theodore reacted minimally. Stiff was distraught and close to tears, fearing he'd done some serious harm to Theodore, but was steered away by Natalie and Andrew Goode. A doctor caught them on the way out and suggested that the trauma might have caused elective mutism, normally limited to children who, because of a dominant mother, would punish adults by defiantly refusing to communicate. (Natalie just thought Theodore was in shock and didn't want to talk yet.) The doctor also explained to Steve Stiff, to allay his concerns that he'd caused an injury, that although Theodore was catheterised, this was not a needle stuck into Theodore. It was just a tube fed through (and not attached to) the penis where an inflated bulb kept it lodged in the bladder. Stiff was glad he had chosen computer studies and hadn't ventured into medicine. The thought of feeding a tube up someone else's privates made him screw his mouth up in distaste; his privates screwed up in distaste automatically. He pondered how they drained off the bags and was about to lift the blanket and take a look, when he stopped himself as he stooped. They left the hospital on the Friday and went to the pub for a sneaky drink before returning to work in part to expunge Stiff's guilt over the catheter incident. Peter Mack could have assisted here because whilst in the same hospital recovering from a chest injury, he was in the adjacent bed to another patient who was almost dragged out of his bed when the patient's mother, after kissing her son goodbye, managed to get entangled in the catheter tube. Fortunately, the patient fainted, but the mother needed a cup of tea and a long period of consolation before she could leave for home. After that, Mack kept any visitors a decent distance from the line into his arm and the drain in his chest, with a heavily muscled forearm holding up a hand the size of a shovel, a pretty effective stop sign.

Over their drink, they agreed that next week, they would visit him in shifts and drew up a rota on a piece of paper, updating each other in work the next day, to keep a steady daily flow to and from Theodore's bedside. Whilst a sensible practice, Natalie quietly felt that it was the start of a distancing process in order to harden themselves should the worst happen, like a gradual depreciation before the final write-off. The growl and grumble of the TVR's V8 engine as she drove home matched her mood.

Later that afternoon, Theodore gazed out of the window that was beshitted by seagulls as there had been no real rain for some time. The seagull crap had crusted, and further coats had been dropped from above. The lack of rain and a water shortage would ensure the crust would increase in volume. The smeared windows caused the sun to glare, and the pungent smell of sweat that hung suspended in the air added a stale acridness to the atmosphere. The creased and tangled bedclothes did nothing to improve the environment. Although no one would notice the difference in his body language, Theodore lapsed into a sedative-fuelled sleep, and it wasn't long before his stress-filled mind was activated. In his dream, his eyes snapped open, and he was in the corridor. He didn't know how long the corridor was, but he could just make out a shape at the end gradually getting larger as it approached grumbling its strange dirge. He took guard and patted his imagined bat up and down and then held it balanced almost parallel to the ground as he awaited the delivery.

Theodore's mother swam into his vision.

'Just ignore it, Son. It'll go away. Just banish the nightmare. There's nothing to fear.'

'I can't, Mum, I'm too scared.'

'Banish it, Son, banish it.'

The vision of his mother faded, and the larva approached. The larva grumbled closer and reared up as if on hind legs. The suit peeled downwards banana-like and revealed the insanely grinning clown in beige overalls and flat cap.

'Get orff, DANGGG, the bleedin' DANGGG.'

'I'll give you fucking *DANGGG.*'

To the left of his vision, Peter Mack (a much more youthful one in Theodore's dream) appeared holding his own much larger spade. He swung the spade through an arc in execution of the most exquisite cover drive (foot pointing to where the ball will pitch, high back lift and weight transfer from rear to front foot), middling the clown and the suit of the larva and causing them to roll and tumble head over heels into a pit that appeared in the corridor. There was a splash. Mack held his 'bat' aloft as if celebrating a century at Lord's, and Theodore swallowed long and mightily in reality. (He felt and almost heard larva hominivorax hit his shrivelled stomach and the gastric juices effervesce as it was dissolved.) What had the little blighter been doing during the last few days? What had it fed on? Had it eaten through the contents of Theodore's inner ear before exploring the Eustachian tube and being pressed by peristalsis into its own demise? Theodore didn't really care. At the worst, he would be deaf in one ear, possibly temporarily or even permanently. If he picked up an infection, he'd blame it on the assault or subsequent self-inflicted concussion. Theodore felt a tsunami of relief sweep over him.

'Nurse,' he croaked, barely audibly. He cleared his throat and said loudly, 'NURSE! I think I'd like a drink now.'

Chapter 16

The intrepid trio arrived at neurology on the Saturday. Andrew Goode's usual round of golf with Brian Greatrex would be delayed until the afternoon when, to his surprise, he would play like a professional and annihilate his good friend. They arrived just as a burly suited man was crushing Theodore's hand between his mighty paws and bidding him goodbye. He turned, nodded at the three, and thanked them for visiting Theodore. He left without introducing himself, out of self-effacement, not rudeness.

'Ah, Goode and Stiff,' Theodore quipped. Natalie's fruity laugh echoed through the ward. The occupants of other beds turned and stared. Some honked and clapped as if they were seals in a circus.

'Aw my God, I wish I'd thought of that,' a serious Steve Stiff muttered.

'You will, Oscar, you will,' joked Andrew Goode.

Natalie, ever the inquisitive female, asked who Theodore's other visitor was and was unconvinced when Theodore said Pete was his mother's friend.

The neurology resident wanted to keep Theodore under observation and perform tests after such a dramatic turn round.

'I'll say dramatic, he used to be a miserable git before,' blurted Steve Stiff. A nudge from Natalie on one side and a look from Andrew Goode cautioned Stiff. Theodore was not offended and smiled in appreciation of Steve Stiff's attempt to lighten the strange atmosphere that is present in a neurology ward. Theodore agreed to stay for an additional week under observation and undergo tests as necessary. He wasn't particularly bothered because he could blot out the normal background noise of a neurology ward by sleeping on his right side. He was also apprehensive about returning home to live in his violated space. To be honest, he was looking forward to a week of being attended upon (and visited). He hoped that just maybe Angel 3 would work on neurology and he could confirm his curiosity about whether she still wore a flower above her ear. There was general bonhomie and positive feeling around the hospital bed until an officious staff nurse chivvied the visitors away and off the ward in preparation for the tea trolley (gone were the days when visitors were offered tea during their visit).

Alone again, Theodore wondered just what the larva had fed on before finding his way down the Eustachian tube. Had it just fasted? Was eating the way through his eardrum sufficient nourishment? Did hominivorax have a diet, or would they (like a dog) be a glutton while food was available? Had it bored his inner ear completely to the bone? Theodore had visions of the resident placing an otoscope into his left ear and, shortly after, saying 'My Goodness!'. Well, Theodore had to wait; he didn't feel a great deal of discomfort, apart from a distant headache that he put down to the assault and his own head banging.

Theodore was happy to take his injury and discomfort as part of the project collateral, if he could close the whole thing down as if nothing had happened (apart from the damage to his eardrum). He was concerned about what had happened to the other charged headsets. This was the issue that prevented closure. Oh, how he wished he'd just bought the EMP device for £300 and played with it until bored. He was deeply afraid that the headsets would be distributed or that somehow hominivorax would start to multiply in the UK *and* the responsibility would be placed at the door of Theodore's laboratory. Theodore feared that his action could ruin Andrew Goode totally (surprisingly, he didn't really care about himself). If Theodore realised where the headsets and the larvae were now, he could estimate the likelihood of the little blighters realising his fears.

In the week that followed, Theodore experienced the first-hand delight of being in one of the many wards that formed the major part of the hospital without the concomitant benefits of regular strong medication. He had been moved from Neurology and would be moved again from ward to ward and earned renown among the nursing staff for misheard comments because he had this habit of leaning on his right ear, thus muffling the sounds, and his lip-reading skills had not developed beyond base level.

Probably the best example was as follows:

> Nurse (early morning): 'I've brought your tablets, Mr Grouchier.'
> Theodore: 'Cabbage? I didn't order any *cabbage.*'

The ward giggled in unison at the thought of cabbage for breakfast or the nurse putting down the little pot of pills and pulling up a saucepan full of boiled cabbage from under the medications trolley and spooning on to a plate for breakfast. A couple of patients who were detained for some period often asked for cabbage for breakfast as the new response to 'Good morning, Mr X, What would you like for breakfast?' which was normally 'Egg, bacon, fried bread, beans, fried potato, mushrooms, black pudding.' The nurse by the trolley would tap her foot impatiently while the requested menu was reeled off before responding, 'Right then, porridge it is. Sugar?' (OK, but don't call me sugar), causing the foot-tapping to increase in tempo.

The general wards of a major hospital is where you can summarise the whole of a life in a short period of time from pain, fear, relief, boredom, change, acceptance, death, sorrow, and continuity. Theodore wished dearly to escape from the realisation of this philosophy. He just wanted to be back at work and possibly share a convivial drink with friends, which he'd done very little considering his fifty or so preceding years. He wanted to catch up on the friendly side of socialising that he had thought beneath him for so long. He missed his cricket; this was to cause him further anguish when he realised that England were on the verge of sealing a test series victory. Finally, he knew he was as fully recuperated as one could get because he had reached that level of comfort where one can break wind as freely in a hospital bed as one can in one's own (institutionalisation is where one is disturbed by breaking wind anywhere else).

At the same time, Theodore finally awoke from his ordeal. Skel had finished his day at the office having spent a satisfactory day conning people into giving him money by making the most of his pathetic demeanour. He hadn't washed his hair, and the crusted contusion was visible to people as he cringed against the shop front with knees hunched up. They had been generous but not enjoyed their usual feel-good factor of generosity. Skel didn't give a shit. He had noticed another conman who had a much superior modus operandi. The conman was respectably dressed in a business suit but wore a hangdog expression of someone who'd experienced a misfortune. He would approach people with a sorrowful expression and explain that he had been mugged and that his wallet and everything had been taken. He said that £20 would see him home and that he would repay the loan and that all they had to do would be to call his office (it was a major insurance company in the city) and he would pay it back the next day. He'd also managed to acquire (by luck or research) the name of a real employee of the company, which would fog the trail. With his hangdog expression, smart suit, and the genuine feel of the story, this conman was earning up to £500 a day. Skel was enthralled; he wondered if he stuck to one area or if he moved about the streets and varied his story. He followed the conman back to the station where coincidentally he had left his rucksack. When the conman went into a sandwich bar, Skel followed him. With rucksack over one shoulder, he grabbed a sandwich and a fizzy drink, which was more a camouflage than a meal. He blatantly sat at the same table as the conman. After nods of acknowledgement, Skel leaned towards the conman with his most lupine expression, 'Nice sketch, my cocker.' The smart conman was simply a one-man operation, which was his own invention. He didn't look for a minder; he also thought that Skel might be an undercover officer, admittedly a well-disguised or selected one. He thought it unlikely that any law enforcement agency would recruit such a specimen. He bluffed, 'I don't know what you mean,' while trying to look like an office clerk. Skel said that he understood, but possibly the conman might like to hire a lookout, who'd point out the marks and give warning or all clear signals. All this partnership cost would be 10 per cent of the takings. (Skel would up this once started and successful. He wouldn't suffer any risk.) The conman using a name of Chris David said they would try an experimental week with Skel as his eyes, ears, and minder. Skel would lurk nearby with his polystyrene cup and earn additional cash that he would share with Chris David quid pro quo. (Ironically, Skel knew some Latin. Chris David had Business Studies.) A skinny Skel's hand grasped a wet Chris David's hand, and the deal was done. Skel swept the remnants of his sandwich into the rucksack and simultaneously decided that he ought to quit the drugs while there was financial profit to be obtained. He knew that quitting drugs meant pain and hunger, but it would be worth it, as previous drying out had meant that two days of excruciating pain, coupled with the inability to get comfortable, vomiting, and diarrhoea. He needed a plastic bucket, a fistful of Brufen and Paracetamol, some cans of soup, and the patience of the squatters with whom he had moved in. If this worked, he would sell his stash and be clean for a while. Unfortunately, for his plans, the surviving larvae had found the remnants of his sandwich.

Skel located Chris David (Skel suggested that henceforth he would be just CD) outside the mainline railway station. He was surprised that CD hadn't just told him to get lost or not bother turning up, but there again maybe CD needed the partnership. The day proceeded really well until Skel hadn't noticed a bunch of men who'd been on a thwarted trip for some concert or another that was cancelled. They had been drinking heavily and took exception to him lurking with his polystyrene cup. There was a bit of name-calling, and Skel made the mistake of calling for CD, who came over warily and enquired the nature of the problem and was promptly put flat out on his back by a punch. Skel tried to scurry away, but before he could rise to run, he was booted along the pavement by the men to the accompaniment of a football chant. This could have been explained by high spirits, but what followed next encroached into loutishness. One of the more malicious of the men had picked up a broken bottle and playfully (so he thought) stuck it into Skel's skinny buttocks with an encouragement of 'giddyup you sponger'. (Theodore would have been aghast. His opinion was that concerts at cricket grounds and one-day cricket itself were ruining the spirit of cricket, and with people of this ilk, his opinion might well be justified.) The howling wail of a police car siren caused all to disperse, with the exception of CD and Skel. A still dazed CD was taken for questioning, although Skel was released after a brief interview (Skel looked pathetic and CD could act and therefore was suspicious). Skel went to the squat and decided it was time to lie low and face cold turkey (apart from the remnants of the sandwich that he'd stuffed in the rucksack). He crammed two Brufen and two Paracetamol into his mouth to combat the oncoming bone-grating agony and swigged a mouth full of cold soup from the tin. He dragged a blanket from his rucksack and wrapped himself against the shivers that would be forthcoming. Attached to the blanket was a couple of the more resilient of the larvae. They were overjoyed that they were put in close proximity to a food source, even though Skel's buttocks might seem like a meagre one. Skel thought through the next few hours that this reaming of his buttock was part of the cold turkey, so he suffered without complaint, while he munched painkillers, slurping at cold soup and occasionally sleeping fitfully. The rest of the larvae in the rucksack perished and shrivelled into husks. The headsets remained unaffected; his buttock was seriously infected.

The squat was raided two days later. The owners were Arabs who wanted to sell and had finally realised that enough was enough and the occupants were forcibly evicted. There was much cheering for the members of the public while the healthier squatters were removed, but this quickly died down when a stretcher bearing Skel was hoisted into an ambulance. The mess that was Skel's right buttock caused even the most experienced paramedic on the scene to gag. In the ambulance, Skel was given a new blanket. The blanket with the pupa attached was to be incinerated. The time period before incineration was sufficient for the flies to emerge and escape into the smoggy atmosphere of the capital. Skel's buttock had acted as a foster home for a new generation of screwworm. It was a day or so before CD turned up at the city centre hospital, he had managed to locate Skel and sheepishly turned up at his bedside.

'I have your share here. I don't want to seem obvious, but I haven't seen you for a while. Where should I put it?' Skel lay on one side and was so full of antibiotics and sedatives that he merely nodded towards the small cabinet. CD was reluctant and looked around before making a move, which wasn't discovered until Skel checked his rucksack some two days later, when the loss caused him to howl with injustice. Unwittingly Skel had managed to turn someone else's life around via his roll. CD had a certain amount of accumulated money, CD managed to pay off his creditors and clear the County Court Judgment, the roll caused a change in role, and instead of Skel playing CD, the CD played him. At last, Chris David could settle down again and be normal; he could lead a bit of a standard existence. The debt that was the albatross that hung around his neck had been released. The future years saw David manoeuvre himself through various positions, accepted into one of the major accountancy companies, then a partnership, and then being invited into a position within the regulatory body for overseeing the financial services of the city. All the time he progressed through his roles, he had a certain amount of paranoia that his conman past would come to light. He also feared Skel would come to light too; no doubt he would spill the beans or insist on payment to keep his silence. But this was far in the future, back in the near future. Skel left hospital clear of his addiction and with the worrying prospect of making a half-arsed attempt (literally) at getting a job to earn some money. He had no savings, but possibly after he explored the amount of disability benefit to which he might be entitled, he could start redressing the balance.

Chapter 17

The first generation of wild UK Cochliomyia hominivorax mated, and the females had found a tethered and maltreated horse that was the ideal host to create the second. The horse featured in the national newspapers in the following week, its horrendous wounds published and also available online for those with gruesome appetites. The owners of the horse were filmed on their way to magistrate's court with their features obscured by pixelation. The magistrates were almost forced by public opinion into a custodial sentence, but it was neglect rather than downright cruelty that was the cause of the animal's plight and subsequent destruction. During the sultry summer, hominivorax flourished. Nurseries varied from road kill to abused and wounded domestic or wildlife. It wasn't until a female laid eggs in a patient who was under the so-called care of a private care home that there would be serious attention drawn.

Theodore had gone home on the Sunday evening; the fruit looked sad and mould covered. The house was humid and stuffy. He made a cup of tea, but the milk was curdled, and he poured it down the sink. During his stay in hospital, Goode had arranged for Theodore's garage door to be replaced with a more secure model. He'd also arranged for the bill of repair to be sent to Theodore's insurers. Theodore carried the mug of black tea through to the lounge and looked at the rows of books standing to attention, like a row of soldiers awaiting inspection. His laptop had been left on the table and obviously been snatched by the burglars, so the only way to occupy his mind was via a book. Theodore marched up and down, scanning the rows seeking something that would provide a bit of escapism or possibly nurse him surreptitiously into a hopefully dreamless sleep, although the spiritual version of Peter Mack had appeared to have banished the clown dream and it hadn't recurred in his two weeks of observation. After walking up and down, he finally selected Irving's *Cider House Rules*. He knew the novel was about an orphanage, and Theodore felt he'd been an orphan for the past twenty or so years. He read a sizeable chunk of the novel before finally dropping off to sleep with the lamp still blazing. Theodore empathised with Dr Wilbur Larch as a fellow scientist, taking the correct decision to save a life, because as a scientist, he could. To top it all, Wilbur Larch had only had sex once, whereas Theodore hadn't had sex at all! Theodore did beat Larch on the beer consumed front, but on the ether (and the gonorrhoea), he was definitely a loser. It was in this state of mind that Theodore fell into a deep sleep, albeit for only three hours or so. It was the 'Sometimes I deliver a baby and sometimes I deliver a mother' that he took into his dreams.

The sun bursting through the window woke him from a surprisingly dream-free (or dream forgotten) sleep. He reached over and switched off the bedside lamp. He decided he would get up and face his own challenge, despite his fatigue. After a quick look at the clock, he realised he could still catch the first bus and even had time for a quick shower. He had no appetite for any sort of breakfast, which was lucky because he didn't really have anything edible left in the kitchen.

It had been three weeks since the incident in his workshop. Theodore decided to get on the bus and try a day at work. He would need to stock up with food on the way home. His loss of appetite and confinement had made him gaunt and spectre-like. His shirt hung on his shoulders and gave him the appearance of a scarecrow. His trousers were creased and needed a belt, and he looked pale and unwell. The scars on his head were still pink and angry-looking, which was accentuated by the way that parts of his head had been shaved, by an unskilled razor-wielding nursing aide, and was now growing back like poor thatch work. The bus snorted and hissed at him as he boarded. He showed his season ticket to the driver, who had driven Theodore before, but didn't recognise him now, so he carefully examined the ticket. The passengers acted as usual: Mantis munched, Little Red Riding Hood hid her hair, and Uvula talked loudly about taking his girl to Spain for a holiday and ordered her to eat properly and not to stress out. (How could any girl who was a friend of the Uvula *not* stress out?) Theodore found that if he rested on his elbow and covered his right ear with his hand, he could successfully blot out the hubbub as he was now totally deaf in the left ear. He endured the rest of the journey and kept a low profile when he saw Steve Stiff board. After the initial uplift of recovering in hospital, a cloud of depression hung over him. He hadn't felt like eating and didn't feel like exchanging any pleasantries with Steve Stiff. Theodore forced himself from the seat as the bus pulled up outside the research facility. He waited as Steve Stiff, personal stereo earphones still in place, alighted. Theodore stumbled from the bus, the sun blinding him momentarily, while in front, Stiff strode towards the entrance of the facility. Theodore took a little longer to get there, as he felt a bit reluctant to greet the working day with a smile. He checked that he'd remembered to pick up his security pass and looked wearily at his picture on the pass that bore little resemblance to how he looked at the moment. He paused and gathered himself before stepping towards the security barrier. A security officer watched him approach the barriers but visibly relaxed when Theodore beeped his way through.

Theodore changed into his white coat and realised there was not much for him to do. He went to the canteen ostensibly to make a cup of tea, but seeking not a conversation, but just company. There was no one about, not even Steve Stiff, who by rights should have been taking one of his many breaks for vending coffees (unpaid for). He took the mug of tea and went down the corridor and peered through the window set in the door with a tatty A4 label pinned to it, typed with a mixed font that read 'Puter Room' (this was Stiff's humour). He was miffed to see Natalie and Stiff standing close to each other and rigging up a laptop that looked very similar to his own. He didn't know it, but Steve Stiff was demonstrating to Natalie how to take a forensically sound digital image of a laptop before they examined the contents. Theodore started worrying that Steve Stiff's computer wizardry might discover his project. After rattling the door and trying to open it the wrong way, he finally burst into Stiff's lab.

'What's going on here and where did you get my laptop from?'

Although they had heard the door rattling, both Natalie and Steve Stiff were shocked at Theodore's dishevelled entry and, in a subconsciously defensive attitude, had stepped guiltily apart.

Steve Stiff said, 'Relax, TG, the police handed it over to us after it had been found in a lock-up in town, a lock-up that they suspect belongs to their prime suspect in the break-in at your gaff. They want to see if it has been used since the break-in, and it may be a chance to show off our forensic skills. There may be a spot of business in it for the whole shebang.'

Theodore would be put in a bit of a predicament if he demanded that they return his equipment and delete any images taken. He could ruin the facility's chance of getting forensic contract work via the police. He decided to let Steve Stiff continue making a forensically sound copy of the hard-drive and the logs that recorded whether a USB device had been connected to the laptop. Stiff had not really cottoned on to Theodore's anxiety and was only bothered with any files or cached elements that had a modified date after the aggravated burglary, i.e. had it been used by the perpetrators and had they given anything away by visiting their own social networking pages, or keyed in their own bank details? As a bit of a joke, Steve Stiff asked, 'TG, how do you know that it's your laptop and not a similar model? They do make more than one of this model, you know.'

'Right!' said Theodore. 'I'll show you by logging on,' and he grinned superciliously at Stiff.

Steve Stiff had already noticed the image was completed and saved, so Theodore wasn't going to contaminate any digital evidence. The initial display of the forensic software showed the hierarchy of the systems files and he had noticed that there was a user named Theodore Grouchier together with all the associated files required for a system that had multiple logons.

'No need, TG. I can see it's your box and that someone has powered it up since you were set upon.'

Stiff handed back the laptop to Theodore saying that he had a working image to play with and that the information he sought was for intelligence on the potential whereabouts of the perpetrator, not evidence in court. Theodore felt a bit sheepish and together with Natalie looked at Stiff's navigating the initial stages of information gathering. Steve Stiff had found that the system had been booted and shutdown a couple of times and that someone had tried to guess the passwords of the existing users and the administrator. This seemed to have caused a lot of deletions, but the system had been powered off while a job had been running a program that was writing an ever-increasing file of meaningless characters to an output file that just filled up the free space on the disc. The program would delete the file on exit to free up the space. He also had seen that someone had interrupted normal start-up to run an operating system from compact disc but hadn't really done much else. Stiff poked his nose into the deleted cache, part of which had been unrecoverable because of the disc filler, but he was able to recover partial details of the cricket sites Theodore had visited. Stiff then noticed a deleted file marked as encrypted by the forensic software but the free space hadn't been overwritten by the disc filler.

'OK, TG, watch me open your secret file!'

Stiff assembled his password-cracking tools that specialised in the standard offerings of word processing software, spreadsheets, and small databases. He smiled at Theodore as if this was a friendly single wicket game of cricket with a little wager.

Natalie, looking at the tension on Theodore's lined face, became a little concerned that Stiffy was overstepping into Theodore's privacy. But Theodore kept his peace, although he clearly wanted to tell Steve Stiff to mind his own business.

'Stiffy, you are such a snoop!'

'Hey, Steve Stiff, private investigator, sounds sort of cool.'

'More like cul, you silly ass!'

'Eh?' said Theodore.

Theodore was starting to get very weary after all that he had been through, being his first day back at work. He looked close to collapse.

'C'mon, you boys, what are you trying to prove?'

'Eh?' said Theodore.

'Theodore, you are becoming a stuck record!'

'Eh?'

Theodore was hoping that his own encryption would beat the cracking tools, but he knew that Stiff, whilst a young upstart, was no fool and probably knew far more about computers than Theodore did, especially programs using Dynamic Load Libraries (DLLs), which meant you could borrow bits of common code in the programs and applications built and distributed. The one thing that Theodore might have on his side was that he wrote his plan in plain text using a simple editor. When he had finished the latest version, he would copy it to the clipboard and encrypt it with a small program he'd written with a very long pass key. He used the ASCII alphabet, which meant that rather than twenty-six characters (fifty-two upper case) and numeric and a smattering of special keyboard characters, the alphabet was 255 characters. In addition, he added a few characters that would encrypt to null, which were seeded among the encrypted text. These null characters would be ignored when Theodore's program ran is decryption routine. The use of nulls is a useful weapon in the armoury of encryption versus cracking. Every character of the pass key would shift to a new alphabet. Theodore used a long pass key based on the first letter of a saying with variations of special characters instead of spaces, and of course, he had a complex document that he'd encrypted. Stiff had a set of dictionary crackers that could pluck the DES block from a binary document until the cracker got a match with the password. An easy password was cracked within a second; longer dictionary passwords may take a minute. A dictionary cracker would include substitutes (Theodore, Th30d0r3, THEOdor3 etc . . .) and would not last long with Stiff's operating the keyboard. Also, with certain documents, they would respond with incorrect password, whereas Theodore's technique wouldn't tell you it had failed but would just display the document with gobbledygook characters, so you had to read the document before you could progress to the next attempt. Theodore realised that if he had put a paragraph of garbled characters as an introduction, he would have infinitely increased the chances of correct decryption.

A simple version of Theodore's encryption using a limited alphabet in unscrambled mode would look like this. Encrypting THEODORE with the pass key of NATALIE would give GHXOOWVR by reading down the first column until row N and looking at the letter under column T giving the G and so on.

A	B	C	D	E	F	G	H	I	J	K	L	M	N	O	P	Q	R	S	T	U	V	W	X	Y	Z
B	C	D	E	F	G	H	I	J	K	L	M	N	O	P	Q	R	S	T	U	V	W	X	Y	Z	A
C	D	E	F	G	H	I	J	K	L	M	N	O	P	Q	R	S	T	U	V	W	X	Y	Z	A	B
D	E	F	G	H	I	J	K	L	M	N	O	P	Q	R	S	T	U	V	W	X	Y	Z	A	B	C
E	F	G	H	I	J	K	L	M	N	O	P	Q	R	S	T	U	V	W	X	Y	Z	A	B	C	D
F	G	H	I	J	K	L	M	N	O	P	Q	R	S	T	U	V	W	X	Y	Z	A	B	C	D	E
G	H	I	J	K	L	M	N	O	P	Q	R	S	T	U	V	W	X	Y	Z	A	B	C	D	E	F
H	I	J	K	L	M	N	O	P	Q	R	S	T	U	V	W	X	Y	Z	A	B	C	D	E	F	G
I	J	K	L	M	N	O	P	Q	R	S	T	U	V	W	X	Y	Z	A	B	C	D	E	F	G	H
J	K	L	M	N	O	P	Q	R	S	T	U	V	W	X	Y	Z	A	B	C	D	E	F	G	H	I
K	L	M	N	O	P	Q	R	S	T	U	V	W	X	Y	Z	A	B	C	D	E	F	G	H	I	J
L	M	N	O	P	Q	R	S	T	U	V	W	X	Y	Z	A	B	C	D	E	F	G	H	I	J	K
M	N	O	P	Q	R	S	T	U	V	W	X	Y	Z	A	B	C	D	E	F	G	H	I	J	K	L
N	O	P	Q	R	S	T	U	V	W	X	Y	Z	A	B	C	D	E	F	G	H	I	J	K	L	M
O	P	Q	R	S	T	U	V	W	X	Y	Z	A	B	C	D	E	F	G	H	I	J	K	L	M	N
P	Q	R	S	T	U	V	W	X	Y	Z	A	B	C	D	E	F	G	H	I	J	K	L	M	N	O
Q	R	S	T	U	V	W	X	Y	Z	A	B	C	D	E	F	G	H	I	J	K	L	M	N	O	P
R	S	T	U	V	W	X	Y	Z	A	B	C	D	E	F	G	H	I	J	K	L	M	N	O	P	Q
S	T	U	V	W	X	Y	Z	A	B	C	D	E	F	G	H	I	J	K	L	M	N	O	P	Q	R
T	U	V	W	X	Y	Z	A	B	C	D	E	F	G	H	I	J	K	L	M	N	O	P	Q	R	S
U	V	W	X	Y	Z	A	B	C	D	E	F	G	H	I	J	K	L	M	N	O	P	Q	R	S	T
V	W	X	Y	Z	A	B	C	D	E	F	G	H	I	J	K	L	M	N	O	P	Q	R	S	T	U
W	X	Y	Z	A	B	C	D	E	F	G	H	I	J	K	L	M	N	O	P	Q	R	S	T	U	V
X	Y	Z	A	B	C	D	E	F	G	H	I	J	K	L	M	N	O	P	Q	R	S	T	U	V	W
Y	Z	A	B	C	D	E	F	G	H	I	J	K	L	M	N	O	P	Q	R	S	T	U	V	W	X
Z	A	B	C	D	E	F	G	H	I	J	K	L	M	N	O	P	Q	R	S	T	U	V	W	X	Y

This particular code can be cracked by frequency analysis. For example, the most frequent letter in English written usage is 'E', so if you make the assumption that the text is written in English you can say that the where an encrypted letter appears most, it could be a representative of the letter 'E'. This tactic is useful, but if the encrypter uses more than one alphabet, it requires the length of the key to be guessed, and therefore, the longer the key, the more difficult frequency analysis becomes, and as mentioned, Theodore's code used the ASCII alphabet with all special characters increasing the permutations to 255. He also had a key that scrambled the alphabets into different orders. This was similar to the Enigma machine in certain ways with the rotas being replaced by electronically stored alphabets. A moment of worry ran through Theodore's mind with this challenge. Would he find the source code that he used to compile the program that encrypted his project schedule? Theodore had been certain he'd copied it to a USB drive and deleted the source code. Even if Stiff found the source code and worked out the process, he would need the pass key, and Theodore wasn't going to volunteer it.

After an hour, Stiff had given up on his quick wins, gradually getting more and more disappointed. A bored Natalie and a relieved Theodore had already wandered off to the canteen for coffee. Steve Stiff found a brute force cracker that didn't give the message 'Unknown Encryption', and it seemed to be running. He joined Natalie, Theodore, and Andrew Goode in the canteen. Andrew Goode had explained that the local constabulary had offered the facility a proof of concept trial run for cost price, which meant that Andrew Goode would not make any profit from the exercise. He was outlining the up-and-coming test where a pig would be killed and abandoned as if a murder had occurred. The carcase may be moved away from the scene of its demise. The police would deliver the pig's carcase to the laboratory and request date of death, an estimated time (very unlikely), and additional theories and findings to provide leads for the police. The report produced by the experts available to Goode would be the hinge of a possible contract to provide forensic services locally and possibly further afield. Andrew Goode said that Natalie and Theodore should jointly compile their findings into a report with recommendations. Steve Stiff asked how long he could be producing the report based on the image of Theodore's computer.

'You have forty-eight hours for a draft report based on data with a modified date exceeding that of the break-in to Theodore's property.'

'OK, I don't think I can offer much, but I've got a great challenge with one of TG's files! I didn't know TG was a computer geek as well! I only wish he'd secured his garage door to a similar level.'

Chapter 18

The hot summer persisted, and life at the care home wasn't made easier by the unreliable air conditioning and the reluctance of the staff to run around opening and closing the windows at the beck and call of the patients. The staff employed here didn't like the responsibility of looking after people at all, especially people who were vulnerable or difficult. Each member of staff had been keen to learn the restraint manoeuvres that they were taught during the first month of induction and would often compete with each other to see who could take down and suppress a misbehaving patient the quickest. If a patient wasn't misbehaving in the communal lounge or anywhere else, they would pick on one until he or she became stressed, and then one of the staff would be able to practice their moves. It was the recent recruit with the strange look in his eyes and the fondness of tending to patients on his own who didn't participate in the 'team building' as the rest of the carers. The charge nurse, Jason Bluett, was concerned that he mighty be a plant from a newspaper or some investigative journalist on a factual television series. Jason decided he would assign each of his team to observe as discreetly as possible the habits of Craig Harris, the new carer.

Craig Harris was given a new identity and other supporting documentation that conveniently covered up his past. As a child, he had been convicted of being party to bullying of at least one child to the extent of torture, then torture being the significant factor in the death of one of the children. The court decided that he and his co-defendant hadn't intended the death of the child, but manslaughter was their finding. Prior to this conviction, he had been responsible for the disappearance of many local pets and other animals. His early victims were small animals such as mice and hamsters that he would launch into the local canal from a bridge via a catapult after tying self-constructed parachutes to them, a 'watch with mother' sort of re-enactment of D-Day. After launch, he would pick up his air rifle and shoot at the creatures on their sometimes slow and sometimes not so slow descent. If a boat was approaching the bridge, he would fire the animal directly at the boat as it chugged towards him. He would aim at either a passenger or possibly a crew member. With no obvious target, he would pick up his air rifle and aim for the windshield or one of the windows at the front or side, if it was a narrow boat. Some of the narrow boats had gaily painted water jugs and other metal-ware that Craig sometime preferred as targets because of the satisfying ping they made on being struck by a pellet. After scoring a hit, he would duck down below the parapet, occasionally peeping out to see if there was a reaction, one that was in excess of the usual fist shaking and robust language.

Craig acquired a partner in crime because a bored boy had seen him appearing just as lost as he was along the canal. It was a drawing together of lonely ships in the doldrums. His new partner was a rather large, backward, and abandoned boy by the name of Horace who attached himself to Craig because Craig didn't shout at him, beat him, or shove him out of the house with endearments such as 'Get out from under my feet, you useless lump of lard!' Craig had the capacity to do far worse. For the first few outings, Craig and Horace shot cats with ball bearings fired from their catapults. Horace's catapult had been supplied by Craig, an act of generosity that caused a genuine look of hero worship to dawn on Horace's soft and dopey face. After a successful strike, the corpse of the cat was collected, dismembered, and dissected until curiosity was satisfied. They ritually buried or cremated what remained with the exception of the tail that had been severed and retained to adorn a childish sort of totem pole that stood at the entrance to their den, hoping to ward off intruders. Their den was located on a bit of unused land behind some lock-ups; curious dogs were kept away (for some reason, the scent from the totem pole drew them like a magnet) with stones thrown or propelled, but not to injure the dogs as Craig had an empathy with canines. There were other strange rituals associated with their partnership that mixed black magic, cowboys and Indians, and other influences on young boys, such as smearing of blood on walls, the mixing of each other's blood from fresh cuts, and much avowal of oaths of loyalty. It was the escalation to a human victim that would lead to their subsequent arrest and appearance in court, which was unusual because cruelty to animals seemed to rate higher in the mind of the UK public than cruelty to humans. This observation was supported by the foundation of the RSPCA (Royal Society for the Prevention of Cruelty to Animals) in 1824 whereas the National Society for Prevention of Cruelty to Children (NSPCC) was chartered at least sixty years later.

Whilst they didn't *directly* kill and certainly didn't dissect the child, they beat and cut him over a period of imprisonment lasting three hours. Craig was fascinated with the way the flesh parted like a ripe fruit under the pressure of his knife. Then there was the pause with just enough time to see how deep he had cut before the wound filled with blood. By some stroke of fortune, they missed major blood vessels. Horace was just fascinated by friendship, albeit a strange one, he would do *anything* for his friend, now hero. Craig and Horace were caught literally red-handed by a police constable, who reacted quickly to the radio alert about a child being abducted by two older boys. The experienced police constable given the type of call knew the likely dumping places were this to develop into a worst case scenario, i.e. canals and close by waste land. His hunch struck gold at the first site he came across with the gory, foul-smelling entrance. In addition, being an experienced constable, he was able to restrain the two boys with one hand, despite the slickness of their bloody wrists, while he called for assistance on his radio. Using his handcuffs to link the two culprits, he released the victim, who he noted was unconscious, but still breathing.

'We'll need an ambulance, pronto, with a big sewing kit,' he announced down his lapel radio.

Keeping an eye on his two captives, the constable rolled the victim into the recovery position after checking that his airway was clear. They awaited the whoop of sirens with anxiety felt by all but because of different reasons. The child was to die, apparently from shock a day or two later, much to the grief of constable, who was unable to take part in the trial.

Because of the lack of CCTV images to show the public, this case didn't make as much headlines and therefore attract the furore that a subsequent case in the north of the UK made. Craig managed to heap as much of the blame as he could on Horace whose expression of stupor didn't generate any argument to gainsay Craig's version of events. When the abandonment by his family, treachery by his partner in crime and the general lack of interest in him finally dawned, Horace decided to exit his miserable existence by forcing strips of bedding and other cloth down his own throat. The coroner equally horrified and amazed by the volume of material he was able retrieve from poor Horace, it was like a magician pulling knotted, coloured ribbons as an illusion, but in this case, all the ribbons had a similar colour, and there wasn't any real knotting, and, of course, this was no illusion. It was a horrible way for anyone to experience their last day on earth, and even the horror of the coroner relating the facts in court left Craig indifferent to Horace's demise. Craig knew for some inner sense that he was better equipped to deal with his punishment. When he met fellow detainees, he fought the weaker ones and submitted to the stronger, but only after making a point by resisting. Craig was a survivor, assisted by his belief of superiority over the others. He thought of other beings as mere objects, and being objects, their feelings and pain didn't register through the outer husk he'd grown over his soul. He was the antithesis of someone who should work in a care home and had his past been known or the proper checks been undertaken. This should never have happened. However, while he appeared, if not a model care assistant, he was certainly better than average, but he had his personal psychological Achilles heel, and this was the urge that came over him to gain pleasure from the infliction of misery on others. His pleasure perversely enhanced if the misery was inflicted on the weak. Craig had mitigated this lust by remembering his disgrace at being arrested and imprisoned, and while under supervision, he didn't succumb to the urge, although it nagged at him when he was alone, especially at night.

Having acquired the role as care assistant and working shifts, Craig's lust came back with a vengeance as if a voice was congratulating him on his abstinence and endorsing an indulgence. Craig would hover round the dormitories and occasionally let himself into a patient's room with the pretence of observation, but sometimes, he couldn't resist the urge to touch and then the squeeze the body beneath the blankets as if testing the ripeness of the produce at a greengrocer shop. The occasional lurking presence of Jason or one of the other carers meant that sometimes he would just straighten the bed linen and exit the room. The cat and mouse element added spice to his lust, taking it to a higher level. What he was seeking (as a bonus objective) was the chance to take the whole of Jason's team down when Craig let his lust free. The power in his self-belief had grown and was still expanding even the thought of his own capture couldn't confine his urge. Craig felt that his own urge was on a higher plane than that of Jason, who he thought was a mere bully.

Craig didn't have long to wait for a target to focus upon. Lizzie Day had been a patient committed by her family, who had been exhausted by caring for her hyperactivity coupled with her learning difficulties. The parents were in their late forties; Lizzie was still a teenager, with a mental age of an eight-year-old. Lizzie was strong and stubborn, which coupled with her other attributes made quite a supervisory handful. Her parents were not strong and wilted under the relentless innocent energy of their daughter. The tearful Days left a puzzled Lizzie at the care home, hoping for a break to recharge their batteries. The Local Authority had concurred with the decision and recommended the care home (which was new and joint venture between the local authority and a private healthcare company). One day, Lizzie had been her usual challenging self when a relatively inexperienced carer named Wayne King had antagonised her. Due to his lack of experience, he was unable to counter her strength and obstinacy, and as a result, Wayne was left pinned under Lizzie, who was riding him around like a hobby horse. He had half-heartedly attempted a restraining manoeuvre but hadn't been quick, determined, or trained enough to subdue a rampant Lizzie. 'Ride a cock horth to Banbury Cwoth,' Lizzie lisped, like the child she was, just captive in an adult body. Wayne was also babbling as if joining in but then started snorting. 'Hmmpfh, Hmmpfh,' grunted Wayne, which was a similar chorus to the one Theodore had uttered in the confines of his own garage. Wayne couldn't reach the panic chord as he couldn't get Lizzie to ride him close by where it dangled in a corner near the window. Wayne wouldn't have the ability to pull the chord with his right hand as his collarbone and a couple of ribs had been broken by Lizzie's jockeying. Jason and Beth (another carer) discovered the rodeo after about five or so minutes. At first, they were amused by Wayne's plight, but when they saw he was in difficulty, a deft armlock by Jason encouraged Lizzie to dismount Wayne. Jason hoisted the armlock higher and twisted sharply. Lizzie collapsed to her knees, her face buried in the rough carpet. 'Jathon! Thtoppit, Thtoppit, Jathon, you're hurting me, Jathon, you bathtard.' Beth tugged at the panic chord, summoning the rest of the shift to the lounge. Beth, Craig, and a black youth carer nicknamed Cannonball marched Lizzie into the restraint room, where she was held in a device similar to a straight jacket and pushed on to her back and secured to the bed, after Beth had removed Lizzie's clothes and wrapped her with a hospital gown. This should have been done by female staff only, but they needed Cannonball's strength to hold Lizzie down, who was swearing and struggling. Jason signed for a sedative, which they gave her in a drink.

It was three hours later when Craig, having let himself into the restraint room, used his knife to slice the bindings from Lizzie. It was a Japanese ceramic chef's knife, extremely sharp. The manufacturers had been requested to add iron filings to mix before it was baked in order to give it a signature for X-ray machines at airports.

He would let others puzzle where she had got the knife from and how she managed to manipulate it to slice through the bindings. Craig would also let them wonder how Lizzie had scraped together the nous to force the window and throw all her bedding and clothes out of the window and leap on to the bundle, in order to cushion her fall. Craig had forced the window and leading a groggy Lizzie to it given her an encouraging shove. After seeing Lizzie sail from the window and hearing her make a solid thud as she hit the ground, Craig left the room and tripped over to the charge nurse's office and politely tapped on the door, before opening it sufficiently enough to poke his head through.

'I'm off, now, Jason, if that's OK.'

Jason grunted acknowledgement as he haltingly and clumsily tried to complete a report on the afternoon's events that he had been hunched over for the last hour. The shift was also short on numbers because Wayne had been hospitalised and one of the night shift (who'd admittedly arrived early) had accompanied Wayne to Accident and Emergency. Jason knew that waiting for Wayne to recover and then taking him home would be a good skive instead of working a normal night shift. He had appreciated Craig staying on for a few extra hours. He just wished he didn't have to complete all this bureaucratic bollocks. His tattooed hands with their stubby fingers just didn't seem right pecking at a computer keyboard.

Leaving the care home, Craig looked furtively to and fro before hoisting his rucksack over his shoulder and making his way to the rear of the building which backed on to some fields and a bridge over a motorway. Craig located a winded and confused Lizzie and hoisted her to her feet, despite complaints about her leg. They stumbled off across the bridge and into a small wood where a stream once cut through (the heatwave had reduced the stream to barely a trickle). Craig occasionally stuck the knife into Lizzie's buttock or upper thigh as an encouragement; being a chef's knife; stabbing wasn't its purpose, so little damage was done. The sedative and exhaustion of the previous eight hours had taken a toll on Lizzie's resolve. The fight had been taken out of her, and Craig's lust for blood and inflicting pain was burgeoning to new dimensions.

'Pleathe, pleathe, pleathe,' chanted Lizzie through her tears. Craig mimicked her and jabbed the knife into her after each word as if punctuating a short sentence. He was looking for a suitable place, and the lights from the motorway gradually fading in the distance had forced him to retrieve his torch from the rucksack. Lizzie felt the Craig's distraction subconsciously and made a bid for freedom. Craig watched her stumble among the trees and followed her at a steady lope, like a scene from *The Last of the Mohicans*. He pursued at a distance, keeping an eye on her like the predator he was, allowing her fear and exertion to tire her. His sudden appearance as if by magic caused her to lose any desire to resist her fate, almost like the effect Count Dracula had on virgins. Craig wasn't interested in stealing her virginity. He was going to steal her life. As Lizzie stumbled to a standstill, Craig leapt on her like a lion. The sheets that had been stripped from the bed and then torn into strips were ideal for providing tethers. He tied each wrist to a separate sapling. Lizzie needed prodding into a suitable position (in this case, kneeling, head bowed), which with his knife was easily achieved. Her exhaustion awkward position meant she soon sagged, causing the knots to tighten. Craig's first cut aroused him. He then sliced again, and his arousal became more pronounced. If Lizzie had screamed or just whimpered, he didn't hear. He sliced more, bit as if trimming a joint or finely carving a goose. What caused Craig to leave the scene wasn't even known to Craig. Something just told him to walk. His surgical slicing of the Sunday roast hadn't caused much blood splatter on his clothing, although the knife had a considerable coating. Craig needed a place to rinse off, and given the drought, this wouldn't be a convenient stream running through a picturesque glade. Craig knew that within two miles, there was a village cricket ground. He also knew that there would be a stopcock to water the precious area of lawn called the square. After flashing his torch periodically, trying to locate the stopcock, Craig got fed up and just kicked the door of the pavilion and found a shower. He showered off most of the blood but had little with which to dry himself. Fortunately, whilst cooler at night, the heatwave would mean that he wouldn't suffer from hypothermia.

Nobody tried to enter the restraint room for another day, and when Jason wondered what had happened to the key, he knew this was going to be the end of his time at the care home. When the stories hit the papers, Craig phoned up to say he wasn't returning to 'a place where such atrocities happened.' The whole of Jason's shift would have their photographs published by the tabloid press for the enquiry that subsequently took place, with the exception of Craig.

Chapter 19

Andrew Goode had been refining Steve Stiff's report on the digital image taken of Theodore's laptop. Stiff had used the pre-formatted report that was an output from his forensic software. This template type report would require more explanation and story around the hard technical facts. But even a well worded report would not provide any clue that might lead to an arrest. Goode added introductions and explanations of some of the jargon, generally providing a story that could be read in court to members of a jury. The bare facts were that someone had tried to start the computer by switching it on, and then was faced with usernames and passwords, and had made an amateur attempt at breaking in. Subsequent power ups and use of function keys to get to the BIOS settings had been made, but no alterations to the settings had been saved, and the configuration wasn't saved. No other devices were connected to the computer. He changed this to read that no evidence was found that showed other devices were connected to the computer. Oh how difficult this would be in the future to get Stiffy's good work explained to a judge and jury (without offending him). He hoped that Natalie and Theodore would help Steve Stiff to get his science understood by the non-scientific. The conclusion would be that the computer gave no clues to suggest the whereabouts of the perpetrators of the crime committed at 13 Acacia Avenue.

Andrew Goode's mind was also on the approaching weekend, a weekend comprising mainly of golf, good company, and beer. He was interrupted by a 'phone call from his contact at the local police station. He pushed Steve Stiff's much-emended report to one side and hoped that Stiff wouldn't find it before he could explain all the pencil work. The police had decided to abandon the exercise with the pig carcase because there was a real murder case that would be fit for purpose as a proof of concept to use the facility as a forensic resource. This meant that the pig earmarked for the exercise would now exchange roles to be a hog roast for a barbecue that the local CID had planned (because it was after all perfect weather for barbecues!). Goode was bemused as he felt that he was being given a brush off, but the detective inspector, hearing his doubt, explained that the Thames Valley constabulary had a case on their hands that was puzzling their forensic team. The Thames Valley boys would appreciate additional opinion and support on the examination of the infestation of a corpse discovered in a field near the motorway. The DI would pick Goode's team up at 8 on Monday, assuming all would be ready to go. Andrew Goode hung up and immediately dialled Theodore's extension and requested that he bring Natalie and possibly Alan Turing (junior) to his office (Steve Stiff would have been delighted to be mentioned in the same sentence as Alan Turing). There was a jolly trip to beautiful Buckinghamshire in the offing. The three arrived within ten minutes, curious to find out what was exciting Andrew Goode. On their arrival, Goode gave a briefing about the coming Monday. He had received nothing from the Thames Valley police in the way of faxed photographs or preliminary reports from scenes of crime officers. All Goode knew was that it was a corpse infestation and therefore it would require Natalie and Theodore. But he also had an inkling that Stiffy would be useful for any computer logs that might be available or for simply taking notes. Goode also wanted to demonstrate that they had a multi-aged-group team as well as multi-skilled team. When Stiff also offered to bring along his older brother to provide a smoother age range stratification, Natalie just trod on his foot. They exchanged theories for twenty minutes or so until Andrew Goode said that he was meeting his good pal for a lunchtime pint and suggested that they all adjourn to the Folly (public house).

At the pub, Andrew Goode introduced his pal Brian Greatrex to all. They exchanged pleasantries, but Brian kept making double takes at Theodore, who couldn't believe his misfortune. Hopefully, he wouldn't remember where they first met. Eventually, Brian voiced his reason.

'I'm sorry, but Andrew said your name was Theodore, but I'm sure I've met a relative of yours before. You don't have a brother called Kevin, do you?'

Theodore hadn't heard Brian speak because Brian was seated on his left, so after explaining his injury and getting Brian to repeat himself, he answered remarkably calmly, but truthfully, by saying that he was an only child, although not adding a smile or a laugh, and made it sound a little bit artificial and not totally convincing. Brian Greatrex nodded and then gave an amusing recollection about the strange man who couldn't act, ordering a sample of headphones, paying cash, and collecting in person instead of free delivery.

'You should have heard what my manager Shirley said and seen her impression of him. She's a bit of a wag,' Brian said, causing all to chuckle with the exception of Theodore, who had turned his deaf ear towards Brian and tried to forget about Greatrex's manager. He fervently hoped she wouldn't make an appearance. Greatrex noticed this as he looked aside at Theodore and then realised that if this was the same person who was present for the headphones order, he had gone through serious stress and weight loss. Even then, something still bugged him. If he had the number of this Kevin Sedgley-Ahern, he would have dialled it, but he didn't. A hush settled over the party for a minute when the 'Dublin dabbler' arrived with the non-drink, throwing companion.

'It must do wonders for his hair getting a regular beer shampoo,' Mumbled Steve Stiff just loud enough for all to hear, except for Theodore, who said, 'Eh?'

'He'd get more than a beer shampoo if he dabbled with someone else if I were going out with him. I'm strictly a one man woman,' voiced Natalie.

'Well, I'm a no woman man and have been since university,' added Theodore, pleased that he'd had his right side to Natalie and was able to pick up on the conversation. Not that he'd entertained many women before university, being made more difficult because he went to a boy's only school.

Andrew Goode said that he thought his ex-wife was a one man woman, but he thought she meant a different one and then after that, a different everyday. He also said that once after working late, he got into bed to be greeted by a slurry voice saying, 'Hurry up before my husband gets home.' Andrew Goode cast his eyes down into his pint having killed the conversation stone dead.

Brian blurted out with a suggestion that they talk about something else, 'How about golf!' *to* which all present except Goode closed their eyes and took a deep intake of breath.

'Golf is a good walk ruined,' proposed an unoriginal Stiff.

'Pronounced by someone who has never wielded a club,' retorted Goode.

'Clubs, bats, and racquets, the modern cave man, Ugg, Ugg, come here, woman!' Natalie mimicked, causing almost a U-turn in the conversation.

Greatrex added that he wasn't sure if it was an addiction or an affliction.

'Might do you some good to take up golf, might take your mind of dabblin' with other women.' A sullen sounding voice came from behind them.

'My dabblin' days are definitely behind me!' Her companion shrugged.

'Yeah, and I'm a Russian,' muttered Natalie, not loud enough to be overheard.

'Surely, you're not with that hillbilly accent!' said Stiff and then ducked when Natalie raised her drink as if about to throw at him.

'You better watch it, boy, with the purty face, or I'll make you squeal like a pig!' she added, and then all turned in amazement when Theodore piped up with, 'Piggy Sneed, piggy, piggy, piggy, piggy, OINK, WEEEE!' Because of his deafness in one ear, Theodore spoke much louder than he intended. Natalie burst out laughing, which was made worse by an indignant Steve Stiff huffing, 'I don't get it. What's so funny about that impersonation and who the flip is Piggy Sneed!'

Natalie responded that he ought to read a few more American authors, and he would get what Theodore meant.

'Oh, it was just something a youth used to yell at me when I used to occasionally run the gauntlet of the local yobbos,' announced a naive, but honest Theodore.

'But I've seen the collection of short stories in your bookcase. You're pulling our legs!' retorted an amused Natalie, who thought that Theodore must have read it, to interject at such a moment. Theodore kept his peace, and Natalie winked at him in a conspiratorial manner.

'Ahhaaa, you've seen his book case! Nudge nudge, wink wink, say no more, say no m-o-o-ore.'

Andrew Goode stared with amazement at Steve Stiff.

'Stiffy, I am shocked that you know who Eric Idle is and how you know anything about Monty Python!' To be fair when Goode was young and Monty Python was live on the television as a series, it was still 'alternative humour' (although humour is just humour, even if it is just silly) Monty Python flourished in popularity and shortly became an institution. So much so that almost anyone can perform a reasonable facsimile of the 'parrot sketch'.

Andrew and Brian got up and shook hands. Brian left after with a wave of his hand to the other three having agreed to meet Andrew on the golf course early Saturday morning. Simultaneously, the couple behind rose to leave after the woman sniffily muttered something about the 'quality of patrons in this establishment'. The man sheepishly rose and straightened his 'T'-shirt, which read 'Heart of Gold—Nerves of Steel'.

'Yeah and Knob of Butter,' commented Steve Stiff, just loud enough for the couple to overhear. The man smiled to himself and nodded; he thought he would get that comment added. Natalie was amused but didn't understand the double entendre. Stiff replied that possibly she ought to understand a few more English colloquialisms. He had to explain to Natalie and Theodore that knob of butter could be interpreted as the man's organ of generation was manufactured from butter. Goode, out of the blue, said that butter could also mean a goat and that the man with the 'T'-short was definitely a horny old goat. However, he continued, now was the time to get back to work and pack equipment, cases, laptops, and notebooks for Monday. After this was done, maybe they could all finish early. They all left and piled into Andrew Goode's Volvo estate.

Chapter 20

All four with various cases had assembled in the foyer by 7.55. Even Steve Stiff was early, possibly because he had left the pub early just as things had started to get into serious beers. He had taken part in a cycle ride with some friends on behalf of a cancer charity. The extent of the sunshine this year meant that cycling was massively popular. Given the sunshine and dehydration, the post-bike ride beers had started to go down really well. They had chatted to some girls who'd also taken part, and the party was getting merry. Stiff had been called names as he left, for leaving the party early, but he knew that while he might miss a damn good sesh (session), he didn't want to miss a damn good career chance. It was not all regrets because he'd asked for and given the mobile phone number of one of the bubbly girl cyclists. She had laughed when he said not only would he be stiff in the morning, he'd probably be so for the rest of his life! She said she was a part-time hack for a local rag. Stiff didn't pay too much attention and didn't really hear because he was interested in her eyes and character. A big Vauxhall drew up in front of the building, and the four descended the steps to meet a large, but pleasant man who introduced himself as Detective Inspector (DI) Broome and said he would drive them to Aylesbury and back. It was a large saloon, but for comfort sake, the equipment boxes needed to be stored in the boot. Part of DI Broome's role in the expedition was to judge the report they provided and make recommendations to the chief constable. After introductions, when DI Broome said, 'No jokes about "you must be a brush with the law," *please'* (*Eh?* said Theodore), they got in the car and headed off to the motorway. To escape the boredom of motorway driving, they took it in turns to hum or sing a theme tune from a police-based TV program. DI Broome kept quiet and concentrated on driving and keeping to the speed limit, much to the disappointment of Natalie, who wanted him to squeal round a corner leap out, and shout, 'Book Him Danno', and Stiff, who wanted the DI to floor the pedal and put on the blues and twos. Andrew Goode just wanted to do a Jack Regan in *You're nicked*! Theodore leaned his head against the window and with his right ear covered could block out the gaiety. Natalie nudged him after she'd had enough of watching him be antisocial. 'Hey. Mr Grumpy, join the conversation.'

'Eh?' said Theodore.

'Police TV Series themes tunes, sing, whistle, or hum one or pay a forfeit, and don't pretend you can't hear me.'

Theodore just prevented himself from saying, 'Eh?' and started with the theme tune from *No Hiding Place*. When all 'gave up', he told them, although Goode argued that he thought it was the theme tune from *The Valiant Years*. So Theodore did that one as well, just to demonstrate the difference. Both were series televised when he was young, and Theodore remembered the signature tunes as if it was yesterday. He was about to rest his head when Natalie told him that he didn't get out of it that easily and that he had to do another one, a bit more modern this time. *Dixon of Dock Green* was quickly recognised by all except Natalie. 'C'mon, boys, give a Yank a chance,' she drawled. After a moment or two, Steve Stiff sang a 'Who' song, and Natalie said, 'Easy, CSI!'

'Ahaa,' sneered a smarmy Steve Stiff, 'New York, Las Vegas, or Miami?'

'Who are you? Who-who, who-who, it's Las Vegas.'

At about 10.30, the Vauxhall pulled into Aylesbury police station, where they met the investigations team and made introductions. All five were given a copy of the draft autopsy transcript, which under the header external appearance started, 'This is the body of a well-nourished female.' And it continued, 'There are infestations from Calliphora vicina' (bluebottle blowfly). The significant part of the report concerned the atypical lesions that looked like calliphoridae infestation, but these lesions were infected, normally, calliphoridae clean out the infection in wounds. The report continued for many pages, including the weight and appearance of various vital organs. Natalie and DI Broome were unaffected by reading the report. Andrew Goode and Steve Stiff had gone green around the gills. Although without viewing the attached photographs, Theodore had paled when he read about the infected lesions. He was pretty sure that he knew what was responsible for the lesions.

The wounds appeared to have been caused before death, the eggs being laid in some of the slicing wounds in the buttocks and upper thighs. The victim had struggled and survived for some time by sheer determination. The nastiest lesions were where the insect couldn't be brushed off while in the process of oviposition, and Lizzie had been tethered. The way Lizzie had been bound prevented her swatting the persistent flies away.

The cause of death was loss of blood and exposure. A worried Theodore looked at the photographs of the body and the close-ups of the lesions. He shuffles them from left to right hand, getting increasingly concerned and absolutely convinced that they had been caused by hominivorax.

'Mr Goode, Natalie, could we have a break for a discussion about preliminary findings?'

Both Goode and Natalie were curious as to why he was being surreptitious, and Goode noticed that Theodore hadn't called Steve Stiff over. If Theodore's theory was correct, then it wouldn't take long for the coincidence to come to light that their facility had been breeding hominivorax up until three weeks ago. He feared that Steve Stiff might give air to the findings, as he was a lot younger (actually Steve Stiff was a professional first, so Theodore's fears were unfounded). There could be inferences of slack security or something similar. Andrew Goode thought that Theodore was being far too paranoid. There hadn't been a normal spread of infestation outward from the facility, there had been no cases locally to the facility, and, talking to the Aylesbury police, there had been some suspicious infections on local animals. It seemed like it had originated in the London having arrived either from the airport or the docks. Still Theodore wasn't mollified. Goode pointed out to Theodore that the government interest wasn't in the detail of what they were funding and that they just quoted that so many thousands were funnelled into aid for Africa.

'Anyway, I am comfortable with the controls being robust, especially the integrity of my colleagues.'

Theodore explained that the paradox regarding the infestation, which meant that the victim (Lizzie) had been a host for hominivorax before she had expired, was that the more accurate indicator was the Calliphora vicina. These would only lay eggs on dead flesh. Given Lizzie's injuries, she would have been alive for two days before vicina moved in. The hominivorax were irrelevant, an horrific experience for Lizzie, but irrelevant for forensic purposes, except the instar might give an indicator when Lizzie was abandoned as opposed to when the flesh started decaying, attracting the more common calliphoridae. Leaving the infestations aside, the important evidence was that the lacerations that criss-crossed the victim's body seemed to have been inflicted by an extremely sharp blade, like a scalpel. Even when hominivorax had infested a wound, there was little damage to the epidermal layer. There were several specimens of third instar of hominivorax that Theodore recognised immediately. There were no pupae, meaning that it was less than a week from start of infestation to discovery.

The report that was co-written by Natalie and Theodore, emended by Andrew Goode and finally proof-read by Steve Stiff, was factual and didn't omit the lesions from larvae that were thought to be hominivorax, but the most pertinent evidence was the lacerations, and next steps were to obtain the blade and locate the owner of the blade that had inflicted them. The Thames Valley CID were already sweeping the area for Craig Harris. They hadn't taken long after interviewing Jason Bluett and looking at the restraint room to establish who their prime suspect was, to start the search. The sliced restraints were taken for cut comparison with Lizzie's wounds. Experienced officers were amazed that how such tough restraints had been so easily cut. This was a special knife. Good quality images of Craig were available from the security system at the care home. These would be transmitted to all police forces and would be broadcast on national television, if a quick arrest wasn't made.

It was less than three days before organised investigation procedures were interrupted when a transcript regarding the hominivorax lesions and recovered larvae and the lack of pupae had been leaked to the local press. In addition, a junior reporter had undertaken a little bit of Internet research into the nature of the screwworm fly and realised what had been discovered and promptly provided the lineage to the tabloid press for a considerable bonus that publishing in the Aylesbury Journal would never equal. The Aylesbury police were furious but couldn't establish whether it was civilian employees or outsourced cleaning staff who'd obtained a photocopy. The leak was something that could wait; another investigation could be conducted to remove the leak from Aylesbury at a later date.

The mastheads that greeted everyone who stopped at a news vendor or local shop were typical.

'Man-eating Maggots on the Loose in the UK' (This included a large blow up of the third instar displaying all the accoutrements for cutting flesh. It was quite horrific.)

'Lizzie Day Eaten Alive by Scourge of South America'

'Could Care Home Have Harboured Horror Creatures?'

Chapter 21

It was Steve Stiff who purchased one of the tabloids and brought it into the facility and left it in the foyer. Theodore got really angry (which shocked Steve Stiff considerably).

'Just what do you think you're doing? Mr Goode does not need anyone to put two and two together and make five. There could be all sorts of inspections and audits as if we were in some way responsible. We could all be out of work!'

Theodore was also badly shaken, and whilst he thought it unlikely that his batch were the index cases behind the UK colony, he couldn't rule it out somehow. (He'd only known of the demise of one hominivorax. There were several others, and two were needed to start breeding). A chastened and full-eyed Steve Stiff gathered the tabloid and took it to the nearest shredder. He awaited Natalie's arrival to cheer him up, as if he wanted to bury his face in his mother's apron. *Miserable bastard,* he thought and almost sobbed. Steve Stiff would never believe it possible that Theodore would risk smuggling hominivorax eggs outside his laboratory. Natalie breezed in, and Stiff almost ran to her. She could see he was a bit upset and slightly red around the eyes. Stiff announced that he'd offended TG with the purchase of the newspaper and then leaving it in the foyer. He looked so puppy-eyed that Natalie took him by the arm, and they went for a coffee. Natalie bashed the machine twice, one free vend for each. Theodore knew that the eggs he'd taken were able to grow into a full-blown male or female hominivorax.

'TG was right. I wasn't thinking, and I don't seem to have a handle on what's important,' he sniffed. Natalie scowled. There was no need for Mr Grumpy to take it out on Stiffy. He was naive and thought only of the benefit that publicity would bring. Theodore was being a little bit oversensitive about the whole thing. Possibly he'd been suffering from the injuries inflicted, especially as he still suffered from deafness on his left side.

Natalie mellowed just before Theodore walked into the canteen and in a sort of fatherly way (he wasn't experienced at it) put his hand on Steve Stiff's shoulder and tried in a gauche manner to explain himself. Natalie glared at him until he voiced his apology for being a bit sharp.

'Look, Stephen, erm Steve.' Stiff eyes lit up in disbelief. 'I've been a bit paranoid about the work I've done with hominivorax, and then there's a spread of the little creatures. I took it out on you, and I feel bad.'

Natalie and Stiff were gobsmacked. Theodore left the canteen and went to the toilets. He locked himself in a WC, sat down on the seat, and held his head in his hands. 'What have I become? A scientist who lies.' He wished that he had been hit a lot harder by the spade. It might have given him an escape route from his guilt.

Theodore stayed in the WC for some time. He really didn't believe that his actions had caused the outbreak, but it was a bit coincidental, and now he'd offended Stephen and Natalie had turned frosty on him. He felt wretched and alone. Previously, he had exulted in his insularity, and now he was weakened and wanted a supportive shoulder, preferably one belonging to a steel-eyed woman. How on earth did hominivorax spread to the capital without any infestations on the way? Had he caused it? If he explained all that he had done, what would it achieve? How could he get his camaraderie back with Stephen and Natalie? Theodore, being a scientist, was not used to unanswerable questions. He wanted to weep. A bang on the door shook him from his preoccupation.

'TG, it's me, Stiffy!'

Theodore marvelled at the resilience of the young. He was also a bit envious of Stephen's magnanimity, unusual in youth.

'I'll be out in a minute. I have a bit of paperwork to complete.'

'Hoo Hoo, gotcha man, don't write on the walls.'

'My God,' thought Theodore, 'this lad is fireproof.' For a minute or so, Theodore wished he had married and one of the children of that marriage was a son like Stephen. He then heard the tap being turned on, and two or three seconds later, a small shower of water sprinkled down on him. Stiff had learned this prank at university, where some of the students got so paranoid about having a shower when they were seated on the toilet, that trips to the toilet were never announced.

'Oy, you, you . . .'

In Andrew Goode's office, he took a phone call from DI Broome to say that he wished the team he'd taken to Aylesbury hadn't been so knowledgeable about the worst sort of parasites which meant that the tabloids would be so joyous about publishing in order to frighten the public. The public perversely bought the papers that frightened them, and because of it, scary headlines made sound business reasons. He was also pleased to announce that there had been an arrest by the Thames Valley CID of Craig Harris.

Craig Harris had been in possession of a chef's knife, admittedly clean as a whistle but surprisingly suitable for comparison purposes. There would be no giveaway nicks on the blade because the blade was so precisely manufactured, and therefore, cuts would be too clean, meaning it would be difficult to explain to a jury that the cut was unique *because* it was too clean a cut. Craig Harris relaxed on his cell bed. He was no fool and knew he had to be convicted before his previous offences could be revealed, and if anything leaked out, he would ask his lawyer to claim a mistrial. Whilst taken to and from questioning, he had once been tripped going upstairs, and being handcuffed had not been able to protect his head. Two burly uniformed officers heaved him, none too gently, to his feet by each elbow. He wouldn't have a happy time in custody, but he knew he was mentally tough enough to endure it. It was about one o'clock in the morning that Craig Harris witnessed the six-foot-plus pink rabbit who opened the cell of a perpetual drunk and disorderly (D&Ds are not appreciated because they take up cell space as if it were a free doss house, cell space that could be used for a more serious offender). The pink rabbit shook the drunk awake and repeatedly hopped around the cell, slapping the offender, or if he fell to the floor, kicking him with an oversize fur covered foot, not thought to be lucky. This was done until the man was sufficiently awake to yell abuse, when the rabbit hopped away and closed the cell door. The rabbit suit was laundered frequently because of the hazards associated with using this treatment on perpetual drunks and having to clad a sweaty night shift police officer. Craig Harris laughed to himself. His offence was not of the type that would warrant a visit from the pink rabbit.

Theodore joined Natalie and a cheekily smiling Steve Stiff in the canteen. Goode wandered in and enquired if there was any work going to be done today. Joking aside, he wanted to ensure that any correspondence with the press went through him. Andrew Goode couldn't afford a professional Public Relations Officer (or a pro, PRO) getting a leak from any unsuspecting members of staff. He knew that any loose talk would provide a field day of aspersion in respect of a company that is conducting procedures on a particular specie and then, when it appears that these procedures fail, is called in to fix the failures. A bit like a company spilling nails in the road and then selling puncture repair kits.

For a concerned man, Andrew Goode was collected and determined. He knew his procedures hadn't failed. He would fight harder to retain this business than he ever did for his miserable marriage. Theodore, as his main man, was known to be a stickler for procedure, and anyway, they were irradiating the flies to sterilise the males. This outbreak comprised flies that were fully reproductive. It would be a total distraction from the resolution of the issue to associate his facility as having nurtured the creatures that fed on Lizzie Day.

While Goode was seeking to control contact with the media, in the reception area, Lovejoy was having difficulty with a bubbly girl asking questions about recent events. The girl was using her feminine ploys to try and manipulate Lovejoy, but she didn't have much luck. This security man was not for turning. He persuaded her to take a seat or she would be ejected from the premises. Lovejoy used his experience and training to 'placate the subject' by offering an easy option and an unpleasant one. Only two options were ever offered, and there was no negotiation. Lovejoy did not let on that he couldn't eject the girl physically from the premises, he could only ask the police to do so, but he mustn't let the girl know that he had reservations. When she didn't respond quickly enough, he forced the play by calling over his shoulder to reception.

'OK, control, ensure all of this is recorded. Ma'am, you must leave now. I have the authority to eject you from the premises.'

Lovejoy had been trained. Babs, the bubbly journalist, had received an unpaid internship. She slumped down into a chair and was suddenly subservient. Lovejoy was magnanimous in victory and, after thanking her, retreated behind his bullet-proof glass, quite content until Steve Stiff bumbled into the reception for no real reason apart from his bonhomie after the recent exchanges. By coincidence, Babs was the girl from the cycle ride, who had given Stiffy her phone number. She is surprised and couldn't believe her fortune in seeing Stiff. She could mix her professional assignment with social reasons (although the fact that Babs wasn't being paid for the work didn't stop her from thinking she was a professional).

'Wooo Hoo, Steve Stiff, is your bum still sore?' she shrilled across the reception. 'And why haven't you sent me a text or phoned, you toad?'

Lovejoy quickly marched out from behind his screen and said that he would only allow them into the hospitality zone, not any further. He was briefed earlier by Mr Goode, and like all ex-military men or women who are proud of their service, he never forgot or disregarded a briefing.

'Objective—no one talks to the press, but me, understood? I repeat, no one but me,' Goode said, echoing the words in his head.

After Lovejoy's retreat behind his ramparts, Stiff poured two cups of water and whispered, 'What are you doing here, are you stalking me? 'cos if you are, that's cool. I never thought I'd ever acquire a stalker.'

Babs was a rarity for the time, in that she was a hack that tried to report the truth and had not *yet* had the decency in treating the public, or their private lives dashed out of her by the pressures of an unscrupulous editor wielding a foul tongue. She told Steve Stiff the truth that she was a hack' 'I *told* you after the cycle ride' she had said a little petulantly and with the 'I want' bottom lip slightly protruding. (Steve Stiff could clearly envisage her as a child). She realised that Stiff didn't know that a hack was a journalist (in his mind, a hacker was someone who messed with computer code, not necessarily with malice aforethought), so she explained that she was an intern for the local newspaper, which was owned by a national tabloid, basically meaning that she was an unpaid reporter, although she got expenses, of which she had not incurred any.

'Oh good, you can bung me a grand as a source. Anyway, I thought an intern was someone like Monica Lewinsky.'

Stiff rabbited on without pause for comment. Babs wrinkled her nose at him and his implications. They had both been very young at the time of the scandal, but there was much information available on the Internet of the period concerned, for keen youngsters to 'research'. In respect of expenses, there was far more focus on this topic these days, and whilst not having worked a long time at the paper, she had heard some of the stories about the good old days, where expense claims were even more legendary. One story was about two reporters who meet each other while walking in different directions down Fleet Street and one says to the other, 'Can't stop now, old boy. I'm in a taxi'. Mr Murdoch's purge of Fleet Street had assigned that era to folklore. The bungs to other sources did not seem to have so much management control.

'Ah well, sadly I'm not allowed to talk to the press without Mr Goode being present, even for vast sums of bunce.' Babs made cow eyes at him and said that being such a junior, she was hardly the press and he could give her an insight. Her eyelashes fluttered at him. Lovejoy peered at the two of them from behind his screen and picked up the telephone, his eyes squinting with suspicion. Within a minute, Andrew Goode made his appearance into the reception area and gave Stiff a bit of a pointed look. Babs leapt to Stiff's defence, babbling that she didn't know that Steve worked here and she was following up on a lead given by her editor to try and ease her way into the facility. It was coincidence that they had met before on the cycle ride. Goode listened more to their explanations and thought, 'OK, maybe we can make use of this opportunity and pre-empt any adverse publicity.'

'Young lady, I appreciate your candour and enthusiasm. Therefore, Mr Stiff, how would you like to give the lady a guided tour of the facility. Start by getting a visitor's pass from Mr Lovejoy for her and bring her to my office, where we'll have a brief talk over the history of the place before we see the labs. Miss, bring your notepad and/or recorder. We might have an article for you, although no photographs are permitted to be taken within the facility, and just to give us comfort, would you leave your mobile phone with Mr Lovejoy?'

Babs had been prepared by the editor of the local rag, by the unfortunate but apposite name of Crawley (nicknamed Creepy by his staff, but never to his face), to try and get Theodore or any of the scientists to talk, but especially this bloke Grouchier, because it had been picked up in many articles that he was the victim of a burglary where his garage was raided and also worked at the facility that looked it might get a contract after the trip to Aylesbury and the subsequent stir that had happened. Babs was led into Goode's office, and she pulled a notebook and a notepad (one electronic, the other ring-bound paper) and got ready to scribble or type. She hadn't brought a voice recorder because she liked talking to people, not machines. She also (like nearly all of us) hated the sound of her voice replayed from a recording machine.

Steve Stiff started off nervously, but then his confidence grew. He explained that he was really the computer technician but he was also able to undertake digital forensics. He hoped to acquire his certificate of competence on telecommunications equipment, before the end of the academic year. He stressed the importance of the word 'forensics' being associated with a court of law, meaning that with something as open to spoiling evidence as a computer, it was vital to secure the computer and take an image to work on. Stiff said the key point in digital forensics was procedure not interrogative software. If it was a laptop, take the battery out, if it was a desktop, pull the plug out from the wall, and if it was a server, disconnect any uninterruptible power supply (UPS) and then pull the plug out of the wall. Stiff realised his enthusiasm was getting the better of him, although he hadn't caught a signal to cut short because 'This is really boring, you geek'. He wound up with a summary and suggested that he ought to handover so that Natalie and Theodore could give an overview of their fields of expertise, although both attended the same university at similar times. Goode picked up the phone, and shortly afterwards, Theodore and Natalie entered the office, both sporting a similar frown. Steve Stiff quite smoothly gave a précis of the briefing he'd given and handed over to Goode, who asked them both if they would give Babs a guided tour after a brief explanation of the how forensic entomology could be of assistance to a murder investigation. Natalie and Theodore explained that a human corpse would be a food source for various insects that would lay eggs that would hatch and the larva would feed on the decaying flesh or organs (if they were exposed). The growth of the larva and the specie would give indicators of the location and date of death. They both noticed Babs looking slightly nauseous, and while not sympathetic to the sensitivities of members of the press (who are not renowned for their sensitivity), they could tell that Babs was a bit of a newbie. It didn't take a great leap of logic to understand what Andy Goode's tactic was. Theodore suggested that it was time for a break for coffee and that he had to make a telephone call. 'Perhaps Natalie and Stephen Stiff could complete the guided tour of the laboratory?'

Stiff and the two females departed on the sightseeing tour, and Theodore came very close to smiling at Goode. 'Head them off at the pass, Sheriff?'

Goode turned the corners of his mouth downwards and shrugged in a very Gallic manner.

'I have a couple of presentations, and hopefully, she will take the bait and produce a story that might help all present in addition to preventing any red herrings.'

Natalie and Stiff introduced Babs to the marketing research team, who were far more enthusiastic and not so staid as 'these boring science boffins'. It was Goode's idea that the marketing research team would provide enough fluff and tinsel to overpower the forensic department's presentation. Their presentations didn't produce nausea in the audience. There were a lot more graphs, colour and positive speak, less bullet-pointed phrases, and statistical facts. When Babs returned to Goode's office, she had a little more colour in her face than when she'd left. In addition, she carried an armful of colour slides. She held out a firm small hand to Andrew Goode to say goodbye and thank you. Babs picked up her equipment and left with a cheery wave, and Steve Stiff escorted her out through security and assisted as a pack animal.

At the front gate, Babs thanked him by giving him a peck on the cheek. She was clearly impressed, but Steve Stiff was hopeful and optimistic for a little more. Stiff was also impressed with her and not a little smitten as he trailed behind her. Whilst he was a bit worried that he looked like an excited puppy, he cheerily vowed to send her a text or call before the end of the day. He was still waving and walking backwards, and when he encountered the steps at the entrance, he stumbled in ungainly fashion into the security and reception area. Lovejoy was amused and shook his head in kindly fashion (for a security officer) at the youth.

Babs left a waving Steve Stiff and headed back to the house she shared with friends. After making a mug of instant coffee, she started on her story with her notepad open, and the presentations arranged fanlike alongside for prompts. She had also drawn a storyboard with arrows and rough sketches, so she had a framework before writing first draft. She constructed the story using carefully crafted sentences and lovingly caressing the adjectives into place and making changes only that improve. A nicely crafted scientific factual piece was emerging, her fingernails ticking on the screen like an erratic clock, pausing only to consider whether she ought to get a keyboard, because the wear and tear on the screen might cause a problem later (she didn't earn sufficient money to keep replacing digital equipment, if only she could sell this piece!). Two hours later, she had rattled off 2,000 words, quoting from the presentations given and the observations she had made during the interviews and tour. She concluded, 'This is a professional outfit that will provide sound evidence. The procedures are robust and the staff dedicated, if only care homes were run by these people.'

After another hour, Babs had finally grown weary of rereading her article, polishing it, and enhancing the adjectives. When one of her house mates let herself in, Babs leapt up and took her bag from her. Using bribery of a coffee, she cajoled her into proofreading the copy. The house mate had been suckered in but was quite happy to help out. She knew that Babs was struggling with her choice of career and her share of the rent. Some twenty minutes later, she raised her eyes and said, 'Babs, this is good and straight. Are you sure it will go down well as an article? I'm no expert, but are you sure about the reference to care homes? Anyway, I can't think of anything to improve it.'

The next day, Babs took her story to the paper having downloaded it to a flash drive. She was ready for yet another review by the subeditor. After an hour or so, all seemed ready to publish after the subeditor sent Babs off to lunch with an inappropriate pat on the buttocks. He was going about setting when he noticed Crawley and managed to buttonhole him to draw his attention to the story. The subeditor expressed his opinion that it was a good article, certainly exceeding the reports on the 'coffee mornings' or the 'residents call for traffic calming' and all ready to go at Crawley's nod. However, the closing line about the care homes raised Crawley's doubts, and he held the article while he phoned the editor of the parent company in London. This particular editor had his ear close to the ground and knew that the national paper had some tricky dealings and friends in funny places. Crawley, for his own sins, had a friendship with his local member of parliament who thought that the funding initiative for the care homes was a good thing for the economy. Unfortunately, when investigated, it was just an accountant's ploy at pretence profit where the whole organisation ran at a loss (and paid no tax) until it was forced into receivership where the tax payers would bail out the care home. One suspected that there might be mutual interests involved with owners of a national newspaper and directorships of care home companies. The national editor congratulated Crawley, saying that certain friends of friends, etc. would be pleased with his information and suggested the intern is hounded out to stop her using any systems or other resource available to the paper to back her story. 'Once she's gone, water it down, and print anyway, you can have the lineage money'. After the handset was replaced 'See to it Creepy'. The national editor will get a lunch and other quid pro quos, Crawley his lineage bonus, Babs would get the boot.

It was two days before Babs was called in to Crawley's office, and she was given the hairdryer treatment that probably exceeded those given by the Manchester United coach, for writing such a wimpish marketing puff piece. She was already sure her article would get no further because of the time delay after the subeditor seeing Crawley.

'What's the matter? Couldn't dig hard enough for the dirt? These guys are bunging the old bill, I'll tell you.' Crawley paused to draw breath. 'You are going f*ck*n' nowhere, you useless, spineless, arse-licking tart. Were you blowin' goody-goody, hoity-toity, see my lab, goody-goody Goode under his desk?'

Babs tried not to react even though tears were starting to sting her eyes, partly from the shock, but also the whisky fumes carried on the hot air. An instinct told her that this was exactly what the editor would like, possibly even more than a sex act. She gathered her strength and pressing both hands on Creepy's desk forced herself up on to her feet, causing the chair to tumble backwards with the force of her thighs. Babs leaned forward and drew her right fist back. Crawley cowered, cravenly. Babs just pushed her fist towards him and twisted it into the classic two-fingered gesture to which she gave an extra flip, with a finger each side of Crawley's nose.

'If you want to me to write fiction, I'll become a novelist or starve. A journalist should only express the facts, Creepy. My first character will be moulded on you.' She jabbed her forefinger at him. 'You are a stagnant pool of distaste, a Shylock, a Goebbels, a Uvula!'

'You'll never publish anything and you'll never earn a living as a journalist!' he snorted. Babs just raised an eyebrow as a response. It was sufficient. She left the room, a banner of whisky fumes from Crawley's breath trailing her. She departed the building, tossing her security pass on the table in front of an astounded receptionist. Babs was an honest, but worried young woman for her career.

Chapter 22

After the comparative success of proof of concept, the chief constable of the Wessex force decided to award the contract to Goode's facility. The contract was to be signed in the reception of the facility with the media present, which was causing Lovejoy a bit of a headache. All participants were smartly dressed, with the exception of the members of the press who were taking notes and photographs (some media members were dressed as if they expected to be sent to Afghanistan at short notice). Stiff was leaning from one side to another and seeing if he could catch a glimpse of Babs. There was no sign of her. There were no awkward questions, and everything ended almost as an anti-climax, apart from the lightning flashes from the cameras. Stiff was miffed. After all the publicity razzmatazz had died down, it was curious to note that a local senior reporter (because of his age) had hung around, especially after Goode had invited all to the folly for a glass or two and canapés. When have members of the press refused a free drink? The reporter lurked and took photographs as well as scribbling notes. He reached for his mobile and made a call that was almost military and far too short for a member of the press. Theodore ushered Steve Stiff to the celebration, clucking like a mother hen. He didn't like this sort of political meet and greet and false bonhomie and also added 'that nice young girl might be there.' Steve Stiff thought Theodore came close to winking conspiratorially. 'What is wrong with TG? His grumpiness has taken second fiddle recently.' The party headed off to the Folly with Goode, Natalie, and Steve Stiff leading the advance. Lovejoy and Theodore kept a close eye on the suspicious journalist, and when he sneaked past a turnstile with his camera, they nodded as fellow conspirators and followed, Lovejoy enjoying the first chance to use his skills since returning from Iraq. A small red light was flashing behind the bullet-proof glass in the reception area, as the reporter had placed his hands on the glass top of the cabinet that concealed half of the turnstile. His palm print was scanned, causing a second light to blink in sync with the first. One camera had now switched to one frame per second mode, and the second security officer on watch was now controlling the CCTV panel manually. The reporter crept into the canteen to the amusement of Lovejoy, who beckoned Theodore into hiding with a forefinger across his lips and a twinkle in his eyes. The reporter crept out of the canteen like a poorly acted Inspector Clouseau. Lovejoy waited until the reporter managed to get into one of the laboratories and then they pounced. The ease at which Lovejoy restrained the reporter was very sobering to Theodore after how he'd been so dismissive to Lovejoy earlier. ('This man could paralyse me and make it look like an accident.')

Lovejoy contacted the police and mentioned DI Broome's name which ensured that two cars turned up speedily. The officers were led into the canteen, where Crawley was sat crestfallen and looked a little scared of Lovejoy. Crawley didn't complain about his treatment but, on being arrested and escorted from the facility, gave Theodore and Lovejoy a wide berth. On Theodore's suggestion, they seized Crawley's mobile phone and dropped it into a bag. Steve Stiff would have been pleased to note that they took the battery out of the phone. Lovejoy said that it was all recorded on CCTV and now as he had switched to the backup disc would make the main disc drive of the security surveillance system available to the officers unless they wanted him to create a DVD of the last twenty-four hours, from the relevant camera positions. The officers agreed a DVD would suit but kept the original disc out of circulation, for the time being.

The timing of the shift change meant that Lovejoy could also attend the beano at the Folly. He offered Theodore a lift, and hopefully they could get there before all the battered prawns had been eaten. Lovejoy parked his Land Rover close to a TVR which he admired, and Theodore explained that the car in question belonged to Natalie. Lovejoy glanced quickly at Theodore and wondered whether Theodore knew how special that particular model was. 'Oh yes,' responded Theodore, 'it is rather special.' Lovejoy knowingly nodded but made no comment. He would drink one pint and dump the landy at home before walking to his own local for beers and reminiscences with some ex-service chums. He was keen to draw swords with a couple of ex-squaddies who'd teased him for taking a uniformed security officer's role. He would have something to share that would justify his choice of work, rather than starting up his own team-building business based on army training techniques. When Lovejoy had located the crowd from the facility, milling around the buffet, he was quite surprised that Theodore had managed to push his way to the bar and was frantically mouthing to Lovejoy, 'What would you like to drink?' He was also surprised that Theodore had a similar taste in beer that he had. They chinked glasses, and Steve Stiff meandered over with a glass of cider with clumps of ice pinging merrily away. A wedge of lime (an unnamed ship) was battling for survival between Scylla and Charybdis. Theodore updated Stiff about the arrest and the fact that the officers had confiscated the phone, after he had taken the battery out.

'Oh Wow, cool', responded Stiff in typical fashion.

'I thought you may be pleased,' responded Theodore.

Lovejoy had become interested in digital forensics and looked at Stiff with a little more respect. Stiff was a little bit garrulous, enthusiastic, and a little merry with drink but engaged Lovejoy at the same time, who was wooed into staying a half hour longer than intended, but steadfastly refused the offer of another drink. Stiff promised to bring in the prospectus. Once again, he propounded the importance of procedure over technical investigatory software. This made much sense to Lovejoy, who, with sincere apologies, made his exit to the car park. He had much to discuss with his own buddies over a pint. He couldn't wait to garage his Land Rover for the night.

Three young ladies entered the Folly, one of which was Babs, who looked forlorn. Stiff was waxing lyrically about computers to anyone who would listen, and he noticed the subdued party in the corner. He wandered over, ice cubes chinking in his cider glass like a wind chime.

'Hi ya, what's going on? I thought they would have published your piece by now?' he cheerily interrupted their misery.

'I've been fired by the editor, who made horrid accusations and said I was put up to it by your boss,' howled Babs. Her friends looked glumly on while reaching for tissues and then both trying to dry her eyes at the same time. The effervescence had been shaken out of Babs, and the sparkle gushed from her and carried on a torrent of tears.

'What!' For once, Stiff refrained from making any flippant comment intending to lighten the scene. This was definitely not the time. He got up, strolled over to the buffet, and filled a plate with vegetarian sandwiches and samosas from the table. He returned and placed the plate in the centre of the table and settled down while Babs related her last day confrontation with Creepy, a sob interjecting periodically. If Babs had known that Creepy was being interviewed as she spoke, she might have felt somewhat less aggrieved.

The gentlemen of the press were getting stuck into more drinks, courtesy of Andrew Goode's tab. (Goode, well aware of the capacity of the press to soak up liquid refreshments, had agreed a limit of an eye-watering £500 with Chris, the landlord who'd ensured extra staff were on duty.) Andrew Goode was a gentleman of sensitivity and observation. He knows from Theodore and Lovejoy that a man from the local press had been arrested for trespass but had picked up the misery emanating from the young journalist who was conducted on the tour of the facility. He nodded to Chris for a bottle of white wine and three glasses and set it beside the sandwich plate for the girls to share. 'Mr Stiff can sort himself out with fizzy apple juice' was his only comment. 'Oh, your boss is so kind,' wailed Babs. Her two companions had caught the mood and were crying silently. Stiff sat bemused, subconsciously rattling the gradually dissolving ice cubes in his watered down Wessex Whippersnapper sparkling cider. Stiff's ebullience with assistance from the Soave (he tried the joke that the wine was named after his character) brought the party round the table to better humour.

'Well, fuck your editor,' blurted Stiff a little too loudly, a recharged glass of Whippersnapper and ice now half-empty.

'Oh, I don't think she'll do that now!' hooted one of the house mates. She was a matronly sort with a matronly chest. Stiff turned round and looking up saw Natalie and Theodore looking down at the party, about to announce they were leaving. It was not certain whether Theodore caught 'f' word or not (surely he would have commented?). Natalie urged them to get another round in before the press finished off the tab. 'And don't get too drunk,' a grumpy(ish) Theodore added as a footnote. Both were standing close and cast a fond look at each other before leaving.

As soon as they had gone out of the door, Stiff got the three girls to follow him. He put his finger to his lips as they stood by the door. The three were trying to guess what was the purpose when the deep-throated roar of the TVR caused Stiff to smile in satisfaction. The TVR burbled in satisfaction at tick over. He ushered them back to the table, and Stiff caught Chris's eye for another round.

'Well, he doesn't look the sort who'd own a car that sounded like a fighter plane. He looks more like a bus wanker,' announced the girl who had a hoot for a laugh.

'Well, actually it's her car. You shouldn't jump to conclusions about cars, just because you may be a sexist,' snootily retorted Stiff with a smirk of satisfaction.

They talked for another hour or so, and finally Stiff plucked up courage to ask Babs out for a date on Saturday. A day ticket would take them round Wessex for £7.00 each. They could take in the sights, have a spot of lunch by the river, or go cycling, given the recent weather. No thought had been given to alternatives, should it perchance rain. Babs accepted and opted for the day ticket 'to spare your bum, Stiffy.'

'There's nothing wrong with his bum, from where I'm looking.' This was declared by the one that Stiff was to name 'The Hooter with the Hooters'.

Later on, the four stumbled from the Folly with arms either over shoulders or extended to place the hand on the shoulder in front, like troops being relieved after a long spell on the trenches. They headed back to the rented house where Stiff accepted a coffee and at first a peck on his cheek. Then the two other housemates insisted on giving Stiff a sloppy kiss each for being their knight in shining armour and walking them home. Babs looked a little suspiciously or possibly a bit jealously at both but was also grateful for them bringing her out of the dumps and also for putting up her share of the rent until she got another job.

Saturday morning saw the sun scintillating off the car windscreens and into the eyes of Steve Stiff and Babs, causing them to raise their hands for shields as they waited patiently at the bus stop. They were waiting for the bus to take them to the Roman city that is the county capital of Wessex. After about twenty minutes, the bus wheezed and performed a sort of curtsey as it ground to a halt beside them. After buying the tickets, they saw it was rather full and had to share a set of four seats (two arranged opposite each other) with the little old lady that Theodore sometimes assisted. Babs and Steve Stiff wriggled into place, and when they were settled, the LOL decided to engage the young couple in conversation. She folded the local newspaper and stuffed it unceremoniously into her wheeled shopping basket. Putting her hands on her thighs, she drew a breath and leant towards them with a slight whiff of eau de toilette.

'Oooh, it's disgusting what happens in those care 'omes. You wouldn't catch me going into one. I've got me own plan.' (She'd obviously been reading an article about it in the paper.)

Babs said, 'Things can't be that bad. Surely you won't want to commit suicide rather than go into a care home although some may think this is the better option?'

'No, I'm not gonna top meself,' LOL responded. 'I've got a much better plan than that. I ain't goin' into no 'ome.'

Babs and Stiff sat silently for a while and waited to see if the LOL elaborated and sure enough.

'I've got an old double-barrelled shotgun that my Roger used to shoot rabbits wiv on a Sunday morning.' She gummily rolled her jaw in thought for a while. 'It's taken me ages to saw the barrels down. Bleedin' tough they were.'

The LOL paused after every sentence, almost for effect, while Babs and Stiff were sitting open-mouthed, until they exchanged glances and shut them. The bus halted at a stop and, after a pause to let passengers off and on, lurched away. As if prompted, the LOL spoke up.

'Yus, I'm gonna do a bank job, take the shooter in, and just get them to hand the loot over. I might even let the ceiling have one barrel—just one mind—in case they rush me.'

Eventually, Babs couldn't hold on to her silence. 'You can't do that. They'll catch you and send you to prison!'

The LOL looked pityingly at her and shook her head, just a fraction.

'That's the 'ole bleedin' point. What would I do wiv the money? Prison is cosey, and you get looked after wiv television and all that, much better than being ignored or even abused in a care 'ome. That's my point. You won't catch me in one of them gaffs—hypofermia an' all.'

Babs's mouth opened and closed a few times, and Stiff snorted. Hypothermia was not at the forefront of his mind, given the season. The bus chose the moment to grind to a halt, and the LOL dragged her shopping basket across Stiff's shins, before setting it on the wheels, ambling, and mumbling as she made her way to the exit. In front of her was a youth also waiting to alight. He had his jeans at half mast so that the top 35 per cent of his underpants were clearly visible. It was also clearly visible that he thought he was a gangster. The LOL had to reach up to tap him on the shoulder and having succeeded in getting his attention loudly announced, "Ere, you want to pull yer strides up. Not every bugger wants to see 'ow good yer mum launders yer skivvies.'

Interestingly the youth hoisted his jeans up and got off the bus without glancing back. It was definitely not wise not to engage in debate with LOLs.

Babs and Steve Stiff continued the journey, looking at each other and exchanging happy smiles. The bus pulled into a numbered bay, grunted, and shook itself to a halt as the driver cut the engine; the doors hissed open and discharged their charges into the glass and limestone of the recently renovated bus station. The pair left the bus, and Steve Stiff reached for Babs's hand, and seeing his sheepish action, she slipped her own into his, and they walked, arms swinging, into the nearby shopping centre. They window-shopped for a while, Babs wistfully looking at shoes while Steve Stiff rolled his eyes. Other stores caused them to pause and exchange opinions. There was a tobacconist, possibly the last in Wessex, selling aromatic pipe tobacco and luxury cigars and cigarettes. Neither of them knew anyone who smoked, so they wondered how the shop stayed in business. They wandered into the abbey, which was fully functional and had been used as a place of worship for over a thousand years. It was also open to visitors from 9 to 18 on a Saturday (which was good because they wouldn't have liked to blunder into a fully fledged religious service). After spending a half hour staring at the gothic arches, vaulted ceilings, and stained glasses, which had been restored despite the efforts of Henry VIII to raze or erase the establishment, they departed after depositing some loose change in the restoration fund collection box. Back outside, the sun had lit the stonework of the abbey like a massive honeycomb confectionery. They took a couple of pictures using their mobile phones and meandered off with no real destination in mind until, by chance, they stumbled across and stopped at a cycle shop, of interest because of their recent bike ride. This shop stocked various road and mountain bikes, but what drew the eye was a rosso-red-Ferarri-designed road bike, complete with rampant black horse logo and polished aluminium chain rings and cranks. Just as they were watching, the manager of the store lifted the bicycle from its rack and presented it to an obviously love-struck potential purchaser, causing the polished aluminium to glint in the sun. The purchaser, a man in his late twenties or early thirties, didn't look like an archetypal cyclist. His spiked gel hairstyle would be compromised by a cycling helmet; his polo shirt bearing the Subaru logo indicated a petrol-based sport, but this didn't mean he didn't have the *right* to own a bicycle.

They left the shopping centre and found themselves by the river Avon, sunlight sparkling off the ripples, making the river seem as evanescent as a 20-metre-wide diamond necklace. They joined the footpath-cum-cycle track and enjoyed the stroll punctuated by a merry jingle of a bell as a cyclist sought to pass. They had been holding hands for about an hour, almost non-stop. A half hour later, they saw a riverside pub with its colourful parasols beckoning to them, offering refreshment under shade. Babs's sat down while Steve Stiff sorted out drinks and a menu. Both ordered a pint of Whippersnapper. 'Whippersnapper for the Whippersnappers,' joked the rotund manager. Then they shared a ploughman's lunch, which, to be fair to the manager, would have fed a ploughman with a serious appetite, although the accompanying pickle contained odd bits of fruit as well as vegetables, on the menu. The manager called it his tropically spiced chutney. A large colourful narrow-boat chugged steadily by. They both watched it awkwardly navigate a bend in the river, when it had disappeared from sight. Babs looked into Steve Stiff's eyes. Apropos of nothing associated with the environment (apart from Stiff), she said, 'Stiffy, why do you dye your hair?'

'You mean you don't find it attractive? And anyway, why do you wear make-up?'

'I don't wear make-up, and it's not that it's unattractive, but I bet you've got nice hair, anyway.'

'You sound just like my mum.'

'Ahh, you still live at home, then.'

'Excuse me, don't jump the gun, but, yes, my folks are quite good to me, and I need to pay off my student loan and all that stuff. My mum is fantastic, although she does go on about me messing up the shower and screams indignation if I stain a towel or there's the odd drop of paste on the shower base. Oh and the usual things that mum's witter on about: Are you wearing clean pants? Have you eaten? You're not going out like that, are you?'

Stiff's response caused Babs mood to turn gloomy.

'I'll probably have to go back home, tail between my legs. I can't afford to sponge off my friends. It's not fair. What a bloody silly notion that they would take me on as an intern and then convert it into a salary after a probationary period.'

She sipped her cider, hoping it would ward off her low spirits. The only thing that cider wards off is constipation.

'I can help out, if you need money,' Stiff generously offered.

Babs swiftly changed the subject, thus evading a response on Stiff's kind offer. She settled on the following.

'That old lady, you know, the one on the bus, who had the whiff of embrocation. Could you imagine her arriving at the bank on her electric scooter?'

'Yes, actually, it would be the getaway vehicle.'

'And then she gets off and shuffles into the bank, with the shopping bag that holds the sawn-off shotgun, with a crocheted doily as a covering, or at least something crocheted like a baby's blanket.'

'I bet she would wait patiently in the queue until it was her turn to be served. By the way, what is a doily?'

Babs ignored his question.

'And then she would peep over the top of the counter (the LOL isn't very tall at all) and demand the contents of the till.'

They both imitated the voice of an old lady trying to imitate how a bank robber would make the demand, like a Vinnie Jones, a Bruce Willis, or a Paul Newman (*esto es un robo*).

'I bet she hasn't even got the strength to cock the shotgun!'

'She has to ask for help from someone in the queue behind her! And when the gun is cocked, she thanks them politely and fires a shot, and the recoil causes her to fall over backwards!'

'The shot causes her false teeth to come loose and the plaster of the ceiling to crumble and starts a miniature snow fall that lightly dusts her like a snow queen's mother.'

They enjoyed compiling the script for the little old lady. Babs had been committing some of it to her mobile. They drained their drinks, rose in the hazy afternoon sun, and realised they could pick the bus up when it stopped at the New Bridge over the river. They left hand in hand.

'A doily is an ornamental plate stand, normally circular and named after a London draper,' she snootily added, but with a smile that Steve Stiff was finding increasingly touching and increasingly difficult to restrain from touching her lips.

'Smart-arse.'

Chapter 23

During the coming week, panic struck the home counties, especially among the stock breeders and dairy farmers, who were having enough problems with the drought (but admittedly not as much as the arable ones). There were fewer and fewer farms in the South East because of land prices, so they didn't have the impact they used to (fewer farms, fewer tractors to block the capital's thoroughfares). On the Wednesday, several farmers had driven tractors to Whitehall. Some had brought cattle and sheep, and some had trailers full of manure, which were dumped in Whitehall. There was a ripe smell, causing the Prime Minister's nose to twitch when he stepped in front of Number Ten to address the press. It was the late afternoon, and the manure had ripened in the heat. After a few platitudes he added, 'Of course, we take threats to our live stock farmers' interests very seriously. We will consult the leading experts in the field to provide advice on the appropriate course of action.'

'Prime Minister, like regulators, did with the behaviour of the banks?'

The PM scowled at the freelance journalist. He knew he was beginning to lose control of the conference.

'Oh yes and the attitude of HMRC in respect of tax efficiency!'

Another journalist had picked up the thread. The PM's fear of control loss were confirmed.

'And the water companies' neglect of the infrastructure causing another hosepipe ban!'

'Yes and the awarding of the Olympics security contract to that firm, ho ho!'

The Prime Minister rolled his eyes and pushed his hands out as if propping up an invisible wall (he came close to raising them in surrender) to calm his audience and judged his moment to announce that he knew where the expertise existed. He assured all that the crisis would be resolved before the autumn. Because of the amount of camera flashbulbs being triggered and out of the bright lights required for television, he made a rapid and strobe-like retreat. A few more flashbulbs fired before all performed a form of U-turn and disperse.

The newspapers had a field day with the PM's retreating figure, front pages with headlines such as 'PM FACES THE FACTS', 'HIS NEXT COURSE OF ACTION—RUN AWAY!' and 'PM MEETING THE ISSUE HEAD ON!' already being composed.

Andrew Goode's mobile phone rang within three hours after the press conference. The caller explained in a gruff, but matter-of-fact, voice that the government needed his facility to assist with this issue. Goode tried to explain that the funding was cut and he had taken the appropriate action and trimmed his team of experts and didn't get any returns from that kind of work anyway. He thought, 'That's typical I've taken strategic decisions and now there's a change of the collective mind.' However, his rebuttal was short-lived when he was chilled by some of the facts that were related about his business and strained financial situation. This was delivered in the same unfeeling, insensitive tone. The caller also told him, in almost a bored manner, about the award of the forensics contract that might just suddenly dissolve because of certain press articles that might be published giving coverage to slipshod procedures. It wouldn't really matter if there were little substance behind such stories, the contract would be pulled anyway because of the lack of due diligence. 'Of course you may wish to merely go bankrupt.' This was said in the manner very close to that of a waiter at a stylish (reserved seats only) restaurant who when confronted with a minor complaint from one of the diners on Goode's table gave a slight bow and merely said, 'Of course, sir, one could always eat elsewhere.' Andrew Goode wasn't afraid, but he had a dose of apprehension that kept him from telling the caller to stick his offer where the sun didn't shine. So he mentioned the costs he would incur diverting resource. The voice down the phone sounded comforted now that they had started negotiating in the manner of an Arab souk. A substantial 'grant' was available for the investigation and resolution of this particular 'stock viability incident'. After ending the call, a nervous Goode cursed Theodore for not having a mobile phone. He needed a little bit of comfort that an expert (even a grumpy old Bath bun like Theodore) could offer. Even Natalie's mobile phone was diverted to voicemail. He was about to call Brian Greatrex, but a sudden jolt of fear caused him to stay his dialling thumb. The caller sounded like he could easily arrange for call logs to be obtained and examined (which was not phone tapping and therefore not subject to the Regulation of Investigatory Powers Act). Goode did not want yet another friend being dragged into this perceived storm in a teacup. He was going to need the support of Theodore and Natalie as it was. It could wait until they discussed it in his office. He hoped that they wouldn't question Goode's requirements too much, especially when it appeared to be another U-turn on behalf of the government, but he thought that Theodore would either refuse or just co-operate, whereas Natalie would argue ('bloody women thought Goode', but not maliciously); he would prefer space to argue and persuade rather than listen to the terse response that Theodore would give.

The next day, Theodore and Natalie were summoned to Andrew Goode's office for a meeting. During the meeting, Goode explained the background and suggested how they could meet the requirement of appeasing public opinion, but also dealing with the real threat that Cochliomyia hominivorax presented. To both Goode and Theodore, Natalie's response was a surprise. She suggested that they just go to the press and announce that Andrew Goode had been threatened by a government official to bury the threat of CH. (Theodore frowned at the abbreviation Natalie was using. He hated abbreviations.) Goode rather patronisingly explained that this was not like *All the President's Men*, where some good investigative journalist can bring down a government but rescues himself when he says that he wishes it could. In the UK, this sort of event can allegedly lead people to commit suicide in a strange manner, such as tying one end of a length of coiled rope round one's neck and the other end to a sturdy oak before jumping into an open-top sports car and accelerating away until the limit of the rope length causes virtual decapitation before one is plucked from the driver's seat like a recalcitrant wisdom tooth. Natalie shook her head in disbelief for a moment. However, having experience of being the wife of a US serviceman, she had heard the comments that US servicemen made about the perfidious albion and to 'beware the Brits'. Although a strong and determined character, there was a little apprehension that caused her to swallow as if this could be for real. The US version with the CIA, NSA, and FBI seemed so straight, correct, and upfront, whereas the British version was meiosis in fact. Seeing Natalie's brief look of concern, no one commented that she had a sports car and may be more of a target.

The solution all agreed on was that Theodore and Natalie made a television appearance on the BBC's Country File to explain the habits and limits of the damage that Cochliomyia hominivorax could do. It was a very useful coincidence that the program was filmed in Wessex so there was not much distance to travel and the studios specialised in wild life and programs with a rural focus. Andrew Goode returned the call to the number of the calm, but menacing voice that rang him, suggesting that possibly he could arrange a slot for his experts on the Country File program as soon as conveniently possible. The voice at the end said he would make it happen by tomorrow with transmission at the weekend and terminated the call. Andrew Goode suppressed a shudder and hoped he would never have to do any business with this gentleman again.

At the television studios, the rehearsals didn't take a great deal of effort apart from the fact that Theodore looked so taciturn and wooden, requiring the cameraman to keep Natalie in shot, which was the preferred option, anyway. The director-cum-producer of the program controlled his cameras like a conductor. He anticipated when Theodore would have a scientific fact to deliver. He then would get this on camera and then switch focus to Natalie for interpretation into plain English. Intelligent, articulate, well-dressed, and attractive women are a sure-fire winner for directors. During the program, they explained, 'Care with open wounds on livestock is paramount. Call your vet if there is anything unusual about any wound, clear any larva from the wound, and retain one for identification. The good news is that the females only breed once, so if careful attention is made during this summer, then there is little ongoing risk from these pests, which are not native to the UK. Definitely far less risk than foot and mouth, swine flu, and BSE (Bovine Spongiform Encephalitis).' The interviewer interjected, 'Do you mean mad cow disease?'

Theodore then replied, 'Oh that's not my speciality. You'll have to speak to my colleague, Natalie, about that, but I'd like to add that I think this represents less of a risk to the farming community than badgers.'

The interview was edited just in time before Theodore's comments were broadcast because a potential scare story would have puttered out in an anticlimax. This also meant that no one caught on camera the clip that Natalie delivered to Theodore, which caused his eyeballs to rattle in his head. 'Eh?' he spouted as his head rang. The whole studio was rolling around hooting with laughter, both at Theodore's bemusement and the look from Natalie, whose eyes were sparkling like crushed ice in sunlight and also the capers that studio crew could have when their whole working life had a potential of being editable.

Back at the facility and having forgiven Theodore, even though he didn't mean the implied insult, Natalie thought that, as an extra precaution, sterile male CH (Theodore gave her a withering look) flies should be released into the home counties, ideally at the epicentre of the outbreak, and Goode agreed this was a good choice because it would look like something positive was being done and it would be good public relations. This would also satisfy the caller to Goode's mobile (the one with the polite but menacing implications). Andrew Goode decided that it would be a good idea to send Natalie and Theodore to London with his blessing, ensuring that they should seek plenty of chances to plug the name of the facility. Goode also suggested they make the trip on a Thursday, stay over in the capital, and make a weekend of the whole affair, although he wouldn't fork out for the hotel. Theodore wanted to go on the bus because it was cheaper. Natalie thought the train would be better (although far more expensive). Natalie wouldn't drive the TVR into London for various reasons. Theodore thought that the bus would be more private because of the gangway restriction that inhibits people marching up and down at will, also there is far less children on the bus. He couldn't offer any substantive evidence to back this statement but knew it to be true (children have the knack of irritating Theodore at will, thus making him even more taciturn). He would also have in his care a metal case holding two containers of sterile male flies.

Early Thursday morning at the Wessex mainline station, they continued their bickering about which mode of transport was more suitable. Nearly all the seats were taken as the train pulled away from the platform (they were sitting facing each other at a table with four seats). To add to their ill humour, twenty minutes later, when the train pulled into the Wessex capital, a mother and her two children boarded and shuffled up the coach. The two children were shepherded into the vacant seats, the older boy beside Theodore and the younger girl beside Natalie. Before the train had covered ten miles, the children burst out in chorus in the endearingly persistent way that children, between the age of five and eight years, possessed.

'Mum, we're hungry. We're hungry. We're hungry.'

Theodore looked pointedly at Natalie with a 'see, I told you so' grimace. After a few renditions and without any discussion, probably just to silence her offspring, the mother delved into the capacious carpet bag that she managed to tote along the coach. She fished out two parcels of cling-film-wrapped sandwiches that have been overfilled with a form of chocolate spread. The chocolate spread was easily identifiable because it had been generously applied and was trying to ooze from the clear wrapping and in a couple of places had succeeded in doing so. Natalie looked askance with concern and desperately searched in her handbag for tissues. Theodore fixed his best scowl on the brat that sat next to him and defied him to encroach beyond his section of the table. The children tore open the package and proceeded to smear chocolate over their fingers and faces and on the table. Shards of bread were left scattered on the table like battle victims, trails of chocolate had the appearance of old blood spatter, Natalie and Theodore had shrunk back in fear and were compressed against the window and its frame. This move was encouraged by the mother, producing two plastic bottles of cola and placing one each in front of her offspring. The carbon dioxide in both bottles could be seen gathering in a brown froth at the neck. The effervescence was enhanced when the girl next to Natalie knocked her bottle over; the seal just managed to hold. Natalie was starting to tremble. She was wearing her best suit for the televised release because she thought that they were going to perform at the House of Lords. She wore what she thought the upper classes in Britain would approve of, in such surroundings. Natalie also thought that Theodore should have hired a suit and not worn the one that looked such a poor fit. However, a tatty suit is often the hallmark of a scientist. Steve Stiff would have called it scientists' street cred. Natalie's thought process was disrupted by the girl next to her reaching for her bottle of cola and grasped it round the neck. The child's right hand was reaching for the coloured top and had clasped it when Natalie gasped in horror, whilst, young in age, this child was experienced at breaking open plastic cola bottles at the first attempt. There was a split second of silence, followed by the hiss of aerated, brown, sugared water gathering strength to spume forth. Natalie moved with the speed of a cheetah and, with the dexterity of a card sharp, gripped the child by both shoulders and simultaneously twisted her through ninety degrees just as the geyser burst forth. The spurting flume gave a generous coating to three or four people who were in range. The mother got (appropriately) the mother load. The spray slowed to a gush that flowed down the child's forearms. While her brother was squawking with laughter, she was dissolving into tears, the lace sleeves of her pink princess's dress were being stained as if by diarrhoea, she leapt from her seat and went for comfort, smearing chocolate and additional cola over her mother, and tissues were offered from all corners. Meanwhile her brat of a brother was shaking his bottle of cola, as if to provide an encore. Theodore ripped the bottle from the boy's grasp and posted it into the flip-top litter bin that fortunately was within reach between the inverted 'v' where the backs of two seats joined. (As he did so, Theodore took the opportunity of putting his elbow into the chest of the boy with sufficient force to cause him to whine). The cola bottle noisily disgorged its sticky contents within the bin and all within earshot of the commotion nodded their approval for Theodore's prompt action. The journey continued in silence with everyone avoiding eye contact for another thirty minutes until the family arose to alight at the next station, presumably their intended destination. Theodore stuck out a foot and caused the boy to stumble as he made his egress. He turned and looked accusingly back, but Theodore coldly stared him down. Natalie spent ten minutes and a considerable amount of a pack of tissues clearing the detritus. The cola helped break down the chocolate; the corpses of the bread battle victim absorbed some of the cola, but the treacle coating of the table meant that Natalie almost stood on the seat to avoid contact with the table, until they got to the London terminus. Theodore got a filthy look from Natalie when he suggested maybe they ought to have travelled by bus, after all.

The trials and tribulations of one train journey were over. Theodore and Natalie boarded the tube train to go to North London (they had to change at Baker Street). Both tube trains were crowded, but fortunately, no children with apparel-damaging comestibles were travelling on either. They left St Johns's Wood station, where Natalie looked around for the river and the Houses of Parliament, but instead, they headed for the Lord's cricket ground (Headquarters of the Marylebone Cricket Club, not the House of Lords). They were met by the committee members and orderly members of the media, who formed a crescent, generously allowing each other to get a good view of the proceedings. Theodore held the case aloft by the handle as if he were the chancellor of the exchequer heading to present the budget. He and Natalie crouched down and released the catches, taking out the two canisters that held the flies. The two posed for the camera, before, on the count of three, ceremoniously lifting the lid and admittedly, after a bit of shaking, letting the contents fly, buzzing, first hesitatingly, then frantically, and then optimistically to a potentially perfect bachelor's coupling (i.e. unfruitful). London had been without rain for so long that the haze of the flies merged into the hazy blue sky. The heat and aridness was taken for granted. The outfield at Lord's had not been watered for a week and was starting to look like a running track. The MCC membership was huffing and grumbling while paradoxically savouring the floral flavour of a London gin ('there's only one thing you should put in a gin, old boy, and that's another gin'). Theodore tried to explain to Natalie what a travesty that a brown outfield at Headquarters would be in the eyes of a cricketing world. Natalie was eying the square and commented about how fine and well watered this part of the ground was and why hadn't the whole ground been equally freshened? She set off across the outfield, to the consternation of Theodore and the cluster of males, her heels unable to penetrate the almost rock-hard top layer.

'What is that blasted woman up to now?' This was said by a particularly acerbic, red-faced, white-haired, yellow-toothed, blue-eyed male from the class of c1950. His colour combination reminded Theodore of a flag belonging to some banana republic, but strangely, he felt quite at home with this gruff character. Theodore leant back from the circle of males, and to his horror, Natalie looked like she was contemplating stepping over the rope (she had hoisted her skirt above her knees, so there was definite intent) and set foot on the lush green of the hallowed turf. At the last second, she turned around to the comic apparition of Theodore running towards her with his ungainly gait. Natalie giggled loudly as Theodore impersonating a panic-stricken Basil Fawlty staggered towards her. Theodore grasped her arm and dragged her back towards the pavilion, he marching in determined fashion and she trotting behind like a mischievous pony. There was a party awaiting them. A brief speech was made about the issue, today's events, and the prompt response of the facility sending their two entomological experts to deal with the 'crisis' in the South East. It was in this respect, Theodore was awarded complementary membership of the MCC (he was beaming with delight, and Natalie ensured that a good photograph of this rare event was taken for posterity) and got his egg-and-bacon tie. The mysterious caller had pulled strings for Goode. It wouldn't occur to the committee of the MCC. Although Natalie received a gift voucher and a bunch of flowers although, she was less than pleased when she discovered that only recently were women allowed to become members (well 1998). Theodore was tempted to throw some of her comments about cricket back at her, but he remembered the clip round the ear he got at the Wessex TV studios. Theodore showed Natalie around the Long Room and pointed out the cricket ball that killed the sparrow (bowled out by Jehangir Khan in 1936). Then there is the board of fame that holds all the names of batsmen who have scored a century at Lord's and similarly one for bowlers who have taken five wickets in an innings.

Chapter 24

The police released Crawley after interview and an overnight stay in the cells. DI Broome thought it was unlikely that the Crown Prosecution Service (CPS) would have any enthusiasm in prosecuting a local journalist of some experience. His doubt was sound because a skilled brief would make much of the freedom of the press argument and the fact that the trespass hadn't caused any physical or psychological damage (and it was corporate and not personal property). DI Broome tossed the bagged mobile phone lightly in his right hand as if weighing it, wondering if there was anything that the phone could tell him. In the interview, Crawley didn't show any respect for DI Broome or his fellow interviewer. Crawley came across as supercilious and disdainful, even to the extent of hinting at the police being taken for lunch by the National Press, all recorded on tape. DI Broome did not like Creepy, and this made him put the bag holding the phone into the inside pocket and announce he was booking the exhibit out and transferring it for forensic examination. He called Andrew Goode from his mobile.

Broome was in Goode's office, explaining that he would like the phone examined, analysis of calls made and received, text messages, attachments, images stored done, and also, anything that had been deleted recovered, if possible. This would be paid for according to the contract terms. Stiff booked the phone in and signed a receipt for DI Broome to retain until the phone was returned.

Steve Stiff was delighted with having a phone to examine. He knew that he mustn't switch the phone on with the SIM in place as that would start the registration process and would be easy to refute any evidence. He just left the battery in the bag. In addition, he had been exchanging emails with a friend who had landed a job at a company that supplied equipment for mobile device forensic examination. If he came across any issues, he could call for back-up via email. Stiff booked the case in and completed the paperwork, noting the make and model of the device, and started on the first of the requirements. He connected the SIM and the phone to the forensic workstation and downloaded the call information that was exported into text format. He was looking forward to loading this into link analysis software that would convert the string of data into pictures and create a link between matching entities.

After a couple of test runs with the calls made, Steve Stiff felt confident to import the whole data to give DI Broome a bigger picture. If required, he could email the document to analysts at the Wessex constabulary for further manipulation (the police could find out to whom the numbers belonged, whereas it was just a pretty pattern to Steve Stiff). It took Stiff through until lunchtime to get the data into a presentable form, and rather than make a printed presentation to Andy Goode, he would email him and arrange to talk him through his work, before making it available to DI Broome. Stiff and Goode were seated behind Andrew Goode's desk and had the chart produced by the link analysis software on his monitor. Stiff toyed with the data and adjusted the links to make certain links stand out. He also adjusted the thickness of the link to increase with the number of occurrences a particular number was dialled. It pointed a virtual finger at part of the chart.

'Wait a minute, that's my home number. I haven't taken any calls from whoever this reporter is!'

As Steve Stiff scrolled on through the chart in date order, he was stopped by Andrew Goode again.

'And that appears to be my mobile number. What is this guy playing at?'

Stiff enlightened Goode by explaining that it looked like this device was used to get at Andrew Goode's voicemail recordings.

'What, the bastard's been hacking my phones?'

'Well, it appears that this device has been used to call your numbers and followed by a special character and a PIN number. Then it would connect to your voicemail.'

'But what is my PIN number and how does he know it?'

Stiff explained that the devices came with a default number depending either on the device or on the service provider. The gentlemen of the press shared this information to acquire newsworthy items from people who didn't change the PIN from the default settings. Goode swore again. He picked up the phone and dialled the number for DI Broome. Goode started to rant down the phone about privacy, and DI Broome had to calm him down and explain that he needed to get his guys to look at the information. He would then bring Mr Crawley in for another interview. He ended by telling Goode to keep the evidence in the safe, just in case someone might attempt another trespass on his premises. Goode put the phone down and called reception to brief Lovejoy about developments. Lovejoy was unsurprised, explaining that he felt Crawley was a bit slimey when he restrained him the evening of the bash.

'I do hope he tries to break in, again, when I'm on shift.'

Goode suggested that perhaps they should double security until this issue was resolved one way or another. He asked whether Lovejoy could use his contacts to fill this short-term requirement.

'Can I offer the same rates, i.e. for here and not for other security providers?'

Goode replied that it should go without asking but he would only pay that rate for security staff with experience and expertise similar to Lovejoy's. Lovejoy knew where he could get suitable temporary staff at short notice and locally.

Steve Stiff compressed the data he had extracted from the mobile device and encrypted it, requesting that DI Broome call for the password to open the compressed file. When Broome called for the password, he said that he'd get someone on to matching the phone numbers dialled from the device, but it would be probably tomorrow when he would have any questions or need more information. Steve Stiff was quite excited; he wanted to get squad cars sirens blaring and lights flashing, out on the street, but these things had to move methodically, and really things could wait, especially as the device was locked in a safe and the evidence could be reproduced, for use by the defence as well as prosecution. Instead, he left his room and equipment and pulled his mobile phone from his jacket, because of the Faraday cage that Stiff had begged Andrew Goode to install. Mobile signals were difficult to obtain in Stiff's 'Puter' lab. He scrolled to Babs's number and pressed the green icon. He couldn't mention anything to Babs, even though it was bubbling inside him like a geyser ready to burst, about the success of a mobile device examination. Steve Stiff hadn't realised that the mobile device from which he had been extracting the data belonged to the man who gave Babs such grief before forcing her to resign. Perhaps it was better that he didn't as it might have raised questions of impartiality. His enthusiasm was dulled when the phone wasn't answered and the voicemail kicked in. He left a short upbeat message and headed back into this room. The telephone extension rang. It was DI Broome who had been transferred through, and while he was pleased with the data, he was puzzled by a file that the analysts couldn't read. Stiff asked for the filename so he could do further work and apologised that he sent it through without checking it was legible or, posted a transcript.

Steve Stiff was back at his workstation and looked at the stubborn file, wondering what it contained. It first reminded him of his cockiness, then his confusion, and finally his contriteness about how he was unable to crack Theodore's bloody text file. He sent an email to his friend with a query about securing private areas on the mobile device's memory, and there was a piece of software that he could install on the forensic workstation to run a brute force attack (if it was PIN protected) or a dictionary attach (for a password-secured file). The email response requested the phone's make and model, and once that had been sent, Stiff got a reply from his friend saying he would see what could be done. He drummed his fingers on the table and couldn't think of anything to do while he waited for an email. A trip outside and another short voicemail to Babs killed all of two minutes. Stiff sat down and thought why some of the stuff was just in plain text (like the calls to Andy Goode's phone) yet some of the stuff was encrypted (maybe it was just bank account passwords or something).

It was after 17 when DI Broome and a stout Detective Constable Spice pulled up at the local newspaper office. DC Spice, as DI Broome before him, had been put through the mickey taking mill in the 'job'. His colleagues had made the jokes about the Spice Girls, and the he was the latest addition to their comeback concert—Plump Spice. One of the requirements of being a copper was that you had to take it or leave. At the offices of the local paper where normal routine dictated that the officers would invite someone for questioning in a more subtle manner. This normally meant 'Is there a private meeting room we could talk?' But Creepy's superciliousness had got under DI Broome's skin so much that they barged past the reception (they briefly enquired where Mr Crawley's office was located), having flashed their warrant cards. The security in a local newspaper wasn't supposed to be to Orange Book Standard.

'Oooh,' the receptionist said, 'this could be interesting. I might stay on a bit later to see what this is about.'

Of course, it was part of a receptionist's job description to keep up to date with developments within the office, especially gossip, and to ensure this information was circulated in a timely manner. Creepy went a bit green when he saw Broome enter his office. He terminated the call he was making and smarmily asked how he could be of assistance.

'To be honest, Mr Crawley, as I'm sure you are, it would suit us all if we were to hold this conversation at the station. I'm sure you'll accompany us, to avoid any awkwardness with your staff. We can say we are going for a friendly pint.'

As they passed the intrigued receptionist, a not convincingly casual Crawley announced, 'Your round, I believe.'

An offended DC Spice responded, 'And you're a lying bastard', Just loud enough for only the three to hear.

The receptionist called out, 'I'll have a gin and tonic. Where are you going, the folly?'

She rapidly gathered all her associated clutter and logged off. She was eagerly scampering off to the car park, leaving a bemused night commissaire.

'Oh yes,' said DI Broome. 'Definitely the folly.'

Within thirty minutes, all three were in an interview room. The DC was operating the twin deck tape recorder. On the table was placed an ashtray, a packet of cigarettes (neither Spice nor Broome smoked, but both had a cheap cigarette lighter in a pocket), and plastic cups of vending machine coffee. It was believed throughout the station that the coffee in the vending machines had special additives that stimulated confession and honesty, confession being the most important result. (The vending machine coffee was seldom consumed by the officers). A pale and concerned-looking Crawley sat opposite them and snatched the occasional glance at the file under Broome's hand, which was subconsciously patting it as if it were a family pet. Slight smiles played across both officers' faces. The opening gambit of the first few questions passed reasonably easily (they were confirming Crawley's name and address), but then Broome asked about his mobile phone, and although Crawley corrected him about the functionality available on the device, he was a bit sheepish. Crawley drew heavily on his cigarette and awaited the next move.

'So you agree that this is your phone, sorry, device, Mr Crawley. For the record, Mr Crawley has nodded his assent. Therefore, can you please explain the following . . .'

Broome skilfully managed to get a confession from Crawley that he had hacked Goode's phone 'but that there was nothing there, only his personal stuff!'

Both decks on the interview recording machine were turning steadily, holding a copy for both the prosecution and the defence. Both coppers glanced at each other with satisfaction at the confession made. Broome pressed on.

'Ok, Mr Crawley, thank you for being so honest about the calls made, and that just about ends this interview. However, I have some questions about a file on the memory of your phone.'

'What file is that Inspector Broome?'

'Mr Crawley, please don't mess about. We were getting on so well. Tell us what you think the contents of the special file are. We can always adjourn now while I get our computer boys to print it out, but you'll have to spend the night here.' He spoke pointedly into the machine: 'This is DI Broome halting this recording, the time is . . .'

After looking at his watch and recording the time for posterity, Broome and Spice rose (Spice was trying not to let the windows of his eyes nor his face show the confusion in his mind. He was learning more about interview techniques, rapidly). He noted that Creepy was looking uneasy and did not want to spend any more time, let alone the night in a police cell. DI Broome nodded to a uniformed officer to take Crawley into a cell and remove his shoe laces and tie.

'Posh and I are going for a well-earned pint.'

They were putting the pressure on Crawley and intended to put him through the hoops after he's had about an hour's sleep. They first headed off to the folly for a coke or an orange juice and then one pint. The idea of the pint was that they could breathe beer fumes over Crawley before starting the interview again. While Broome knew (thanks to Stiff's work) that the files were just a red herring, he wanted to hear what Crawley's opinion was. Stiff discovered that they were compressed music files. The compression is far too efficient for high fidelity recordings as high fidelity music doesn't compress much. Stiff managed (with the kind assistance of his friend on the south coast) to acquire the proprietary codec (coder/decoder) software that compressed voice recordings for call recording equipment to save disc space. This enabled Stiff to play the recordings through a normal media player. Stiff's satisfaction and getting a successful decode was knocked askew when he heard the decoded recordings. (There was the crazy frog, a recording of a butler-type voice telling his master that there was a telephonic conversation and whether to tell the call to fuck orrff, and others of equally dubious humour, and voice-overs from celebrities, etc.)

Broome and Spice drained their pints and noticed the receptionist from the local newspaper nursing a gin and tonic and occasionally scanning the patrons. They leave via a side door.

Back at the station, they arranged to have Crawley smartly awakened (he hadn't had much sleep). He was given slightly rough assistance to the interview room, where again they pressed him to reveal the contents. A tearful, exhausted, and confused Crawley finally told them that he honestly believed that he had acquired these recordings from a source he couldn't name (he had a well-spoken, but menacing voice) and that the recordings involved lunch dates and conversations with senior police officers, the media, and leading politicians. Crawley whines that he has been told to keep them safely in case of future repercussions. The tears were starting to flow down his face, and both Broome and Spice realised that the limit had been reached, even for a hard-arsed journo. DI Broome was in good humour, and he'd like circumstantial evidence to find which numbers Creepy had dialled just before downloading the file. Even if Creepy spewed all he knew, he didn't think that he would get much of a sentence, but he wanted him to be processed as an offender under the Computer Misuse Act, just to put a conviction under an existing law into the face of the hackers, that there is a criminal prosecution awaiting them if they abuse people's privacy using modern technology. Broome got the uniformed officer to take Crawley's fingerprints. The officer even got a crack in about being a newspaper man of the old school. He should be used to having ink on his fingers. Crawley rewarded the officer with a sickly grimace. Spice tossed a coin to decide whether they took Crawley home tonight or let him have a free stay on her majesty's pleasure. The coin favoured Crawley, and he was dropped off at his home in the early hours. The house was in darkness because no one but Crawley lived there these days. Crawley opened his front door and stepped into the musty, stale odour of a house that didn't get aired. After switching on the lights, he flipped down the door to the drinks cabinet that became a small bar and removed a bottle of twelve-year-old malt whisky and its top in a well-rehearsed procedure. He slopped a large measure into a crystal tumbler (he was meticulous at washing his crystal, crockery could wait, but he seldom ate at home, so it didn't matter). The warmth of the spirit flowed through him. He toyed with the idea of picking up the phone and dialling his contact at the nationals. It took him another half bottle to do so, and he was greeted with incredulity, laughter, and dismissal. Crawley's intoxication deserted him, and he looked at himself in the mirror that hadn't been dusted for some time. He saw a bloated, blotched face with a network of broken veins. Crawley drew his hand holding the tumbler back to hurl it into the image but, with resignation, sighed deeply. He found his old school tie and picked up the rest of the bottle of scotch and the remaining aspirin tablets from a cupboard in the bathroom. After tying a suitable slip knot around his neck with the tie, he tied the other end to the bed post. He tested it before splashing a scotch into the glass and shaking a handful of aspirins into his palms tossed them into his mouth and tossed the scotch back. He repeated this until both bottles were empty, said a final 'feck' to the world, and let darkness descend over him, as unconsciousness relaxed his muscles, it tightened the knot of the old school tie.

The local newspaper subsequently organised a collection and the funeral. The subeditor delivered the eulogy. As this was delivered, Babs shed tears. The police, especially after letting Crawley free, and all at the facility, after giving him short shrift, would be upset and puzzled. Creepy's contacts in London didn't give a shit.

Chapter 25

The Thursday local news for the Thames area containing a short clip of the release of sterile male flies from Lord's was watched by Skel, sitting on his bed in his bedsit, who thought he recognised Theodore, but he couldn't remember from where. To be fair, he had only recently cleaned his act up, sorted himself out, got it together again, etc . . . Skel reluctantly levered himself from his bed so he could turn up the volume on the old television. It then dawned on him the familiarity of the dour man on the screen and the circumstances. The name of the facility that had stepped in to meet the scourge of the man-eating (hominivorax) flies did not ring a bell, but when the magic words 'a Wessex-based research facility' revealed its location. Things clicked in Skel's head. He would phone in sick tonight from his current role, shelf stacking on night shift (he would be called 'Friday Skiver', one who expanded the weekend). His online wheeler-dealing in almost anything sourced from charity shops, as and when, could wait. He decided he was off on a little jaunt to Wessex. There might be a little bit of pocket money he could extort from the old fart that he'd seen on the television. Ever the optimist, Skel didn't take into account the risks he might incur from revisiting his old stamping ground. He might be in remission from his drug addiction, but he hadn't acquired any additional wisdom. When he was just starting to turn his miserable existence round to normality, admittedly not on the affluent end of normality, but law-abiding and acquiring a few possessions that he had actually paid for, he was taking a step on the road to jeopardising his recovery. A mere three hours later, Skel left the Wessex seaside train station but unlike most of the other passengers who immediately headed for the beach, promenade, and pier, he paused, took in the surroundings, and looked at a few timetables and local maps that had a conspicuous 'You are Here' arrow, before making up his mind. This summer had been kind to the Wessex seaside resorts, admittedly not having the most golden of beaches or most azure of sea. They had drawn the crowds nevertheless, and local trade experienced a boom period. Skel got his bearings, shrugged his rucksack, a replacement to the one that had transported hominivorax to London, on to his back, and slouched towards the outskirts of the town to where a bed and breakfast could be cheaper to obtain. A man of seventy years or so sat behind the wheel of his idling Jaguar. This Jaguar was his latest in a series of the marque he had owned since leaving school, his sunglasses not revealing the direction where he was looking or the surprise at seeing the man he warned off with his ace of spades. The target had put on weight since the warning; in addition, he had lost that hunted and haunted look which marked him as a druggie. Peter Mack was awaiting the arrival of his sister, who was looking forward to a long weekend at the seaside. For at least two reasons, he was not amused.

It is early on the Friday morning that Skel left the B&B without paying (forsaking the second B) and headed towards the bus station. He got off the bus and walked towards Acacia Avenue to monitor the house, which he broke in, not that long ago. He was working out his script that he would use with the intention of milking some money from this old fart of a scientist. Skel knew that he was not high on the Wessex constabulary wanted list and was unlikely to be troubled by any overeager copper.

Some hundred miles or so to the east, Natalie and Theodore left Lord's (in fact, Natalie had to drag Theodore away) and decided to find a place to eat. Theodore put his treasured egg-and-bacon tie in the silver case. They walked to Regent's Park and picked up some sandwiches to eat while they sat in the sunshine. Theodore suggested that they take a walk along the river and see some more sights. Natalie countered with 'let's get a taxi' and giggled at Theodore's horror. (Do you know how much that would cost?)

'Aww c'mon, Teddy, we can split the cost!' ('Teddy! Teddy!' Theodore fumed, while he hoped he had enough money in his wallet. He couldn't of course take his wallet out to check.) Naturally, Natalie won, and after they left the taxi (a small tip was presented to the driver, who looked genuinely astonished. He was hoping the Yank would be a good tipper, but her bloke was a real Scrooge), they wandered round Westminster, seeking out a pub, and Theodore sank a couple of good pints of real ale. Natalie sat alongside and casually swung one long leg, her shoe hanging by her toes. Despite forking out for the taxi fare and a tip, Theodore was in a state of grace. He had his tie and a tour of Parliament and was savouring a very good pint of bitter.

'Theodore, while we're here, let's take in a show at the West End.' (He noted that the Teddy bit had been dropped.) Theodore diverted his attention from his pint and looked into her grey eyes, which brooked no argument. They took another tube and watched Blood Brothers at the Apollo. Natalie had a sneaky weep at the end, which she disguised by blowing her nose into a handkerchief. Theodore is none the wiser. Just in time, they realised that they could get the last train back to Wessex, rather than book a hotel this late. They scampered on to the platform and into the back end of the train. It did take very long before Theodore nodded off on the train and also on Natalie's shoulder and called her mum in his sleep. Natalie tilted her head on to Theodore's and followed him into a fatigue-induced snooze. The train arrived in Wessex mainline city station, where fortunately it was the journey's end. The driver killed the diesels and stepped from the engine. His last two passengers were sound asleep, emitting the odd snort or mumbled until discovered by the ticket collector. They looked so blissful. He was tempted to take a photograph, but this was a serious disciplinary infringement if caught. He walked to the end of the train checking it was empty before making his way back, almost pleased that they were still in the land of nod.

'Wakey, wakey, sleeping beauties, and welcome to Wessex, time for my beddy-byes, too.'

Natalie blinked and rocked her head from side to side to stretch her neck. Theodore snoozed on. He had managed to locate her hand and had gently covered it. She checked that he hadn't dribbled on her suit and then was a little bit ashamed that she had checked. She nudged him awake and smiled at his confused state. Theodore blinked a few times and smacked his lips stickily together. They left the train, and the machine gobbled up their tickets as they passed through the barriers. Fortunately, there were a few taxis waiting for fares. Natalie hailed one and shepherded Theodore in. The stuffy perfumed air in the taxi caused Theodore to nod off again. It didn't take long to reach Acacia Avenue, where Natalie helped him from the taxi and to his front door, which she opened with one hand while indicating the taxi driver that she wouldn't be long (she innocently raised two fingers, meaning she would be two seconds) with the other. She tossed the keys on the table and watched him bumble up the stairs to bed and then let herself out of the front door before shutting it and giving it a tug as confirmation. Natalie tucked her long legs back into the taxi and gave the driver directions back to her flat. She had paid the fare and it was just as she was leaving the taxi that the driver said, "*Ere, missus, wot about this box? Don't it belong to your bloke?*'

'Oh yes, I'd better take it, thank you. He would have been pissed to have lost it.'

'Pissed?' the driver thought, and then he realised that with that drawl of an accent, she must be a Yank and that she meant he'd be upset, not drunk. He was also chuffed because he knew that Yanks were natural and generous tippers and a little bit of assistance and politeness would pay dividends (with a lot of British people, this was not always the case). He was not disappointed.

The sunshine gleaming through the window of his bedroom caused Theodore to blink himself awake, and although being officially given the day off, Theodore realised he had spent enough time sleeping and got out of bed, admittedly a lot later than a normal day at work. He thought he might poke his nose in at work, later on in the afternoon, but he was a little shocked that it was already well past midday. He groggily dressed in his usual casual clothes as if it were already Saturday. He decided to mope around for a while, performing odd chores. After an hour or so, the doorbell chimed at Number Thirteen, and when Theodore opened the front door, he was faced with his neighbour Matilda, red-eyed and desperate-looking. She pushed her way in and sashayed through to Theodore's lounge (he caught a sneer on her face as she regarded his old, worn sofa). After a quick summation of the situation, he went into his kitchen and put the kettle on. It was one of those times when the British determined that a pot of tea was just the thing. He heard her sob and trumpet as she blew her nose loudly. How one can walk so snootily into his house and then appear grief-stricken puzzled Theodore a bit. The kettle boiled, and Theodore took the tray and rattling crockery through to the lounge. He still hadn't bought any biscuits.

'Now what can I do for you, Mrs Dipper?'

'My husband's just been found guilty of fraud at the crown court!'

The woman whose acting was desperate moaned.

'I don't know how we going to manage, with the mortgage, the school fees, and loans.'

Theodore was at a loss what to do and gently sat beside her, putting a fatherly arm gingerly out, and awkwardly patted her back, as if she was a dog. She turned towards him burying her face into his shoulder; her voice muffled against his shirt.

'And y'll be sent down for years, and the papers will have a field day at our expense. I'll be the 'Till Dipper and he'll be blamed for having his 'And in the Till.'

Not having much of an ear to humour and jokes at other people's expense even more so, Theodore didn't make any response, but he knew better than to say that he was sure the newspapers would be more mature and responsible than publishing punning headlines. The tea was out of reach on the low table in front of him, and he didn't want to disturb her by reaching for it. What she said next caused him to go rigid as if zapped by a ray gun.

'Now you're famous and rich. Perhaps you would help me. I mean *us* out for a short while. I will of course be very grateful.'

Theodore tried to fathom her rationale for thinking that he was famous apart from his brief appearances on television. *Surely* she couldn't think that appearing on television automatically meant fame and riches? He sat there puzzled and not daring to move, especially when her hand casually lay on his stomach and then her fingers inserted themselves into the gap between his buttons.

'I would be very grateful if we could keep the house and also not disturb Courtney from his schooling.'

Theodore remained paralysed, and the tickling on his stomach had aroused him and that voice returned again and he picked it up on his subconscious radar.

'There is a stirring down below, there is a stirring down below, there is a stirring down below, down below, in your pants.'

Theodore exhaled when she withdrew her hand from his shirt. Surely she could hear his heart pounding in her ear? There was another pounding organ below his belt which increased in intensity as Matilda's hand casually glided over his belt and settled on his bulge.

'Mmmh,' she hummed next to his chest.

Her hand squeezed lightly, and her forefinger and thumb slowly raised the tag on his zip and tugged it downwards. The trek of the zip over the contents beneath was adding to his climbing arousal, and Matilda took her time. When the zip was at its starting point, she let the tag go, and her hand started the deliberate climb back up over his bulge and started to insert itself into the gap created by the downward journey. Theodore was paralysed. Matilda hummed against his chest a meaningless melody, as if she were ironing a shirt. She gently eased his manhood from the gap and held it like a prisoner. She moved her hand up, paused, and then down. Theodore closed his eyes and the first time for a long time prayed that this was a dream and that he would wake up watching cricket, but his resistance was being worn down, by the steady reciprocation of the hand. Matilda tilted her head and muttered something about 'being very grateful for any assistance' as she kissed him below his ear. Theodore realised he was pinned by her body and held captive in a wrist lock. His will was draining from him. Their languor was disturbed by the voice of Andrew Dipper shouting 'Tillie!' through the door and then again in the hall. Theodore leapt like a wounded gazelle and was nearly dragged back down because Matilda had not released her grip. He wriggled, and reluctantly she let him go. He gawkily stood upright, jarring the table with his knee, and in a panic tugged his zip up in one swift moment, trapping a piece of skin in the process. A muffled howl-cum-yell was emitted, and Theodore doubled over to try and get to the hall before his neighbour could penetrate further to see what was going on between his wife and his neighbour.

'Tillie, I went home, and Courtney told me you had gone next door, leaving him alone with his computer games. Tillie, what are you doing? Why didn't you wait for me at the court? They haven't sentenced me yet, and I'm certainly not a threat to society.'

Dipper heard the commotion and nosed through to see Matilda rising from the sofa, disturbing the table, guilt written all over her face and two distinct dents in the old sofa next to each other, and two cups of tea cooling on the table was positioned exactly in front of the dents. One however, had been tipped over and had disgorged its contents in a puddle, partly on the table and partly dripping on to the worn carpet. Theodore was hopping from one foot on to another like a demented stork, changing from an injured mammal to psychotic bird in a few moments. One hand was tugging at his crotch trying to ease the pain, and the other flapping about as if counterbalancing his dance. It was some bizarre courtship dance of a tropical bird not seen in these regions (even on a David Attenborough television programme).

Dipper surveyed the scene and lost no time in accusing his wife, enquiring what the hell they were playing at. She retorted angrily and said that (quite rightly) Theodore didn't do anything but spilt tea on his crotch (quite wrongly), a quick reaction considering why Theodore was holding the area he was holding. There started a full-blown autopsy of the situation which degenerated into a marital argument in Theodore's lounge. In the meantime, Theodore had hopped into the hall with the intention of struggling upstairs to see if he could release his entrapped organ in the privacy of his toilet. His hop on to the first step was interrupted by the doorbell pressed and the front door pushed open. It was Skel, deciding to pursue his compensation strategy.

'Ah ha, remember me . . . I think you know what I picked up from my previous visit here. It cost me half of my arse.'

'Eh?'

Theodore didn't of course remember Skel because all he ever saw was the shadow of the descending gardening tool before it disabled him. Even now, he could barely focus on the apparition in his hall because of the tears streaking his face.

'Not now, I'm having rather a bad day!' Theodore whimpered as he tried to climb the staircase.

Just behind Skel, another figure lurked, almost filling the doorway.

'Remember me, or obviously not because possibly the clout was too hard. I haven't a spade, but I've a substitute.'

From halfway up the stairs and to Theodore's horror, Peter Mack had leapt with surprising agility and pulled Theodore's souvenir cricket bat from its place of honour in a cabinet on the wall. This bat, a Duncan Fearnley 'attack with Ian Botham', had been signed by the ashes winning team of 198 . . . (it was a bat that Theodore had bought from the Lord's Taverners at the time they had been auctioning quite a few for their charity work). Skel turned around and uttered a challenge that petered away 'What do you want, you ancient old ffff . . . Oh feck'.

Before launching into attack or retreat, the stand-off was disturbed by the throaty roar of a big v8 that disturbed the concentration of the three men, especially when it pulled into the drive. Natalie had decided to deliver the box with his egg-and-bacon tie to Theodore personally. She had also overslept and was hasty in getting round to Theodore's because he hadn't answered his phone and she was concerned about him. (He hadn't bothered to replace the one the police had taken for examination, so he couldn't.) Peter Mack had left the door open, and the whirlwind that was Natalie was upon them, and seeing Peter Mack holding a cricket bat that looked like a toy in his fist, she leapt on to the back of whom she saw as the protagonist. Although she was not particularly weighty, she caused Peter Mack to stumble around woodenly, like Frankenstein's monster. Skel took the opportunity to escape from the affray and scurried around Peter Mack and through the open door into the arms of the police officers who had been following Natalie's car, from a distance. She had been travelling rather hastily, and the throaty roar of the TVR had caught the attention of two officers in a police-only lay-by. Having managed to corner the speedster, it was with added delight that Dawkins, accompanied by his trusty partner from the hospital visit a few weeks ago, came face to face with his 'scrote'. With a typical police turn of phrase of 'Just a minute, sonny', he grabbed Skel and called to his partner to keep an eye on him. Once done, Dawkins stepped into the hall where Natalie was hanging on to Peter Mack while Peter Mack was hanging on to a cricket bat. Theodore was hanging on to his crotch, and Andrew Dipper was hanging on to his wife and occasionally shaking her. Confronted with this pantomime, Dawkins was tempted to call for back-up. Only he couldn't be bothered to attempt explanation to a curious call handler in the response team. It was after all Friday afternoon, and the shenanigans of the weekend had not yet got fully underway. Theodore, pausing for a moment from his battle with pain in his fly, was able to shout at Natalie to get off Peter Mack, as 'He's on our side!'. Theodore hobbled over and relieves Peter Mack of his souvenir cricket bat, Natalie eases up on her rodeo ride and meekly dismounted the mighty steed that was Peter Mack. Dawkins got his partner to drag in Skel and assembled everyone in Theodore's lounge. He (Dawkins) would like to get to the bottom of this soap opera.

'Fuck me, Inspector Poirot. What are the little grey cells telling you now?' Skel challenged as he was dragged into Theodore's lounge.

'Only that you are a . . .' Dawkins's partner stepped in and, clapping her hand over his mouth, whispered in his ear to prevent Dawkins assaulting a member of the public.

Theodore took the opportunity to hobble upstairs, taking his bat with him as he feared it might be picked up and used as a weapon by one person or another. Downstairs in the lounge, they heard a muffled scream, and a minute or two later, Theodore entered the lounge wearing a clean pair of shorts.

'Okay, let's start with you.' Dawkins pointed his finger rudely at Matilda, and she explained that she was in court watching her husband's trial and when his guilt was pronounced, she was so upset and confused that she left court and went home after collecting her son, Courtney, from her mother's house. She dropped Courtney off and needed to speak to someone to whom 'I could blurt out my problems so I went next door, i.e. came here to Mr Grouchier. I saw him on the television and knew he was a scientist. He was kind, made tea, and listened while I blubbed. He even patted my back.'

Dawkins just turned to Theodore and motioned with a rolling of his hand to pick the story up.

'Well apart from what Mrs Tipper said, the only thing to add was that I was comforting her when we heard Mr Tipper's voice, and it looked far worse than it was, so I jumped up trying to pretend that we weren't having a cup of tea and sitting next to each other. That was when the collateral damage occurred.'

'Now we come to you!' Dawkins turned his stare on Skel. 'Well, Monsieur Poirot, I was on break for the weekend at the seaside 'cos I'm from Londahn inn oi. I heard this aggro going on with a scream and raised voices, so I poked me nose in like and that's when this fug burst in and frettened me.'

Dawkins shook his head at the faked accent. He would have loved to get close to Skel and stepped very heavily on his foot. Peter Mack glared. Dawkins didn't give much away, but he was pretty sure he knew who Skel was but needed to talk to the big fella.

'I was just driving past my very good friend's son's house when I've seen this character entering and the front door open. I went in and thought there was a riot going on, so I tried to break it up, then I was leapt upon by this Amazon, and fortunately you guys turned up.'

The Amazon's eyes sparkled with indignation. It was then that she recognised him from when they were visiting hospital. She explained she was delivering Theodore's award from Lord's that he'd left in the taxi.

'He obviously didn't value it much,' she sniffed. Theodore shrugged his shoulders; he was in pain and yet seemed victimised by all present. ('Just please let it be over soon,' he prayed to God in whom he didn't really believe.)

Dawkins realised he was getting nowhere, and the situation was heading towards farce. He honestly believed that he was unlikely to make an arrest in the near future, although he'd be content with giving Skel a slap and calling it quits, but Skel had already offered to get on the next train back.

'I'm on me, Daps, and ahht of 'ere.'

Peter Mack seemed to be the richest source of intelligence regarding the whole incident, but he was not going to say anything, and everyone else but Theodore was miffed for some reason. Theodore was really miffed. Dawkins and his partner turned down the tea offered by Theodore and made their way back to the squad car, not even bothering to caution Natalie (Dawkins would be wary of cautioning that lady with the grey sparklers, without her being in handcuffs). Anyway, that burgundy-coloured beast was so obvious. The next time she was caught speeding, he hoped it would be by another team of officers or preferably by a static camera and a computer. They sat in the car for a few minutes to see if the big fellow looked to follow Skel, but when they thought sufficient time had elapsed, and after simultaneously exhaling a sigh of relief, Dawkins started the car, and they headed for a brief patrol before coffee and hopefully a bit of normal police work.

Dawkins was sipping his coffee in the cafe (where they got police discount). It wasn't long before his partner could no longer keep her peace.

'Sarge, you knew him. You knew he was that scrote from the hospital, and don't forget it was Acacia Avenue.'

Dawkins waited and took a sip of coffee and then said, 'Angel' (he knew she preferred Angie), I couldn't be sure. My peepers ain't what they used to be, but I've never heard a true Londoner have such a crappy accent and use the word "Daps", which is parochial.'

'Sarge, you guessed the other bloke whacked him with the spade, as sort of quid pro quo.'

Again Dawkins paused before he replied, 'Angel, I don't know.' Dawkins screwed his eyes up at Angela and slightly shook his head. 'Do you know what kismet is?'

'Er, I think so, Sarge.'

'Well, if you can imagine your advantages or disadvantages being on either side of a set of scales, the kismet is the additional pain or pleasure until your personal set of scales balance. It's God rewarding you or paying you back before you die.'

'Ah, like Lord Nelson.'

'What, woman?' (Dawkins had dropped the considered pause away and slipped back into his straight talking, but slightly sexist self.)

'Yes, Lord Nelson's dying words. Everyone thinks they were Kiss Me, Hardy. But I think it was Kismet, Hardy, they've done for me at last. It was because of all the previous good fortune he'd had and he was paid back by a French marine, who shot him through the spine with a snipe shot.'

Dawkins wondered for a minute if she was teasing him, but she looked too self-satisfied and not sufficiently devious, and Dawkins had met several seriously devious people in and out of the 'job'. He thought she could have been right, but having nothing committed in writing, we shall never know.

At Number 13, there were three people remaining. The Dippers had headed off home, vowing support and loyalty until death ('Us against the world, love, us against the world'). Peter Mack was sitting on the centre of the sofa, where it sagged under his considerable mass. He was demanding an Irish whiskey for all the trouble he had been put through (admittedly unasked). Theodore remembered the business card of the 'dear person'. He borrows Natalie's mobile, dialled the number, and arranged for a reasonable bottle to be delivered.

'Ah ha, that can be arranged, but I must insist that a bottle of London gin is on the tab, which means I can arrange the deal at cost. Make sense?'

It didn't, but Theodore agreed, and within five minutes, 'dear person' was pressing the doorbell. Peter Mack answered and saw a gentleman sporting a white Panama hat but, more importantly, holding aloft and waving two bottles, one of Bushmills and one of Tanqueray's. Peter Mack quickly invited him in. Taking just enough time for 'dear person' to hang his hat, the two rapidly dusted off some of Theodore's mother's better crystal tumblers that had remained unused for at least twenty years. A couple of measures had been poured and were already being blissfully tasted, one the amber and the other the crystal limpid, when Natalie discovered them.

'Ah ha, you people. Tucking into the decent stuff. And who is our charming guest?'

He responded with a bow and then straightened.

'Sir Jon Hays, at your service, ex of the Senior Service.'

Introductions having been made and various stories exchanged, and reminiscences retold, eventually Natalie overheard Jon Hays saying, 'Of course, dear person, there is only one thing one should put in a gin.'

'And that's another gin!' Both Natalie and Theodore answered in chorus.

Natalie said that she had brought something that Theodore had left in the taxi. He looked extremely puzzled.

'For a member of the MCC, you don't look after your egg-and-bacon very well, do you?'

'Eh?'

She ran off around the house holding his tie aloft like a favour for a knight and was pursued by Theodore as if in a comedy sketch. He decided to abandon the chase and appealed to her better nature, fetching a shirt and blazer. Natalie relented, and soon he had the tie nicely knotted (by Natalie of course) and paraded around for the next two hours or so, not worried about the incongruity of shirt, tie, blazer, and shorts. However, he was poured an Irish Whiskey, which was his first taste ever. After this he was poured a Gin, also his first ever. As he paraded up and down his house, he was reminded when he was a child of five or so, his mother and father entered him in a fancy dress competition during a summer holiday at the Wessex seaside resort. He remembered the hot weather, the smiling and proud parents, the confused and mixed emotions of the children milling round, a grinning man in a bright blazer with a floral breath and being dressed as a hoplite. His march up and down in his lounge was the same that he had performed as a barelegged child some fifty years ago. He stopped and realised that his face hurt because he's been smiling non-stop for three hours, a personal best by some time, since that day on the Wessex sea front.

Even though it was not late, the party started to wind down. Peter Mack ordered a taxi and offered Jon Hays a lift. But he donned his Panama, saluted Royal Navy fashion, and strolled down the street swinging his walking stick from the hook in an exaggerated arc. (He had polished off nearly a whole bottle of gin and, apart from the odd twitch around the mouth, seemed unaffected.) Peter Mack would collect his Jaguar when the whiskey had cleared his system. The taxi arrived to collect Mack, and the silence was complete. Natalie and Theodore stood facing each other. They turned in perfect synchronisation and headed off to rinse the glasses out in the kitchen.

Natalie didn't leave, and the next morning, a new Theodore woke up beside her and suggested that he is making space in the garage that would be perfect for a TVR and also. Would she like to save on rent and get rid of her flat?

She mumbled something about that she would think about it.

Theodore turned his good ear towards her and said, 'Eh?'

'Yes, Theodore, I said yes.'

Epilogue

Babs and Steve Stiff had just set up a joint bank account in the Wessex branch of a bank owned by a European company (they offered the best interest rates). They were shuffling the brochures and assorted forms, when Stiff dropped a handful on the marble floor. Babs muffled her giggles behind a cupped hand. The brochures had been collected and poured into Babs's bag, from where they would get deposited in the rubbish bin without further thought, but a little later on that week They stood upright and gazed into each other's eyes, when a loud bang caused them to jump and look around. The shrieks and 'oh my gods' then filled the whole foyer. There was an epicentre in the foyer from where the noise had emanated. An old lady was lying flat on her back, and all believed she had been shot. There was a shotgun close by, and smoke was curling slowly from the muzzle. Although there was a lack of blood, there was a steady dripping from a punctured pipe that supplied water to the sprinkler system, unfeelingly simulating a punctured blood vessel. The young couple looked in fascination at the reaction of the people in the vicinity, which varied from frozen shock to performing mincing dances of panic, but all a safe radius from the cause. The anti-bandit security shields in front of the bank's tellers (customer service staff) had long since slammed up. Babs was already strutting across the foyer and having reached the source of the incident placed a foot across the lock of the weapon, a sawn-off, double-barrelled shotgun. Steve Stiff was right behind her and had crouched down beside the old lady. He looked at her wrinkled face gradually turning blue, first at the thin lips and spreading outwards, like a light-coloured carpet sopping up wine of a blue rather than red colour. Stiff loudly went through his own version of first aid. Some of the actions accompanying his commentary caused bemusement among onlookers.

'Safety first! Any danger from the environment? No.' A sweeping movement from both arms made him look as if he was trying to swim.

'Is the patient breathing? . . . No . . . check airway.' Stiff tilted the old lady's heads back and peered in.

'Uh OK, I can see an obstruction.'

The onlookers had started to close and were craning their necks in observation around the incident.

'Um, I think I can hook out the obstruction.'

Stiff was still talking aloud that provided commentary to the goggle-eyed audience.

'Oh yuk, it's false teeth.'

Steve Stiff had fished the teeth from the old lady's throat with finger and dangled them in front of the audience like producing a rabbit from a hat, a rabbit with a fair amount of drool glistening in the bright foyer lights. The onlookers who had been craning their necks to get a good view decided to back off in unison.

'OK, the patient is breathing, and I'm putting her into the recovery position . . . erm, I think I'm going to wait until she gets some colour.'

Stiff's patient still had not recovered a pinkish complexion that would be associated with full oxidisation. He had no choice but to try and get some air into her via mouth-to-mouth resuscitation. Given that the old lady's dentures had been removed, he had no choice but to bend his back to the task and take a firm grip on her jaw. He took a deep breath, getting a good hit of embrocation, followed by an aftertaste of eau de toilette and then tilted his head to one side, as if listening to her heart. He then turned his head and exhaled an adequate amount of air into her lungs. Out of the corner of his eye, he watched her chest rise, confirming his exhaust was her intake. He repeated the exercise and then switched to chest compressions. It was unfortunate that one of his friends who'd been queuing for money and quietly crapping himself while events had unfolded plucked up the courage to pull out his phone and took pictures of Steve Stiff in contact with his patient.

'I have completed two breaths and fifteen compressions. We repeat until assistance arrives.'

Stiff announced. Babs had now knelt down beside him and tried to find a pulse. She looked worriedly at Steve Stiff, who finished another fifteen compressions and bent over to deliver two more breaths. The unfeeling prick who purported to be a mate clicked his phone's camera again. Babs screamed at him to call for an ambulance. The shutters being deployed indicated that the police should arrive any second, but they really needed a paramedic, not a copper with a bit of first aid. The bank's doors normally automatically operated were forced aside by Dawkins, followed by an eager

Angela Dickens. They went straight to the centre of the scene where the young couple were knelt beside a supine figure of no size at all. The weapon lay close by, a wisp of smoke curling from one of the shortened barrels as if trying to signal to an unidentified ally.

'Did you see which way the perpetrators went? Is she still with us?' A nod from Steve Stiff was sufficient.

'Angie, get on the horn, and get a meat wagon here, pronto.'

The paramedics arrived and got to work quickly, taking over from Babs and Steve Stiff, who took it in turns like a double act to apprise the paramedics of what had happened. They hoisted her on to the ambulance trolley bed. One of the paramedics was struggling to intubate the lady, and her nerves were worsening with each attempt. It was normally a lot easier to do this outside a moving ambulance, but the people gaping were adding to her anxiety. Two members of the public in dark blue overalls, of the sort worn by plumbers, stepped forward, one taking the tube from the shaking hands of the paramedic with a delicate hand that seemed to be the opposite of how one imagined a plumber's hand should be. He set the head back of the patient and, in one sweet, curving movement, had the patient intubated; a second later, a bag was attached.

'Page three of the plumber's manual,' he announced to all in earshot, and he quietly whispered, 'Why do little old ladies always smell of embrocation and eau de toilette?'. It was not often that a senior orthopaedic consultant of the Wessex Royal Infirmary was on hand from a bit of DIY kitchen fitting. He had watched Steve Stiff's delivery of first aid did not interfere. The boy was doing perfectly well, especially when he decided to perform mouth-to-mouth resuscitation despite hoisting out the patient's false teeth (consultants tended not to perform basic CPR). He had also noted the colour of the patient returning to normal. The unlikely duo took leave of one relieved paramedic while the other who regarded their actions with disbelief bordering on suspicion. It took a lot of practice to painlessly and successfully intubate a patient.

Now the scene deemed safe. The shields were reset back into the counter. Other police, including an armed response unit, had arrived. The armed response unit realising that all that was required of law enforcement was forensic evidence gathering and the mundane note taking of the public's observations disappear in silence, leaving the sawn-off shot, one barrel still loaded, forlornly on the marble. Pages of the notebooks flicking and pencils scratching across the paper filled the next fifteen minutes. It became quickly apparent that the patient and the perpetrator were one and the same. Finally, the shotgun was dropped into a plastic bag and sealed. Despite wearing rubber gloves, which she used for washing up, there would be fingerprints left over from when the little old lady sawed off the ends of the barrels.

The public were ushered from the bank which was to close as soon as the tills had been reconciled and the staff sent home. The battery-powered mobility scooter was left outside the bank for a day or two. The branch manager would arrange for trauma counselling for any member of staff who might request it. During the following week, they were cautioned not to talk to the press, but Babs would get in first anyway with a story that made the national newspapers, with the twist of the little old lady's plan to evade the clutches of a care home and earned her a handsome fee and the heart of a handsome man with funny-coloured hair.